D. M. (Donna) Roy lives in Southern Ontario, Canada. She has had a fulfilling career in the financial field and in those 45 years, she has learned a lot about people. Although experience has been her predominant teacher, Donna has always wanted to write and hoped some day to become a published author. During this new stage in her life, she is now fulfilling her dream.

P.S. If you enjoy this book, then watch for her next one, called *Good Sun, Bad Moon,* Series 2 of *The Messengers.*

For Claude

D. M. ROY

THE MESSENGERS

AUSTIN MACAULEY PUBLISHERS™

LONDON ★ CAMBRIDGE ★ NEW YORK ★ SHARJAH

Ordering Information
Quantity sales: Special discounts are available on quantity purchases by corporations, associations, and others. For details, contact the publisher at the address below.

Publisher's Cataloging-in-Publication data
Roy, D. M.
The Messengers

ISBN 9798889107705 (Paperback)
ISBN 9798889107712 (Hardback)
ISBN 9798889107736 (ePub e-book)
ISBN 9798889107729 (Audiobook)

Library of Congress Control Number: 2023921643

www.austinmacauley.com/us

First Published 2024
Austin Macauley Publishers LLC
40 Wall Street, 33rd Floor, Suite 3302
New York, NY 10005
USA

mail-usa@austinmacauley.com
+1 (646) 5125767

Introduction

Over one million messages are relayed every second, either electronically, by mail, telephone, in person, or by a third party. But what about telepathic messages? How can we track them? I'm referring to that little voice that sometimes interrupts our thoughts, invades our privacy, and even has the capability to alter our decisions; that mysterious little voice that speaks to us from within.

Where do these voices come from? And from whom? Is it just our sub-conscience, a figment of our own imagination? Is the message a cry for help? Could the anonymous messenger be relaying a warning, perhaps a clairvoyant way of saving us or someone close to us from a death-defying fate? Or is the anonymity buried much deeper, beyond mankind's reach?

Perhaps a special delivery being sent by a guardian angel or possibly by a ghost from the past, a ghost who is really an angel just trying to earn their wings? If so, are they real? Or are they just an apprehension of the afterlife that exists in our spiritual minds, not in bodily form?

Definition of an angel according to my ancient *Webster's School and Office Dictionary* (by 'ancient' I mean when it states that the cost to post a letter in Canada is two cents).

Angel, n. *A messenger—a celestial spirit*—a beautiful person.
Resembling angels; angei-ical.

Dreams and visions also have a way of conveying these telepathic messages. In the olden days, some say Native Americans were great believers of dreams and visions and made accurate predictions to the elders of their tribe from these dreams or visions. Some believed that *Tatanka*, who lived in the underworld, and who gave life to the tribe, had turned his spirit body into a shaggy buffalo and saw these tribal nations in his visions. He then relayed his *messages* to the holy man in the tribe through these visions.

Thus, the buffalo became sacred to the tribes, as well as the eagle and the white wolf. They were believed to be messengers for the Great Spirit in the sky. However, the buffalo and the eagle could be killed, but not so with the white wolf. It is believed by some tribes that if you kill a white wolf, he will come back to haunt you, to avenge his death; and if you save him, he will be your protector for life.

It is also believed that the white wolf, mostly identifiable by a pair of shining blue eyes that illuminate in the dark, is a greater force sent by the Creator and that his spirit form is interchangeable. He often uses the powers of nature, like the wind. He is always watching, protecting. He has the ability to sense danger and to transfer thoughts to others.

Tales of this daunting creature spread through the lands, and eventually, a legend was soon created. The legend of white wolf symbolized danger to some and yet to others, he was their protector, their guardian angel. Their *messenger*!

The mystery pertaining to the authenticity of these beliefs, of spirits, ghosts, and angels, may never get resolved. Only survivors of a near-death situation who have experienced the tip of the afterlife may be able to comprehend some of these hidden truths.

However, very few are apprehensive when asked about it or simply refuse to speak about it. Until you have experienced it yourself, you will never understand why. There has been much documentation and many books written on this subject, but what does one truly believe regarding angels? Or these messengers?

My story, *The Messengers*, takes place in Northern Ontario where nature is man's religion and the land is his church, a beautiful land with scenes of majestic, breathtaking landscapes. However, even nature has an angry side that can quickly transform within hours. Blue skies grow menacingly dark and the wind changes direction, rotating to reveal an ugly, cold face.

At first, the spectacular landscape is bathed with gently falling raindrops but within hours of an approaching Norther, the temperature progressively plummets. This is the last warning for travelers to quickly seek shelter while there is still time before the onslaught of the brewing storm. Bone-chilling winds, followed by razor-sharp pellets of ice, bite any bare skin, causing frostbite. And soon, travel becomes dangerous, eventually restricted as mounds and mounds of drifting snow quickly develop.

In less than twenty-four hours after the on-slot of one of these unexpected blizzards, the once-flowing crystal streams freeze over when the temperature reaches minus thirty degrees Fahrenheit. Tall, protective trees bordering the dense forests bend and shiver from the harsh winds, and their ice-covered branches droop, surrendering to the harsh winds.

The nor 'wester leaves no access to roads and pathways and the remoteness challenges the very existence of life. It is only September, normally too early for weather like this! But the north is not a *normal* place. It quite possibly could turn out to be yet another long, lonely winter for any creature living here and a slow, agonizing passing for any unwary visitor who could succumb after starving or freezing to death.

My story takes place in the late 1800s, an era when mountain men were rough and ruthless, Caucasians were referred to as 'White Men' and Indigenous were still called 'Indians'.

It was a time and place where mankind co-existed on disputed land, both fighting the elements of whatever Mother Nature hurled at them and both relying on this precious land for survival while constantly keeping in mind that man, no matter what color or race, was *not* at the top of the typical food chain. A period in time revolving around the dependence of bare necessities for mankind's existence when the natural world is behaving unnaturally!

A period in time when perhaps someday, *peaceful* coexistence will eventually become *normal!*

The Messengers is a dramatic and deeply moving story of two strong-willed individuals, both Indigenous from their mothers' side of the family, and also both Caucasian from their fathers' side, who get caught up in a changing way of life that neither will accept.

Jesse Burns, who was raised in the 'White Man's' world, learns that his illegitimate son (whom he thought was dead) is now living as a Lakota warrior. A father and son, joined together in a strange and deadly kinship by a predator of the wild, a white wolf! Both men are rival enemies who eventually develop a rare understanding of each other while trying to survive in such an unforgiving territory.

This is the first of six fiction novels of *The Messengers* that I have written, six books or related stories that travel through a century of connecting characters and events, challenging your beliefs, your imaginations, by reaching deeper into your souls to leave you wondering if there really could be a spiritual guardian, or *Sicun,* embodied within the human body.

The 'Legend of the White Wolf', alleged by the people from the past, were defenders sent to protect their people from evil, messengers sent from the Great Spirit in the sky, to forewarn them of upcoming danger and hardship. Was the *Sicun,* or white wolf, just a spiritual crux of my character's conscience? Are the *Messengers* just a flight of our imaginations as well? And what about angels, are they imaginary, or do they *really* exist also? Maybe.

Or maybe not!

Prologue

It was June 12, 1860, when the Burns family purchased Trapper Joe's log cabin for a mere two hundred dollars situated on Beaker's Bluff in North Bay, Ontario, Canada. Jesse Burns was only six years old at the time.

His father, Captain John William Burns, was a respected combatant in the Canadian Armed Forces who opted to live off-base with his family. He was married to Warm Wind, a beautiful Cheyenne woman whom he loved and adored since childhood; but because she was not a white woman, their marriage was not recognized by the army, and their union was frowned upon by his peers.

When the Comanches raided their small settlement four years later in the 'Season of The Falling Leaves', Captain John Burns was away on a mission and Warm Wind and her two young children were left all alone during the attack.

On that horrific day, Jesse lost his mother, who was with child at the time, and his younger brother to a brutal slaying. Sensing his mother's fear, the younger, three-year-old child clung to his mother's skirt and wouldn't let go. Jesse was pushed inside the wood cubby and was told to stay hidden. "No matter what happens," she warned Jesse, "you stay there."

Minutes later, ten mean-looking painted warriors barged into their home. Jesse stayed hidden inside the cubby for two days, long after they had left. He cried until he couldn't cry anymore. The grieving boy managed to wrap his mother and baby brother into a blanket and rolled their bodies outside; he buried them under a stone grave not far from the cabin.

Afterward, he often went to the top of Beaker's Bluff and prayed. Jesse lived in the cabin for five more years, *waiting*. And during all that time, his father *never* came home.

During the first year of waiting, the days were long and lonely for young Jesse. But with grit and determination, the ten-year-old boy learned to fend for himself. His mother had taught him well about surviving in the wilds of Northern Canada, where she had grown up. Each spring, they used to go hunting together; they fished from the river in summer, collected and split firewood for the fireplace in fall and during the winter months, they always sat around the warm fireplace and read.

During that year, he found the winter was the worst time for him; he had read every book on the shelf many times and after the fourth time of reading the same book, he was able to memorize every word. During the day, he listened to the wind pound on the wooden door and during the night, he laid in bed and waited for the familiar howl of a wolf silhouetted in the moonlight at the top of Beaker's Bluff, not far from the slumbering, run-down cabin.

When Jesse was hunting during the second year, he stumbled upon a campsite. He called out, but there wasn't anyone around. On the site was an old covered wagon; after checking inside, he surmised that it was being used as somebody's living quarters. An aging, gray mule was penned inside a crude, man-made log enclosure or 'corral'; its ears were perked up and a curled lip menacingly revealed rows of large chomping yellowish teeth.

Nearby, on a tripod made of sticks placed Injun-style (one of the first devices taught to Jesse by his Cheyenne mother) was a steaming cauldron boiling away above a well-made campfire. When he approached the cauldron, he felt the sharp blade of a bowie knife pressing against his throat. "Don't even move a hair, if I was you, boy! This here knife just cut yer skin and cause it's so sharp, you didn't even feel it slice." Jesse only felt hot breath fanning the back of his neck. The crackly voice continued. "What you doin' out here in the middle of nowhere, boy?"

"I live not more'n a mile from here, in a cabin back that-a-ways," Jesse pointed to the left with his eyeballs, while not even moving a muscle.

"In ole' Joe's cabin? Your folks buy it from him or somethin'?" she asked. "Yeah, about five or six years ago, now. But the Comanche killed my family two years back and I've been fendin' for myself ever since," Jesse proudly remarked. "My name is Jesse Burns."

The old lady lowered the knife, deciding the kid was harmless. "You can't be too careful in these backwoods, shouldn't trust anyone out here! *Remember* that, boy!" She motioned for him to enter her abode. "Sit a spell while I fetch us some stew from the pot. You look like you could do with a warm, hearty servin' of food. But first, I'll put some salve on that cut. You jes' wait right here, boy."

The old lady disappeared inside the dilapidated wagon but quickly returned. "I make this here salve myself. It'll heal you up in no time, you'll see." She had brought out a shiny blue jar filled with a yellow paste and applied it to the cut on his throat. Jesse woofed the food down after the old lady set a plate of steaming rabbit stew in front of him. Ruby cackled. "You was sure hungry, boy!"

Before he left, Ruby introduced him to her best friend, the ornery mule. "You have to make his acquaintance proper-like 'cause he doesn't take kindly to strangers. He may look old and feeble like me, but we take care of each other. We been together for more onto thirty years come next spring."

"What's his name?" Jesse asked as they walked toward the mule.

"Stupid!" answered Ruby without even cracking a smile.

That's how Jesse first met Ruby Long Bottoms, or better known as 'the Witch of the North', and her best friend, 'Stupid'. She wreaked of dirty swamp water and her raggedy clothes smelled the same. Straggly gray hair was 'wisping out' from a raccoon hat donning the tail and all, and when she cracked a rare, toothless smile, the leathery skin on her bronzed face creased like veins inside an old buffalo's tough heart.

Ruby Long Bottoms, a descendant from the Ute tribe, truly looked like a witch and even sounded like one when she cackled as she stirred the liquid in the steaming cauldron.

Two days later, Jesse went back to Ruby's campsite. Surprisingly, the cut on his throat had healed, leaving only a slight scar. "What was in that stuff?" Jesse asked.

"I'll show you, boy. I'm rustlin' up a fresh batch as we speak."

From then on, Jesse spent every day with his new friend and she taught him about the medicinal use of plants and trees. Healing methods. And the human body. For the next three years, Jesse couldn't get enough learning from Ruby, his mind was like a sponge.

He found out that she used to be a doctor of medicine until her license was revoked because she was accused of practicing witchcraft on sick folks during an epidemic of smallpox. Her 'brews' were curing people but modern medicine just wasn't ready for her natural remedies yet. She became a traveling witch doctor, living the good life with her best friend and lifelong partner, 'Stupid'.

It had been raining for four straight days and the sun remained hidden behind thunderous, low-hanging clouds. Jesse stayed inside his gloomy cabin, *waiting*. He always hated to *wait*.

After the rains finally stopped, Jessie was on his way to see Ruby when he suddenly heard voices not far from the cabin. He saw a buckboard wagon and two grazing horses. The wagon was heavily loaded with lumber, pieces of piping material, a wooden barrel, and an array of empty glass jugs. Two mountain men were busily running a pipeline from the river near the cabin. They had two galvanized steel buckets, both filled with a bubbly liquid boiling over a campfire and three more wooden barrels also filled with the same clear liquid nearby.

Jesse accidentally came upon them and their guns were immediately drawn, pointed directly at him. He raised his hands, letting them see that he was unarmed. And peaceful. The nearest one pointing the gun at

Jesse's head slowly lowered his weapon and yelled, "It's OK, Merv. It's just some kid."

"Who might you be?" the bigger burly one asked when he stepped clear of the trees.

"I'm Jesse Burns, and this here is my land you're trespassing on."

"Well, is that so? Let's talk over a drink like sociable folks do and maybe we can come to some sort of deal with one another. We pay you for the use of your land and when winter sets in, we'll be on our way. We'll even shake on it, young man. Keepin' it real business-like and all!" He handed Jesse a tin cup filled with the clear liquid. "We'll *jest* have us a drink first and shake on it afterward."

Jesse drank. And drank some more. The yellow liquid was very potent, mostly pure alcohol! He'd never tasted anything like it before. They kept filling his cup. And Jesse kept on drinking until he passed out on the ground. For two days, Jesse was comatose. And when he came to, he literally *crawled* back to his cabin on all fours like a crab. He fell into bed and constantly threw up in a bucket for two more days. He was soo-o sick. When Jesse was able to walk, he went back to tell the trespassers to leave, but they had already cleared out.

"*Moonshiners,* they were! I warned you not to trust anyone out here!" reminded Ruby as she stirred the cauldron of stew. Her wagon was all packed when Jesse got to her campsite.

"Where are you going?" asked Jesse.

"Movin' on before the snows come. It's goin' to be a bad one. Lots of cold blizzards comin' our way. Here's some salve for you until you can make yer own. Stay safe, boy!" Jesse caught the fading echo through the trees. "Maybe we'll meet again someday, boy." The 'Witch of the North' and Stupid were gone. Jesse was all alone once again.

Ruby had been right; it was a bad winter and Jesse wasn't prepared. By November, the temperature had dropped to −20 degrees Fahrenheit and stayed there. Everything froze solid, even the door of his cabin wouldn't open. His food supply ran out one month later; he boiled leather and made a tasteless broth that almost gagged him but he still drank it. There was nothing else.

Before, the winters were never this bad and he could still hunt and ice-fish right through until the spring thaw. But not now, it was too damned cold for man nor beast out there.

December came and went; January was even colder. Jesse managed to catch three small fish in a frozen stream, but that wasn't enough. He was always hungry, and the worst thing about starving is that it doesn't go away. The craving for food consumed him, assailing his mind when he tried to sleep and agonizing him when he conserved his energy by sitting still.

His empty stomach growled like a bear and he doubled over from the pain. The smallest exertion caused his heart to race, and dizziness engulfed him, leaving him shaky and weak. Then he would faint. He even sent prayers up to God, asking for help.

Strangely, he had a haunting feeling that he had been heard by some *majestic* force, an unexplainable force that could never be measured or rationalized by any earthly human being. As the weeks passed, Jesse continued to boil his leather broth concoction and it seemed to barely keep him alive.

One windy night, a noise woke Jesse up; it was coming from outside the door. A whimper, then another! And yet another! Each one sounding weaker than the first one. With a loaded gun in hand, he unlocked the door. Standing outside in the cold, Jesse was met with a pair of blue eyes looking back at him in the darkened doorway.

The whimpering animal lifted his front paw out of the deep snow; blood had stained the white doorstep. The paw was almost torn off and bleeding profusely. When Jesse bent to look at it, long, yellowish fangs suddenly appeared and a deep, menacing growl escaped from the animal's curled-up lips. Jesse stepped back inside the doorway and readily squeezed the gun trigger, unsure of the hurt animal's next move; he was ready to shoot.

About ten feet in front of him was the biggest white wolf that Jesse had ever seen. He cautiously opened the door wider. The pleading looks in the animal's eyes spoke to Jesse. The limping wolf barely made it inside; he collapsed on the floor and closed his agonizing blue eyes. Jesse ran and got Ruby's salve and plastered it on the animal's paw, hoping it would help; the wolf never moved. He never even opened his eyes as Jesse hovered over him. He was dying. The wolf laid there for three days, suffering.

Finally, Jesse pointed the gun and shot the wolf, watching as the wolf drew his last breath. As weak as Jesse was with having no food for eight days, he managed to strip the wolf's hide and cut up the meat, just like his mother used to do to the buffalo. And he ate the heart of the animal raw. When he gained some of his strength back, he had another job to do; his mother had also taught him how to tan a hide. Each day, Jesse thanked the wolf for the food before he ate it. It tasted much better when it was cooked.

Jesse survived the winter and when the spring thaw came, he cautiously answered a knock at the cabin door. It was Ruby Long Bottoms and behind her, the old mule brayed a cheery 'hello'. "See, ole Stupid remembered you, boy." She cackled. "The winter must have been good to you; I think you have grown since I last saw you. Now, I can't call you a *boy* anymore, you have become a strappin' young man."

Jesse invited her inside and she removed her coat, placing it on a sideboard closest to the door while Jesse prepared a meal for her. He set a plate of ribs down on the table in front of her and, being very hungry, the old woman started to dig in with her fork. Suddenly, she pushed it away. "What is this, boy?" It was then that Jesse told her about the white wolf. "I can't eat this! And you shouldnta' ete it either. That wolf was sacred, a *messenger* sent by the 'Man in the Sky' Hisself. And you ete it?"

"I had to! I was starving to death. I did try to save him at first, but he was too far gone," replied Jesse defensively.

The old woman didn't say anything for a long time, then she asked, "How have you been feelin' since eatin' the meat?"

"OK, I guess! Just a lot of bad dreams keeping me awake most nights. One in particular!"

His guest sat very quietly while Jesse told her about the reoccurring dream: *I'm rolling around on the snowy ground and there is a young Lakota brave on top of me. He has a knife in his hand and the blade is against my throat. He is trying to kill me. I look into his angry eyes, his young contorted face, only to see myself looking back at me.*

Then a wolf howls and I wake up.

The elderly Ute medicine woman had closed her eyes and Jesse thought that she had fallen asleep when finally, she reopened them and leaned forward.

"The spirit of the White Wolf is punishing you. In your dream, your offspring is trying to kill you, in revenge of the wolf's death. The wolf is your enemy but he will become *their* friend. He will also dwell inside of their minds until the lifeline gets broken. Be careful. You have insulted the spirit world. By ingesting the meat, you have invaded their world and have become one of them."

"The human world interacted with the world of the spirits intermingled! And now, interchangeable! This spirit could also dwell in your offspring of its choice, recognizable by the shining blue lights emitting from within their eyes. The Spirit will guide and protect them; he will be their *messenger,* no matter where they go. You will have other dreams from the spirit world and your path will be hard and long."

The old woman struggled to get up; suddenly, she had aged and walked with a bent backbone. "Now I must go back to my village, where I will live out the rest of my days. Maybe someday we might meet again in the spirit world, my friend."

Ruby Long Bottoms put on her coat and left shortly afterward. Noticing a doeskin pouch left on the sideboard where her coat had been,

Jesse grabbed the pouch and ran out the door to stop her. But there was no trace of her or her entourage. There were no tracks in the mud where she had walked to the wagon. And there were no tracks in the mud left by the wagon wheels or the mule. Jesse listened and could hear no sounds of the old wagon rolling along the trail either. Only dead silence!

Jesse went back inside his cabin. He opened the pouch and found two more blue jars of salve, a necklace made of rattlesnake fangs, a short pencil that had been crudely sharpened with a knife, a tattered recipe book, and a thick, glass test-tube vial with red liquid sealed inside. On the outside of the vial, a piece of paper was attached, "Only take 2 drops 3x, for 3 days."

Curiosity made him open the book and he glanced through it, finding the recipe of the red liquid. It was a mixture of boiled *swamp* berries, tree bark, and pinecones, and an herb that he had never heard of before. There was also a recipe for the yellow salve found inside the blue jars. He fondly touched the ornate necklace held together with gut-string, and also the doeskin pouch perfectly stitched by hand. Both so expertly crafted!

It was a medicine pouch given to him as a parting gift from someone very special. Jesse never saw the 'Witch of the North' again. A week later, on a cool, crisp day in April 1869, a very determined young man left the cabin and the wilderness behind and went to the nearest fort to obtain information about becoming a foot soldier and find out where he had to go to sign up.

He was following his dream to serve in the Canadian Armed Forces so he volunteered to join the Canadian Militiamen's Cavalry, hoping to eventually be promoted to becoming a horse soldier just like his father. Jesse also knew he didn't want to be alone anymore. At fifteen, being big for his age, he was hoping the recruiters wouldn't question him when he told them he was sixteen. And they didn't.

Part One

In the Month of the Cold, Penetrating Wind, 1885

A pair of piercing blue eyes cautiously scanned the perimeter of an isolated valley below, situated deep in the wilderness of Northern Ontario, Canada. The tall, restless soldier waited, his back unyielding against the cold March wind. Captain Jesse D. Burns sat tensely in his saddle, while under him, the big black stallion nervously stomped the frozen ground from the foul smell of blood drifting toward them. Safely tucked inside one of his saddlebags was his doeskin medical pouch, something he had carried with him for many years.

Directly behind their captain, thirty-two armed soldiers on horseback huddled in formation, ready and awaiting orders in spite of the penetrating wind. Jesse knew that wind. It was a living sheet of gray cold descending from a flat leaden sky singing a death-song, a resonating sound that moaned across the frozen lakes, clearing a wide path as it rushed to claim its next victim.

And once the agitated monster hit land, it took full possession, a giant with no borders, gusting across the dark plains toward the Sioux reservation some fifty miles away to the south while funneling up into the snow-capped mountains to the north. It whistled along the empty, endless roadways and stirred the angry, bending wasteland. It battered the forests, snaking through tall secluded trees. Whispering his name!

It came after him, plucking at his coat, chilling his spine; an unforgiving wind that continually slapped him in the face with invisible wings while cold air relentlessly gnawed at his skin with tiny biting teeth. Jesse knew why he was being targeted as the victim of this wind.

He had never been a superstitious man, but lately, doubt was starting to settle in and his saddle blanket of white wolf-hide had a lot to do with it.

Jesse still waited. He was an impatient man and found it hard to wait. He knew what was coming; it was his job to know, just as it was his job to know the capabilities of each man in his company standing directly behind him. There were few surprises and he liked it that way. And still, he waited.

He shifted his weight in the McClellan saddle to look up at the buzzards riding the cold wind, etched against the leaden clouds. There were at least ten of them, wheeling and continuously circling through the same sector of the sky with a mindless fixity of purpose; it was as if Jesse was looking through a kaleidoscope. The buzzards were also waiting!

A lone rider topped the rise to the south. He was riding hard. Jesse's eyes narrowed, trying to make out the rider as his hand automatically touched the sixteen-shot Henry.44 repeater in his saddle boot, a gun that he could load on Sunday and shoot with all week. It was a good gun, along with his lever-action Winchester, just in case this trip turned out to be one of those 'few surprises' that he so disliked. However, Jesse wasn't expecting a fight, as he hadn't ordered his men to discard their overcoats earlier. And besides, it was too damned cold. As the rider rode closer, he saw that it was one of his scouts.

Corporal Tomas Good Shield, Jesse's best scout, and tracker from the Lakota tribe, reined in his sorrel and saluted. He was a big, robust, dark-skinned warrior who never seemed to be afraid of anything. But right now, he was out of breath and his deeply crevassed complexion had noticeably paled on his wind-burned face.

"Well?" asked Captain Burns.

"We found them, sir," responded Tomas Good Shield in a shaky voice.

"How many?" asked Captain Burns.

"Six. All dead! It's just awful, sir."

"It always is, Corporal. Any sign of the raiders now?"

"No, sir, they're gone. Two days, maybe three at the most."

"Where are Corporal Chase and Corporal Evans?" Jesse asked. "They were with you."

"Well, sir, there was another person still alive. She ran into the trees when we approached. They are still looking for her, sir."

Jesse turned and waved to Corporal Manning, who then moved up alongside the captain. "I'll take Corporal Good Shield and we'll go have a look. In a half hour, bring the men down slowly; that should give us enough time to poke around and check for tracks before they trample things up. And get a burial detail ready," he ordered.

He never looked behind him, he didn't have to. He trusted every one of his men; he trained them, and he knew they would always watch his back. They were good soldiers. The two men started down from the rise. The land was winter-barren, the grass dormant and gray-brown under the thin crust of snow dust; the trees stood dark and desolate, its naked branches reaching out in warning. And the buzzards flew higher while fighting the wind, but they didn't go away. They still waited as the wind pushed and howled even louder.

That damned persistent wind! thought Jesse, as it whistled through the branches and down into the valley where the bodies lay. He could hear it calling his name again, always tormenting.

Tomas had been right. "It *was* awful!" alleged Jesse as he looked around. There was one wagon tipped on its side, the canvas charred. On the back wheel, a male figure was tied upside down, his face burned beyond recognition. The fire under his head was still smoldering while the other wheel on the front of the wagon frantically spun in the wind.

There were four more bodies, all naked, scalped, and mutilated, lying beside a shredded tepee, two white men and two women; the one white female had been with child, the other one was a squaw, possibly from the Lakota tribe. About fifty feet away, Jesse saw the last body. He had been tied up and repeatedly dragged behind a horse and rider until his torn and battered body flew apart. The blood-soaked trail cut a complete circle around the two charred wagons.

"This was another form of torture used by these savages," surmised Jesse as he quickly turned away. The swollen bodies, or what was left of them, were in bad shape. *At least the temperature had remained quite cold and it was too early in the season for flies to contend with,* thought Jesse.

Everything else, their supplies, clothing, horses and two mules, guns, and ammunition, were all stolen. However, the attackers had left the frozen pile of buffalo hides that had spilled out of the one wagon, probably the reason for the raid on these travelers. Jesse looked at the dragged body once again, and then quickly walked away. He pulled out his pipe, filled it with tobacco, and lit it. The tang of the smoke as he puffed away helped disguise the foul smell.

He crouched down as he continued to study the tracks. The picture was clear enough; there were about twenty-five, maybe thirty attackers who had jumped the travelers while they slept, most likely at early dawn. There had been a fight as spent Sharps' cartridges from the buffalo guns scattered the ground and the attackers must have had a few losses as Jesse saw tracks where bloodied bodies were dragged from the sight and loaded onto awaiting horses.

Jesse's suspicions were even more confirmed by the moccasin tracks he found around the bodies, short and stubby prints with the familiar fringe along each heel. And there was an arrow embedded into the wood on the wagon, which was probably left on purpose, another trait of these attackers.

Now, he had no more doubts about who would commit such immoral acts of cruelty, especially to a woman with a child. They 'hit and run' usually at early dawn and always ride with a full moon overhead, only to return home to holler and celebrate their *successful* raiding party. These people have no remorse, no fear. Jesse did not dislike *most* Indians, but he *hated Comanche.*

Jesse felt his muscles tighten as he clenched his fists. He abruptly stood up and chewed on his pipe stem in anger. *Hate* wasn't a strong enough word to describe how he felt about the Comanche.

Memories suddenly exploded inside his brain; memories that he had tried to erase ever since his childhood. His mother's death and the torture she suffered while he had hidden in a wood cubby during a Comanche attack still blackens his very soul. His mother was named Warm Wind from the Cheyenne tribe. They had also killed and mutilated his three-year-old brother when he cried out. His father, Captain John W. Burns had left on a mission with the army the day before, leaving them alone, as he often did back then. Jesse would never forget the savages' evil-looking faces while they took turns raping his mother; she was also with child. What he saw today opened up a deep wound inside of him as soon as he rode into the valley. He had suspected *Comanche.* Yes, he hated them and he always would.

Jesse cautiously looked around him, suddenly chilled. Nothing had changed. The war zone was still bloodied, the land utterly desolate. Above him, the sky was still mottled in dull colors and the waiting buzzards still circled among the featureless clouds, clouds that seemed to roll away to nowhere. And the aggravating wind still howled and plucked at his coat, always reminding him.

Still unforgiving! Still punishing him for what he did when he was a young, starving boy trying to survive the long winter months after the attack! He remembers it like it was just yesterday, even though this coming January, it'll be almost fifteen years since it had happened.

Meanwhile, sitting on his horse nearby, Tomas was regarding Jesse very closely. He knew the torment that his friend must be feeling. He had heard him confess to killing a white wolf, a creature *never* seen by the others. If Jesse hadn't had its hide, Tomas wouldn't have believed him. But Tomas, who was a renowned Lakota warrior, believed in the legend as it was told by his father and by all the fathers before *him.*

The white wolf was believed to be sacred among all the tribes, a spirit that only appeared in their visions or dreams, a *messenger* sent by the Great Spirit Himself. They believed the wolf's spirit would punish its victim by haunting him, even tormenting him. The spirit would never forget. Killing a white wolf was a dreadful thing, but *eating* it was yet another.

Tomas understood Jesse's reasoning for doing what he did back then; he was just a scared fifteen-year-old kid that thought he was going to die during those winter months of continuous snowfall, gusting winds, and never-ending blizzards.

He was alone and starving to death when the injured wolf appeared just outside his cabin door, limping and very weak. The animal had gotten its front paw mangled in a bear trap and was bleeding out and Jesse thought that the wolf wasn't going to make it, that Jesse couldn't help him anymore. So, deciding to put the animal out of its misery, he aimed the gun and shot it.

However, Tomas being a full-blooded Indian warrior who cherished the spirits, would have died himself before bringing harm to any spirit, much less disrespecting them by *eating* their flesh. He believed that the wolf was a messenger, sent by a much greater spirit. Sent to save Jesse's life! Was it his intention to provide Jesse with enough food to last him until the spring thaw? Tomas greatly feared that his friend's fate was now in the hands of the white wolf's spirit.

Jesse, knowing about the legend of a white wolf, had always assumed the legend was just another one of the old tales told by the elderly warriors of the tribe as they gathered in a circle around a roaring bonfire. The stories were filled with mystery and excitement that were always entertaining to the youngsters as they listened in awe. But as Jesse grew older, and he was plagued with overwhelmingly strange nightmares, he began to question the validity of *this* tale.

Jesse quickly turned away from the gruesome scene of the war-torn valley where the bodies lay and walked back to the soldiers just as the burial detail returned, closely followed by the other two, missing scouts. And with them was a little Lakota girl, about seven or eight years old, strapped to Corporal Evans' saddle.

"What's with the little kid?" asked Captain Burns.

"This here is no *kid*, Cap'n. She's a miniature wildcat, sir. It took both of us to get her on the dang horse. She kicks and bites worse than any wild animal I ever tackled with. Look here, she has scratched me all over," complained Corporal Evans.

"We found her hidin' inside a wolf den in the bush. There were big animal tracks all around the den as if the creature was protectin' her, Cap'n," spoke up Corporal Chase. "I reached my hand inside the opening and grabbed her. It was pitch dark in the hole. Something growled at me and alls, I could see was this huge silhouette with a pair of blue shiny eyes starin' me in the face. It looked like a big alpha wolf; that's my guess. I've seen many of them before, but never that big."

"We saw it more clearly when it came out; this one was whiter than snow. When it started after us, we got the hell outa' there as fast as we could. I never seen anything like it before," blurted Corporal Evans.

A cold chill ran down Jesse's spine. "A *white* wolf, eh?"

"Like I said, Cap'n. Whiter than this here snow! I never saw one like it before."

"Never!" chorused Corporal Chase.

"Bring her along! We'll take her back to the army post," stated Captain Burns. Just as the soldiers bundled up for the long ride home, Tomas approached his captain. The child continued to struggle in Corporal Evans' arms. "If it pleases you, Cap'n, I can take the child with *me*," spoke up Tomas.

"Thank you, Corporal Good Shield. I'm sure Corporal Evans wouldn't mind a bit. When we get back to Fort Wilderness, we'll put the kid in the next auction where, hopefully, a Lakota or Cheyenne family will take her in and raise her as their own."

Jesse glanced up as heavy dark clouds quickly formed above him. "We're about done here so we should start to head back home as soon as possible. Corporal Davis, sound the bugle to alert the men to get ready to move out. We'll ride till nightfall, then make camp; we should arrive at the fort by late tomorrow afternoon if we don't run into any more trouble."

Jesse glanced up at the sky again as a gust of wind pushed at his back; he didn't know which would be worst, facing an unpredictable Norther or having to fight off a war party of savages. In the distance, a wolf occasionally howled, making the jittery group of soldiers aware of its presence as they rode.

The soldiers got a break from the weather as the clouds rolled out to the west. At nightfall, the weary outfit had traveled about twelve miles before finding a suitable place to set up camp. After the horses were attended to, a late evening mess was served, but the bugler sounded taps at nine as usual and everyone turned in for the night. Everyone except the posted guards and Jesse.

He had trouble falling asleep again. He stepped outside his tent and listened. The cool damp air turned into a heavy fog and wrapped him in its silent blanket. The darkness was strangely hushed; a wolf occasionally howled in the distance. That was the only sound except for the hissing of the dying fire.

He looked out over the land, a land that was not his; he suddenly felt alien, an intruder, and the land had kept its distance from him. The white man didn't own the land. The Comanche thought they did and fought for it. They were a breed that everyone feared the most. They rode at night by the light of a Comanche moon as they believed it was bad medicine to start out on a raid in the daytime and the silent, bronze-colored ghosts usually attacked at early dawn. And it was the *dawn*, at the break of daylight, that Jesse disliked the most.

Jesse felt his muscles tighten once more and a cold bone-chilling wind sent him back inside the tent. Sleep did not come at once, his mind still troubled by what he had seen that day. Even though he had seen it many times before, it still bothered him, bringing back memories of his past that he so desperately tried to forget.

His body became rigid, remaining unmovable as he hid in the confined space; his liquid blue eyes became slits that gleamed in the darkness, like the eyes of an animal. A feral smell filled the tent; a wolf's howl pierced the night air. And Jesse just *waited!* He knew what was coming.

It was well after dawn when Jesse finally drifted off to sleep, while sometime in the night, a creature had meandered between the tents, leaving large paw prints in the snow. But no one had seen anything, not even the guards and no one knew where the creature had come from.

As they traveled back to Fort Wilderness, Jesse felt that he was being watched. Several times during their trek home, he nervously turned in his saddle and glanced over his shoulder, but he saw no one, other than his troops. He glanced upward and watched a lone eagle circle above them, soaring through the ominous clouds. The dead quiet of winter lay everywhere. The sky lowered even further and lightning flashed periodically, a warning that a squall was blowing in from the north.

On the trail, a line of dark shadows continued to pump the ground as the soldiers rode faster to beat the oncoming storm. The constant cold wind growled at them, making strange and haunting sounds that ran shivers down Jesse's spine, and in the distance, a piercing howl of a wolf seemed to follow them all the way back to the fort. He knew it was the white wolf.

When they finally reached the fort, the young Lakota girl was locked in one of the cabins for the night, fearing that she would try to run away. Food on a tray and blankets were brought to the girl's cabin, pushed just inside the door before it was locked again.

During the night, Captain Burns was awakened twice by barking dogs. In the morning there were tracks in the freshly fallen snow all around the cabin. Big wolf tracks! Jesse checked on the girl and she just scowled at him from the corner of the room. She looked like a caged animal huddled under the blanket that he had given her last night. She looked so small and helpless.

Outside, nearly one hundred mountain men and trappers, as well as Indians from different tribes, had begun arriving at the fort since early dawn for the yearly sale and auction. Most of them milled around the tent that served as a tavern where shots of whiskey that tasted of gunpowder and rattlesnake heads were sold for one silver dollar.

Tepees and covered wagons quickly spread out on the outskirts of the fort gates and more were still coming. It was the only location for several hundred miles where pelts were bought and sold and one could actually spend a year's wages on wares, liquor, and gambling, or other *diversions* amid a noisy carnival-like atmosphere. Differences were temporarily set aside between the whites and the Indians for the sake of business, although an occasional fistfight had been known to break out among them in the past.

Captain Burns walked toward the auction tent that had 'standing room only' inside. He was greeted by a burly man leading a broken-spirited Cheyenne woman away on a leash. Another captive was dragged to the stump that served as an auction block. Her hands were bound in chains and she was kicking so fiercely that it took three big, burly mountain men to get her to the stump.

"Here we have a young Lakota girl," the auctioneer announced as he circled the stump like a cock rooster. "Says her name is *Meadowlark,* but you can call her anything you like. She's very young but soon she'll be able to cook, clean and sew and she's pleasant and agreeable." Meadowlark kicked him in the shins, then spit in his face and swore at him in Lakota.

"Looks like love at first sight," someone yelled out as the men standing around guffawed. Their leering, greedy eyes were bloodshot from the liquor; their beards were caked in mud and food drippings. Gobs of tobacco juice and yellow saliva dribbled from the corner of their mouths. Their long greasy hair hadn't seen a comb in months and they smelled like they hadn't had a bath in more than a year.

The auctioneer planted his hand on the young girl's tiny behind suggestively.

"Don't let this little Lakota bitch get away. It gits awful cold in the mountains, and this little one's sittin' on a furnace. Who'll start the bidding with two bits?"

Captain Burns saw all this. And he saw the sadness in the little girl's eyes. At such a young, tender age, she seemed already broken too, just like that older Cheyenne woman who was sold earlier. Something moved his heart in a way that cut through all the roughness he had learned in his thirty-seven years of living here in the wilderness.

He reached into his pocket and dropped two gold coins on the stump.

"Sold to our own Captain Burns! *Two hundred dollars*!" bellowed the auctioneer as he attempted to curtail the suggestive sneer that suddenly spread across his ugly face.

Part Two

Ten Years Later—In the Month of the White Frosty Grass, 1895

Kaboom! The shot echoed through the hills for miles, then faded, long after the bullet seared through the flesh of the unsuspecting doe. When she fell to the ground, the newborn fawn suckling from her in the long grass almost got trampled on, its survival now in jeopardy. Nearby, a majestic, ten-point buck suddenly turned tail and ran, leaving the fawn to fend for itself.

An eerie purple mist crept over the land like an evil shadow moving with a relentless purpose. The ripping wind bent the long grasses in anger as a soaring eagle wheeled westward until it became a mere dot amidst mottled clouds. On a hilltop overlooking the scene, the silhouette of a large white wolf was etched against the darkened sky. His piercing howl broke the silence. Then there was nothing as the world suddenly went black.

Meadowlark suddenly awoke; she had this same dream many times before during the last few months, ever since she had learned that she was going to have a baby, Jesse's baby. She told him, "I am not one person inside of me now."

And she could not forget what he had said to her just last night. "Don't worry, I will take care of the problem and no one will ever know about this. Everything will be the same as before, you will see."

Those words shot an unexpected pain through her. She stared numbly at him while trying to understand their meaning, trying to absorb what he was telling her. Meadowlark had seen the look in his eyes, heard the granite coldness in his voice as he stood close to her, like a frozen ocean separating their two bodies. She suddenly felt so alone.

When he left, that coldness remained, filling her darkened room and leaving her chilled. She had heard rumors about Jesse and other women that had gotten pregnant while working in his house but she had refused to believe them. The women had disappeared and, in his report, he stated each time that they had gone back to their people. And there was never any mention of babies being born to these women in his reports. Jesse's words kept repeating in her head and she suddenly feared for her unborn child.

After he left her room last night, she made the decision to leave first thing in the morning; even though she had found so much happiness in being with him, and even though she would always love him with all her heart. And in all the years that they had been together, she truly believed that he had loved *her* also. But after what he said, she now had doubts; she thought she could be in grave danger if the rumors were really true.

A woman, soon to give birth, walking alone in unsettled territory and the Lakota village being about a two-day ride on horseback, Meadowlark hoped that she hadn't waited too long as she had many white man's miles to walk before reaching her destination. And as this was October, there was also the danger of 'Winter Man' unexpectantly making an early appearance.

Before anyone awoke, Meadowlark quickly dressed in a doeskin skirt and an oversized, blue flannel shirt with a belt that held a small but lethal, sheathed knife. Then she slid into her warm white capote lined with buffalo hide and to that, she added the red silk scarf with colorful beaded fringes, a special sixteenth birthday gift from Jesse last year.

She filled a doeskin pouch with strips of buffalo jerky, a sack of coffee beans, a packet of sugar, a steel striker and flint, a small cooking pot, and a tin cup. She packed her knee-high winter moccasins in case it snowed and then she rolled a camouflage-colored, canvas ground-cloth to keep out the moisture and placed everything inside. She secured the backpack with a rope, hoping her 'survival kit' wasn't going to be too heavy for her to carry. At the last minute, she grabbed her fur-lined mittens before walking out the door.

She passed through the massive wooden gates of Fort Wilderness that protected the many lodges where the soldiers lived with their families. Lazy wisps of smoke curled through the nippy air from the wood-starved chimneys and even at early dawn, the lodges looked so welcoming. But she was never welcomed in any of them; she was never welcomed anywhere.

Tears welled up in her eyes as she thought of the families living there, all the laughing children. Her unborn child would never know what that family environment was like if she stayed *here*. Her baby would never have a father or even a last name. She had to leave. Her people *would* welcome her, *and* her baby, even if it was a white man's baby.

She wiped away the tears and her proud chin jutted out in defiance. After all, she was the granddaughter of a great medicine man who was the keeper of the sacred arrows and the sacred medicine hat, an honor only designated to a very elite warrior in the Lakota tribe. The sudden movement in her stomach was all the reassurance she needed as she walked eastward knowing that now, with every step she took, she was that much closer to her destination. To *her* family!

Captain Jesse Burns stood on the wooden steps just outside his headquarters office at Fort Wilderness, where he had stood so many times before. He had just finished writing his report and was surprised to see how late it had become. It was almost the end of the day and the orange glow from the sinking sun enhanced the silver flecks in his long blonde hair; he looked handsome, almost distinguished-looking as he kept staring blankly at the three small boys playing a game of marbles in the dust.

At forty-one, he had aged well but those years had not been easy for him. He stood six feet four inches tall and carried one hundred and eighty-five pounds of nicely distributed rock-hard muscle.

Oddly though, it wasn't his trim, uniformed body or that rare smile revealing perfectly even white teeth that warranted a second look. It was his eyes, those dominating blue eyes thickly fringed with long dark lashes; eyes that were sometimes like warm pools of deep blue water reflecting in the sunlight while at other times, they were like chunks of ice bouncing off that same lake, now frozen and cold. Eyes that quickly changed from a liquid blue to a murky gray whenever he got angry, the hard, penetrating stare that almost seemed unnatural and animal-like.

It was a telltale sign to stop messing with this man before it was too late.

Outwardly, Jesse always seemed relaxed and very confident but inside, he was often restless, even agitated. And sometimes the built-up tension he felt quite often pulled rank on him. However, over the years, he had learned to curtail this explosive pressure that wanted to be released from inside his body. His job was so demanding, always challenging his proficiency while at the same time, as a leader, also preserving the high level of respect and admiration that was shown to him every day by his men.

Thus, he had to stay strong, sometimes unfeeling, in front of them. His mission as captain of the fort was to protect the people from Indian raids and to capture troublemakers caught off the reservations, but chasing phantoms in an empty, lawless country was one hell of a way to make a living.

Trying to keep peace among an Indian and a white man was a grueling task as neither party didn't seem to agree on anything, especially ownership of the precious land. When dealing with the Indians, he either had to butcher them or civilize them, during the undaunting task of getting them to accept the white man's way.

Jesse, realizing that he was hungry when he saw the yellow lights gleaming in the mess hall, locked up and walked the short distance to his house. A cold, menacing darkness had fallen from the moonless sky; even the stars were buried behind it. The smell of snow was in the air and Jesse knew that before long, the army would have something more pressing to worry about than keeping the peace, something that only Mother Nature had control of.

He was familiar with the winters here, temperatures so cold that a soldier could freeze to his saddle before he even realizes it, and the winds so powerful that it could suck the air right out of his lungs. Jesse had learned over the years to cope with the frigid temperatures, but the tormenting wind had always been his enemy. And this night was no exception; the wind was already whipping through the tree branches, racing toward him as he crossed the shadowed parade grounds.

Jesse bundled up and quickened his pace as his body pushed forward onto frosted grass, now fighting with driving gusts of cold wind that seemed to suddenly blow in from nowhere. He was almost home. Home to the house that he shared with his wife, Abigail. He was fond of Abigail, but he wanted Meadowlark.

After eating his supper, Jesse retreated to the parlor and sat in his favorite overstuffed armchair situated by a window overlooking the backyard, as he did every night. He picked up his favorite book that sat on the table beside him, but his restless mind wouldn't stay focused on *Moby Dick* tonight, so he flipped through the pages of a magazine, killing time.

Across from him, Abigail primly sat on the couch, her sewing basket lay open on her lap. She wore a long cotton dress stiff with starch and her soft brown hair was neatly pulled back in a bun. Abigail was not a *homely* woman; she was just plain and matronly. And she was every inch a lady, even in the privacy of her own parlor.

Jesse anxiously waited for the mantel clock to chime on the hour. At precisely seven o'clock, Meadowlark's angelic voice drifted across the garden and floated through the open window beside him. His evening *lullaby*! He lowered the magazine that he was browsing through and leaned his head back, closed his eyes, and managed to tune out Abigail's incessant talking. The beautiful music was relaxing him, as usual.

As Abigail chatted on, Jesse occasionally made appropriate responses to give the impression that he had been listening to her. But

Abigail sensed his disinterest and raised her voice when she complained about the dogs that had kept her awake again last night, thus catching Jesse off guard.

He felt guilty for his own lack of interest, knowing that Abigail's idle conversation was her way of making contact in another futile attempt to reach out to him. Jesse had never been able to talk to her about anything that really mattered, and with each passing year, the gap that formed between them had widened.

Abigail was a dutiful wife, a respectable army wife who was married to a very romantic soldier with needs, but it wasn't her fault that she had married the wrong man, that those needs had never been fulfilled. They never really got to know each other and after the death of their only child, a son, in the early years of their marriage, something had died within Abigail.

Afterward, although she seldom refused him, her lovemaking seemed virginal, reserved. She seemed unyielding, but *afraid*. Ever since that day, there was no spark in their marriage and Jesse could never lose himself in her. And he had not been an ideal husband to her, even though he *was* fond of her. Abigail had never been a passionate woman but he knew she did love him in her own way; for some men that might have been enough, but for Jesse, it was never enough.

When the serenade ended, Jesse picked up the magazine again but momentarily tossed it aside; reading was of no use, as he became very restless. Abigail was still at him about the barking dogs waking her up each night. He stood up and announced that he was going to take a walk before he turned in. "Go on to bed, Abigail. I'll see what I can do about the dogs."

"You will be careful, dear," she responded sadly. She had pushed him away from her yet again.

"I'll be fine. Don't wait up."

"Don't be too long. You need your rest, dear," she replied.

In a sharper voice, he retorted, "Abigail, *go* to bed!"

He put on his coat and quickly left the house. The cool night air hit his face as he welcomed the darkness, the isolation. All six dogs of Fort Wilderness found him, wagging their burr-clogged tails. Jesse bent down to pet them but they growled and showed their long white fangs; his strange smell always seemed to repel them at first whenever he approached them.

However, they eventually responded to his friendly, familiar voice and soft touch. He walked on as the dogs quietly paced around him while maintaining a safe distance away from him. The night watchman, who was accustomed to Jesse's nightly walks whenever he had trouble falling asleep, saw his captain and saluted.

An hour had passed and he knew Abigail had finally gone to bed after glancing up at her darkened window just above him. He took a deep breath of fresh air and bid the dogs goodnight before he went inside. He returned to his chair with a glass and a bottle of whiskey in his hands; he didn't want to get drunk but there was something wild inside him tonight, something dark and deeply buried that kept trying to surface. The whiskey helped him to forget, stifled the memories by pushing them to the back of his troubled mind.

Jesse replaced the half-empty bottle, turned down the wick on the oil lamp, and went upstairs to Meadowlark's room. He opened her door, then quietly closed it behind him while taking a deep exhalation of relief. The fragrant scent of gardenias filled the small room. He quickly undressed and climbed into her warm bed, her nakedness caressing his eager body. He took her in his arms and kissed her ardently.

"What took you so long?" she purred. "I was afraid you were not coming."

Her long black hair tumbled over her bare shoulders and her skin shone like gold in the moonlight. Jesse felt more at ease with her than he had ever felt with Abigail. There was no need for conversation as she dug her nails into his back and pulled him down. She pressed her body to his and began to stroke him with warm fingers, her fast breathing heated in his ear. He took her gently but passionately at first, then, with urgent releases of pent-up emotions, they came together savagely.

Jesse held her in his arms for a long time afterward until she fell asleep. He felt temporarily at peace. No more pain. No more shadows or *uncertainties*. He always felt this way after their lovemaking. He had sex with other women, but it had never left him feeling this way.

He loved this woman. She made him feel young again, so alive. He put his clothes back on in the dark and quietly went to his own room, still feeling the peace within him like it was a tangible thing.

He slipped between the cold blankets and tried to fall asleep. But sleep never came right away. The peaceful feeling slowly dissipated. A strong feral whiff, a hint of something bad or evil, suddenly filled his room and the sound of a wolf's howl set off the barking dogs who now gathered just below his darkened window, *waiting*.

Jesse lay *hidden* in his bed, staring at nothing until—his eyes became blue slits, gleaming in the darkness. He also *waited*. He knew what was going to happen, *again*. When the sun filtered through his window hours later, Jesse finally fell into a deep sleep.

Before dawn of the following day, Meadowlark followed the rutted wagon-wheel road that wound a snaked trail between rows of northern pines on one side and a fast-flowing river on the other. Her plan was to follow the river until it forked in a southerly direction toward the hills. Tomas Good Shield often spoke of the Lakota tribe and told her how to get to his family's home.

"You are Lakota, and it is your home also," he expressed with kindness, as he truly cared for the young girl. Just two years ago, when they had gone on one of their many horseback rides together, he pointed out the fork in the road which she should take if ever she went there. She liked Tomas, he was always watching out for her, just like an older brother would have done.

When the sun finally rose, Meadowlark thanked it for its warmth and asked it to give her another good day as she approached the amber-glowing hills that had previously cast long dark shadows across the roadway that she had been following. She climbed the steep bluff, feeling winded by the effort, and looked below. She inhaled fresh cool air into her lungs. She knew the air and it was a good air; it tasted sweet and dry this morning, no smell of snow.

She scanned the sky, looking for clouds and it was clear, but she knew from experience, that the weather could quickly change. She glanced behind her; no one was following her. Not that Jesse would come after her anyway after what he said when she told him about the baby. By her leaving, he probably thought the problem would be solved for him.

However, just in case, she had been very careful about not leaving a trail, as she was aware that Jesse was a good tracker, almost as good as his best scout. And his best scout, Tomas Good Shield, had a reputation of being one of the best trackers in the northern territory, often sought after by others who offered to pay a small fortune for his services. But he had always refused; he remained loyal to Jesse and the army and was *proud* to be called Corporal Good Shield by his peers.

Meadowlark worried about whether she was doing the right thing by leaving, as she thought about Jesse often. She still loved him and missed him terribly. She missed his long golden hair that curled on his neck, his hard, blue eyes that softened when he made love to her, his lop-sided smile and flirty laughter when he teased her, and most of all, his tenderness, a trait that wasn't common among the few white men she had met in the fort and also among the Lakota warriors that she could vaguely remember when she was so very young.

She had accepted the fact that he would never be like her people, that he followed the road of the white man and would never leave his white woman. But was she willing to give up what little she had for the sake of a child? Was she willing to *give up* her child? When she felt a hard kick in her abdomen, Meadowlark *knew* she was doing the right thing.

All day, she walked toward her people, drawn by a magical compass instilled in her mind. The land turned from green to brownish-gold as the sun lowered in the west and the air became noticeably cooler on her face. She vigilantly eyed the sky; a flock of Canada geese flew overhead in a vee formation, hurriedly heading south. She noticed that all the birds of summer had already left and even the small creatures that usually scuttled about had also disappeared.

She walked on dormant land, a place that reluctantly surrendered to nature's command when most living things either stored food or burrowed, preparing for a long winter's sleep. However, there were coyotes and wolves still stalking and the deer and elk were still grazing, but all would soon be in a 'locked room' in the frozen north when the Cold Maker arrives, a predator that could kill with just his breath.

The one thing Meadowlark dreaded most was a winter storm and it wasn't uncommon for a Norther to strike this early in the year, whereas the temperature could suddenly drop to below freezing. And blizzard-like windstorms could cause poor visibility and deep drifts of snow. If the cold didn't kill her, then plodding through deep snowdrifts would, especially in her condition. But Meadowlark wasn't as soft as the white man; she didn't need the things that they needed to survive.

After she had walked most of the day, only her feet complained. She didn't need as much to eat either, although the little one inside her was letting her know of *his* hunger by kicking up his own form of complaint. Wrapping the white capote tightly around her enlarged body and retying the red scarf around her neck to keep out the penetrating wind, she briskly kept walking toward her people.

Tomas took one look at Jesse the next morning and he could tell immediately that he hadn't got much sleep again. "Another nightmare?" he asked Jesse in a concerned tone.

Tomas cared about Jesse and he was fearful about his health. He didn't know how much longer his friend would be able to handle all the responsibilities that he had to deal with on a daily basis. Tomas watched, as Jesse would not yield to his tiredness; he wrestled with the day, hoping it would end soon.

Jesse had reports to complete and his workload lagged; he kept putting them off. It didn't help that the day was raw and gray, just like Jesse's mood. Even the men noticed a difference in him. Tomas felt that it was time to try and help his friend. When they were alone, he looked into his gaunt face and said, "Jesse, I think it is time for us to take a little trip; you need to get away from here, even if it is just for a short while."

Tomas took Jesse to the Lakota village to meet with his uncle, Gray Owl. He was a renowned medicine man and Tomas knew that if *anyone* could help Jesse, it would be him. It was a two-day ride on horseback; they never saw Meadowlark along the way because she detoured into the hills and followed a different route on foot.

When Tomas and Jesse got there, they were warmly greeted by Tomas' people. There was nothing so lovely as the circle of conical tepees that formed a Lakota camp, especially at night. A fire burning in a pit inside each 'tapered lantern' made the canvas glow with a warm golden hue while outside, a thin trail of white smoke snaked upwards, escaping toward the darkened sky from the hole in the center where all the tent poles came together.

On the inside walls of most of the lodgings, brightly painted scenes of courage and triumph were painted, depicting many of their buffalo hunts while on the outside, racks of sliced buffalo meat prepared by the women earlier in the day were drying. The women of the tribe did most of the work while the men kept busy hunting, fishing or just sitting around the main bonfire telling stories and entertaining the young children.

The men were warriors, strong and fearless, ready to die while fighting to protect their families. Lakota braves were the fiercest hunters and the most unrelenting of enemies; the name was always spoken with a mixture of dread and respect.

One of those infamous warriors, now an old man with a bulbous, beak-like nose and wrinkly weathered skin that looked like a well-worn, scarred moccasin was among them. His knowing eyes, even though heavily clouded over with cataracts, were blurred with water weeping from the bright sunshine. The stooped man was waiting outside of his tepee, anticipating the arrival of his favorite nephew and the white soldier-man, the one who Tomas had discussed with him on numerous occasions in the past.

The tight bond between the uncle and his nephew was undeniable. The medicine man welcomed their visit and there was a special feast prepared for them. "Tomorrow, we will smoke the peace pipe and afterward, we will talk. But tonight, we will celebrate," stated Gray Owl in broken English.

Throughout the night, a pair of haunting blue eyes in the face of the yellow-haired *wasicun* plagued Gray Owl, causing him to have a restless sleep.

The next morning, Tomas ushered Jesse into the oval entrance of his uncle's tepee and quickly lowered the canvas flap in order to keep the heat inside. The elderly medicine man sat on a thick buffalo hide hugging the warm fire that his woman had built earlier. Two Faces in the Wind had also prepared a nourishing breakfast of buffalo stew and cornmeal bread, especially for their guests.

Jesse thoroughly enjoyed the hearty meal and politely thanked Two Faces before she left the men alone. He was surprised that she seemed to understand the white man's language so well.

Gray Owl reached over to his left and produced a long, beautifully-carved wooden pipe and stuffed it with a greenish-brown 'tobacco'. The opium smell was very strong and soon filled the tepee. He took a puff, then handed the pipe to Tomas, who, in turn, handed it over to Jesse, going counter-clockwise around the circle they had formed. Jesse coughed a few times and the other two laughed at him.

When Gray Owl glanced over at Tomas with a meaningful gesture, Tomas stood up and also left the tepee, informing them that he was going to go and see his father and mother.

"Now we can talk!" stated the old man as he handed the pipe back to Jesse one more time. Jesse started to feel light-headed and the heat inside the confined space was bothering him. Sweat broke out on his forehead and then across his upper lip; his head was swimming in circles, his body weightless. He thought he was floating in a bottomless river and the rippling water gently flowed over his face. He closed his eyes, no longer able to focus.

He told Gray Owl about his nightmares and how he came to have them ever since he ate the white wolf. He told him about his childhood, his family, and even about the Comanche attack when he was just a young boy. He told him about the ghost of his father and how he always stole his son's socks in the night. Jesse also confessed to the killing of his off springs because of another reoccurring dream he had about the young man dressed in buckskin sprawled on top of him, someone who looked just like himself, a 'mirror image', holding a knife to his throat.

He spoke of the constant howling of the wolf, the feral smell, and the wind, how it irritated him; he told him about Abigail and the death of his first-born child, a son. He also told the old man about his affair with Meadowlark. Gray Owl listened; he never said a word until after Jesse quit talking.

Finally, Gray Owl spoke, "Last night, I had a vision." He shut his eyes and lowered his head and began talking.

There was a big wolf, its fur flocked with white. As big as a man! It wore a single eagle feather behind one ear. There was the wind, then a loud explosion; the wolf fell, uttering a piercing howl as it hit the ground. A crimson stain covered the snow and the wolf changed into a man, a soldier. There was a baby boy, born the color of white but with the heart of a Lakota warrior. He was guided by the wind and lived by the spirit of the White Wolf. A woman was trilling her death-song.

Out of the mists stepped a lone brave carrying a war lance with a white flag fluttering in the wind. The warrior was pale, transparent, like a spirit. The soldier tried to reach the warrior but thick mud stuck to his boots and held him back. He called out but the warrior did not understand his words. A cloud of blue-feathered birds flew down from the sky and circled behind the lone warrior and attacked him. Blood spattered his buckskins and he fell in the snow.

A shadowed spirit-angel came up to him and touched his shoulder and the birds flew away, just as the soldier's spirit flew out of his mouth and his clothes emptied on the ground. The soldier was suddenly freed and only the trilling of the woman's death-song filled the air.

Gray Owl opened his eyes and raised up his head, finally speaking, "It is a hard path that you walk, my friend. But you have always been watched by the wolf's spirit, the spirit who had forgiven the boy of fourteen summers so long ago. You have the spirit of the wolf inside you; you are living in both worlds, making your power stronger. But you wrestle with that power, as a man, and as a spirit."

"Because of your mother's blood in you, you are also a warrior. And when you ride, you ride as a warrior. But sometimes a warrior rides alone upon his horse. Your path leads down a dark, bumpy trail. When you finally come to a ridge; you top that ridge, only to see nothing but another ridge yet to climb. You sometimes envy the freedom of the warrior's spirit trapped inside of you, but feel you must always follow the white man's road."

"So, when the time comes when you stop thinking like the white man, you will ride like the warrior inside you by keeping your back to the hostile wind. And someday, the spirit will become a friend, maybe not to you, but to your off springs. The spirit will dwell inside of *them* also, choosing whom it will serve, gaining more strength, and having the power to transform from spirit to animal or human at any given time. The wolf spirit is persistent. It never gives up. Until the spirit is summoned back to its own world."

The wise old man struggled to stand up and when he did, he added, "I walk with a bent backbone and very soon my time on this earth will be at an end, but I hope to live long enough to see what the spirits have got planned for you. If not, then I will see you in the spirit world in the big sky. And now, I am very tired. Go with peace, my friend."

The meeting was over.

That afternoon, Jesse and Tomas returned to Fort Wilderness. Strangely, the wind was *not* at Jesse's back.

When the sun slipped below the horizon and the landscape's golden-orange hue faded to indigo, Meadowlark, tiring finally, started to watch for a place to stop for the night. She had been traveling over moderately rough terrain but the landscape had been so stunningly beautiful, with blazing sheets of gold flickering across the mountains on one side and a protective canopy of trees framing the gently flowing river on the other.

The changing colors alone left her in awe, causing her to lose track of time. Her backpack had been getting heavier and her joints felt spongy, bluntly traumatized. Thirty minutes had elapsed before she found a suitable place to camp, a hollow in a wind-sculpted rock just a short distance from the riverbank and partially concealed from the wind by young pine trees.

She checked out the area, making sure it was devoid of hidden evils, like foxholes and snake pits, but she found none. Her body didn't have to remind her of the immense hunger she felt. A ration of buffalo jerky and a tiny cup of sweetened broth brewed from a few of her coffee beans eased the pains in her stomach.

As color bled from the earth, a black curtain fell down from the sky. The tall, shadowed pines that surrounded her, now stood invisible, their reaching branches only ghosts that kept whispering to her over the howl of the wind.

She missed Jesse. She knew she would never hear his laughter or feel the warmth of his body against hers while lying in his arms. She knew she would never have the opportunity to proudly present him to her people. She knew she would never *see* him again.

"Did I make a big mistake by leaving him?" she asked the trees. In response, the wind howled back at her by swooshing through their branches in exasperation.

She sat subdued in the darkness for quite a while, her back leaning against the hollow of the big rock, seeking wisdom. Today she had walked the land and the world seemed to grow larger with each step, making her feel like she had accomplished nothing. She was beginning to think that her 'magic compass' was leading her on an endless journey.

Beyond her campsite, wind kept shivering through the long-needled pines, and above her, the overcast clouds had slid away, going south like everything else. Winter stars, sparkling harder and whiter and much larger than summer stars, dimpled the sky, a sure sign of impending snow. Night noises made her jittery. She studied everything around her with care, sensing that she was not alone, that something was lurking beyond her camp. *Watching* her!

She knew she would have to be careful now; a young woman traveling alone was prey to both man and animal in this wild, rough, mountain country.

Meadowlark unrolled the canvas ground cover and slid inside, covering her ears to the forlorn wailing of a lone wolf in the distance. In the middle of the night, something woke her and she thought she heard the soft pad-pad-padding sound crunching in the snow near her. But she never heard it again. Was it a dream, maybe her imagination?

She listened, but still, she heard nothing, only the crackling of logs popping and hissing as they slowly disintegrated inside the campfire. And when the small fire eventually burned itself out, the tightly wrapped *cocoon* felt relatively warm and safe throughout the rest of the night.

Gone! Jesse stood outside the open door of Meadowlark's bedroom three days later. She was not there. Last night at seven o'clock sharp, after returning from the Lakota village, he had impatiently waited for his 'nightly lullaby' to drift through his open window from the garden below, and at eight-thirty, he finally stalked off to bed. But he couldn't sleep.

He didn't know when she had left, but he knew *why*. His words must have been too harsh. He stood in the parlor, feeling lost. *Empty!* He found the house smaller now, almost barren and hollow. Meadowlark had brought life into his home, something *female* to the place, something Abigail wasn't able to do. Now his young mistress was gone, and it hurt.

In the early morning, Jesse left the house and headed toward his favorite place by the riverbank so he could think more clearly. Whenever he had a problem, this was his sanctuary. He crashed through the dormant brush and sat on a dead log near the river's edge. He felt so alone, sealed off from everyone here. The hurrying river helped him think. Life was like this river, unstoppable. All the restless water coming from somewhere and rushing to nowhere.

He watched a fallen leaf ride the current, twisting and turning in the frigid water while struggling to stay afloat. He was like that rebellious leaf, but he could no longer stay afloat; now he was drowning. And Meadowlark was like the bold young sparrow that danced around his feet, only she had been *caged* since she was a little girl, always beating that cage so she could escape and fly free. He suddenly realized that he too, had always felt *caged* and that he also wanted to fly free like that sparrow.

Jesse remembered the first time he'd seen her ten years ago. She was a pretty child, small and dainty. But she never laughed and giggled like the other girls her age. She always stood proud, sort of arrogant, and alone. She was like an elusive, spotted fawn, so loving. So unsuspecting and innocent! But it was the chiseled features of her face and her honeyed flesh that kindled something inside him.

When she reached womanhood with the proper swelling of her breasts and distinct curves of her hips under a slim doeskin dress, eyes hungrily focused on her wherever she went in the fort. He became jealous and moved her from Tomas' cabin which also housed his wife and their four little 'rug rats', to his house to help Abigail; but the real reason being he wanted to keep a closer watch over her.

Over the years, he had enjoyed the sound of her angelic voice; it was like the twilight song of a bird. That was the last thing he wanted to hear every night before he slept. And she was the last thing he wanted to touch. Oh, the feel of her warm skin when he first went to her room! The velvet of her belly held against him filled him with lust. And after they made love, he felt a powerful strength return to his body, as if something had renewed inside him each time; it made him feel younger and more alive.

She seemed to anchor his restless life, made him feel like a *man*. Something Abigail could never do. He loved Meadowlark back then and he loves her even more now. Jesse thought that he had formed a special bond with Meadowlark; how, over the years, they had become one in both spirit and soul, even though their lifestyles and beliefs were so different.

He would go after her and find her. He would plead, even beg her, to come back home. He felt the anger rising in him, as dark and hard as cold granite. He wanted her back and he was going to bring back his young mistress first thing tomorrow. But tonight, he was going to get stinkin' drunk to drown his sorrows.

On the second night, Meadowlark didn't sleep well. She slid into her 'cocoon' bed as usual and because it was much colder than the previous night, she moved her bed closer to the fire and tucked her head inside the ground cover to stay warm. Tomas had always warned her about not breathing inside her sleeping bag as moisture would build up, and if it was cold enough, she could freeze to death.

So, she tried not to breathe, even occasionally holding her breath for short periods at a time or until her lung capacity gave in. She became light-headed. Something wasn't right. Darkness inside was absolute, the air so thick. Pressing down on her skin, pushing her deeper inside the crushing blindness. The air seemed so *hard*, pushing down on top of her while also pushing up from the earth below her, enclosing her. Suffocating her.

Her chest felt heavy like something was sitting on top of her, squeezing her lungs. Choking her! Her nostrils were closing; she could no longer breathe. Her eyes flew open, panic-stricken. In total darkness!

Her arms were pinned to her sides and she couldn't feel her legs. Muscles started to cramp as terror overcame her. She squirmed like a prenatal larva, fighting for space inside the cocoon in order to push herself out. Claustrophobia! She climbed out of her bed, waiting for the panic attack to subside, and decided she had to make other sleeping arrangements.

As it was still quite dark, Meadowlark stoked up the campfire and added more firewood. Using the canvas ground cover, her plans were to make a small tepee. She erected a tripod using strong branches as poles and placed the canvas cover over the homemade A-frame. Before she climbed inside, she tested it for strength and it passed the test of endurance to her satisfaction. By the time she was finished, she was exhausted and when the baby kicked in protest, telling her to get some sleep, she didn't argue.

As Meadowlark's body fought sleep, she eventually yielded to a light slumber. But when she had chosen this particular campsite, she had forgotten the first precaution she was to take before she set up any camp, always checking the perimeter.

Coming awake and slithering toward the heat of the fire, a groggy rattlesnake emerged from his pit in the ground and slipped under the base of the tepee, unaware of its sleeping occupant. It slithered along the outside of the blanket covering the docile form. With small beady eyes guiding the predator, it crawled on Meadowlark's blanket, up the side of her leg, along her arm, and finally found an entrance at the fringed edge. At her neck, it slithered inside, exploring new and warmer territory.

At the same time, beyond the walls of the makeshift tent, came the pad of a soft-footed animal. The snow crunched under its weight as it moved around the tent. It stopped! There came a short waffling breath, like that of a creature tasting the air, sniffing the way a bear commonly does when he's scenting danger. The waffling stopped. Meadowlark was sound asleep, even the feel of the creeping snake didn't arouse her as it slithered along her bare skin, stretching out after it found a crevice to lie in directly under her chin.

Outside, sudden and loud clawing erupted on the tent wall, shaking the canvas in and out as the large creature applied pressure with gigantic paws. The light from the full moon illuminated its dark shadow across the outside of the canvas wall. The woven fabric was scored by the sharp claws raking against it. Meadowlark opened her eyes, something awoke her. The waffling began again; then it stopped. She listened, frozen with fear. She waited! It waited! There it was again, the waffling sound. That foul smell! It *reeked!* She saw the huge shadow move across the wall beside her.

Meadowlark threw back the blanket and quickly jumped out of bed just as her *bed partner* slithered out of the tent the same way it had come in, returning back to the safety of its snake pit. She heard the deep growl and then the retreating crunch-crunch in the snow just outside her tent as the huge shadow padded away. Then a deadly silence.

She cautiously peeked outside and sighted the large shadow retreat, only to suddenly disappear among snow-covered trees. The standing *ghosts* with their skeletal branches, similar to arthritic fingers, reached out into the eerie darkness. Shielding the creature! Whatever it had been was gone but sleep was out of the question for Meadowlark after that encounter.

The morning air was very crisp and frosty; three inches of freshly fallen snow covered the ground and the sun hadn't shown its smiling face yet. Meadowlark's fingers quickly grew numb when she tried to relight the campfire with wet branches. Without the ground cover being underneath her last night, she couldn't seem to get warm.

The dampness had penetrated into her body, leaving her muscles stiff and sore; they fought, disobeying her commands. Icy crystalline glistened on her white poncho and on her red scarf. Stinging needles of icy pellets jabbed at her face so she raised her hood. These were poor defenses against the Cold Maker. She would have to hurry and walk faster today because there would be less daylight now that the snow had arrived. And shorter days meant longer nights.

She also had a dream of falling into a deep fissure in the earth when it got dark and no one ever found her, another strange nightmare that left her shaken when she awoke in the night, just before she heard the clawing noises on the tent wall.

When nature called, she took a detour to the 'outhouse', wishing it had a warmer seat instead of the fallen snow-covered log. She bared part of her anatomy to the Cold Maker's frosty kiss to take care of one of the less glamorous moments of one's life. Dawdling in the 'outhouse' was not an issue with Meadowlark; she quickly got the job done. She cleansed her bare hands in the cold snow, then headed back to the campsite, feeling that someone, *or something*, was watching her every movement again.

She stopped momentarily outside the tent, tracing with her mitten-covered fingers, the large claw marks that had scored the canvas wall. She squatted down in search of tracks in the snow; she saw deep paw prints, perhaps a wolf's, a very *large* wolf. And that would explain the howl and the horrible feral smell.

Wolf sightings weren't common; they were a private animal, a quiet, watchful animal. For decades, wolves and humans lived separate lives out here in the wilderness. Usually, it was more common for wolves to see people than for people to see them. *Unless* he was hungry! Smell was the most primitive and strongest of their senses.

Thus, the smell of food must have attracted him to her campsite; what smells that might have been odorless to humans were ten times stronger to a wolf. But with wolves, every meal was served up with the smell of blood; it wasn't as frenzied as the reaction of sharks in water and, unlike sharks, the odor of humans usually sent wolves running in the other direction. And, as a rule, wolves didn't hunt to kill humans. Their taste buds preferred deer or moose, even sheep when they could get them. And as their population was plentiful in this area, humans were not on the wolf's food chain right now.

Meadowlark retraced the path of her visitor, but there were no tracks leading in or out of the campsite, nothing across the unmarked snow. She had seen his shadow as he retreated into the treed area, a phantom floating over the moonlit snow only to suddenly disappear into total darkness. And he had left *no* tracks! It was as if a big flying eagle had scooped him up in its talons and flew off with him. *What kind of creature could travel in such a manner as to not leave any tracks? Very puzzling,* she thought.

She made herself a quick breakfast, hoping to get an early start. When she drank her coffee, the metal cup was so cold, it stung her skin. In the night, Freezing Moon had struck sparks across the thin layer of ice starting to form on the river. The temperature had dropped to -17 degrees Fahrenheit and by the looks of the sky, it was going to go lower. And soon.

Gathering up her few possessions, she proceeded on the journey to be with her people. She headed south, walking briskly to keep warm. She saw no one; the wiser creatures of the earth had stayed in their warm beds this morning.

Again, she thought about the man she left behind and missed him more and more, knowing that every step she took separated them even further. But this is what she had to do. He said he didn't want the baby, and he also told her that he would not leave Abigail. His words shot her with an unexpected pain as she absorbed their true meaning.

She heard a coldness in him that she had never heard before, running deep inside him. And for a second, Meadowlark thought she saw him curl up his upper lip like a mad dog, then make a noise originating from deep within his throat; it sounded similar to that of an angry growl as he stormed out of her room. That was when she decided to leave, and as soon as possible. Before it was too late!

Still walking south, Meadowlark trudged through the snow, her aching muscles protesting and her stomach rumbling with hunger. The baby kicked her furiously with every step she took; he was hungry too. She wasn't sure how long a white man's mile was, but she knew that her moccasins had covered many of them. She had walked so much the soles had worn thin and her feet were bruised.

At about noon, when the hazy sun was highest, she bowed to her hunger and decided to stop and eat something. She enjoyed the red berries she picked earlier that morning, although they left a bitter taste in her mouth. And shortly after eating them, they unsettled her stomach and she suddenly felt ill. Beads of sweat popped out on her forehead; it wasn't long before she threw up. Waves of vomiting left her weak and shaky. She continued on her walk, even though her legs felt like spongy rubber bands sliding inside her worn moccasins.

Concealed by rows of pines to the left of the weary walker, a large shadow limped along, keeping pace but staying hidden. Meadowlark heard the familiar sound of squeaking snow crunching under her moccasins, like that of dry Styrofoam being rubbed together and then crushed. Her sensitive ears picked up on a faint *echo* of crunching snow. She stopped. The echo stopped.

She sniffed the air; it reeked with that fetid smell again. Someone or *something* was watching her! Stalking her! She had this feeling before, on many occasions. Was she just imagining things *because* she was alone in this less inhabited wilderness? Panic stirred up her adrenaline and made her heart race. Fear was a compound of chemicals stirred into a 'cake mix' of human dysfunction that had the ability to make a mind spin out of control, the difference between psychosis and insanity. Yet, it could be controlled by tolerance and strength. And Meadowlark lacked both right now.

She *needed* Jesse. Many miles later, darkness surprised her. Clouds hid the sky and there was no moon to guide her, no direction from the buried stars. She grew weary in the blackness and her stomach still hurt. Her body rebelled as her strength ebbed; she needed shelter, food, and most of all, sleep. She had to find a place to camp, and soon.

She was so cold, her body temperature falling within a few degrees above that of an average corpse. Her keen night vision was failing as a heavy fog wrapped her in a misty blanket. The dark sky seemed to lower, hovering just above her head. She pressed on through the endless tunnel, desperately searching.

A fierce wind pushed her along and it started to snow, a type of slanting, wet snow that quickly became a blizzard as the temperature suddenly dropped more. One of the first symptoms of hypothermia was mental confusion and the second, labored motor control. She plunged forward, gravity controlled the heavy blocks of cement attached to her legs, instructing each one to take their turn interchangeably. Lift up! Then put down! Next! Do it again!

Meadowlark could no longer see; her eyelashes caked in ice and when her eyes watered, they tried to freeze shut. She kept trying to look down at her nose; it looked white and waxy. She took off her mitten to feel it, but she couldn't feel her nose, fearing that it would fall off her face. Now her hand turned white and she quickly put her mitten back on. Her body fought with the wind, struggling to just move forward and she was making no progress as the snow accumulated fast.

At one point, she fell, dropping the satchel of food, her survival kit; the chance of recovering it seemed unimportant to her now. She struggled to get on her feet again. Walking became intolerable, but she kept plunging forward, stumbling through knee-high snowdrifts. Her moccasins were wet; she could no longer feel her toes either. The strain she was putting her body through made her feel guilty; Meadowlark feared for her unborn child.

Pain ripped through her abdomen, but she defiantly kept moving, hoping to generate some warmth in her freezing body. The stinging jabs of ice pellets felt like they were slicing the skin on her face. Tears welled up and slid down her cheeks, leaving trails that quickly froze. She had lost her way but she knew that if she stopped to reassess her whereabouts, she would give up; then she would surely die. She had heard about people wanting to lie down and go to sleep in the snow but she never understood the allure of it until now.

Intermixed with the sighing of the wind was the crunching of snow *behind* her now, following the thin trail of blood oozing from her frozen moccasins. A stealthy movement, keeping pace with her every struggling step. Meadowlark suddenly stopped and listened. She heard nothing, no one. Only the wind! Was the sound she kept hearing just her imagination? Or was the sound *never* there?

With ears swaddled in fleece, brain in fatigue, eyes caked in ice, she had worse perils to deal with at the moment than an overactive imagination of slithery noises and gigantic paw prints that left no tracks. Just fighting to stay upright! That was a main concern, not to mention the trail of blood. She continued to move forward. Until the distinct crack of a twig snapping unraveled her nerves.

"It isn't *nothing*! It's not *fucking nothing*!" she cried out, yelling to the wind. She tried to run in the deep snow, falling, then struggling to pick herself up again as tears fell, freezing in opaque droplets on her cheeks. She was thoughtlessly threshing through a vast thicket of needle-sharp brush. It clawed at her skin, tore her poncho, and whipped her legs and stomach.

Blindly, she kept moving. Until, whatever it was that had kept her moving, fear, will, stubbornness, pride suddenly ground to a stop; she suddenly stepped into *nothing*. She had tumbled over a sharp rocky cliff, somersaulting about sixty feet down until she landed on a snow-covered, gravel bed below.

Nearby, where Meadowlark lay, water murmured and the snow kept falling on her face but strangely, she felt so warm now. She saw Jesse holding her baby in his arms and he was crying, "I'm so sorry, Meadowlark."

There was a strong feral smell again, something *wild* and very close to her. She *remembered* that smell! Then she saw the shining blue eyes of the white wolf, its steamy breath fanning her face as it straddled her upper body. Meadowlark sang her *death*-song.

Jesse awoke, his *swollen* head was throbbing, expanding, and contracting like bellows. He was ravenously thirsty but his tongue felt too thick for his puffy lips and he didn't think it would let him swallow.

And his bloodshot eyeballs doubled every object when he tried to focus. Strong drink had destroyed his body, clogged his senses. He fought to throw off the blankets and tried to stand beside the bed, only to waver for a few minutes, then topple over onto the floor.

The pounding in his head had worsened, jackhammering over a loudspeaker while a wave of dizziness, a bout of gagging, and finally, a tsunami of nausea erupted from his body. He laid in his vomit, doubled up into a fetal position on the hard floor, waiting for death to take away his pain. Only once, when he was just a kid of fourteen years, had he ever been this sick before. After *sampling* moonshine, he thought that he was going to die that day also.

When death didn't overtake him for the *second* time, Jesse lifted his head and tried to focus again, managing to vaguely recognize Tomas and his twin brother standing over him with a smile on their faces.

"Why are both of you smiling? Can't you see, I'm dying here!" Jesse shrieked, the hollering making his head hurt all the more. And then he realized that Tomas never had a twin brother.

"You're not gonna' *die.* You're just hung over, is all." Tomas answered, trying not to laugh at his captain.

"I'm telling you, I'm dying! I can't feel my body and my head is over there someplace! Just bury me on a platform, Injun-style, so the wolves can't eat me. You hear me, Tomas?"

"You shouldn't of drank so much! You look alright to me; actually, that shade of green becomes you, my friend," Tomas answered as he headed out the door. "I'm hungry! If you feel up to it, come join me for breakfast. I'll be in the kitchen cooking up some hash and eggs," he called over his shoulder.

Another wave of nausea hit Jesse at the mention of food, making Tomas chuckle all the more after he closed the bedroom door behind him, leaving Jesse to sleep it off.

Six hours later, Jesse entered Tomas' kitchen. He sat at the table and held his head up with both of his hands as his senses slowly returned from *Hell*, a place that he never wanted to go to again. But reality wasn't much better now that Meadowlark had left him. He felt miserable, not only in body but also in his heart! The body would heal but the heart would not.

"Tomas, there's something I have to do and I will need your help," Jesse quietly remarked while still holding up his head. "First thing tomorrow morning, I'm going to look for Meadowlark."

A streak of gray settled in the southeast, announcing the beginning of an overcast day. Jesse awoke without feeling rested and when he attempted three painstaking times to get dressed, every muscle in his aching body disobeyed him. He hadn't slept much; worry haunted him all night. An animal's instinct deep inside him kept warning him about time being so precious. And his internal clock loudly ticked away at every second, the repetitious bang hammering at his head until he thought he was going to throw up all over again. He was exhausted, but a thrusting force seemed to be driving him now.

Tomas was already mounted up, eager to get started. He didn't sleep well either. He glanced up at the unsettled clouds; the air had definitely changed, sharper and moister than yesterday. A storm was brewing from the north. Both men were suited for the weather.

Long, merino wool underwear went on first, followed by perforated buckskin pants that allowed the skin to breathe, then army green flannel shirts and layers of lamb's wool socks that reached to the knees; over them were buffalo-lined boots chosen for their warmth and durability. A double-breasted blouse made of heavy blanket material was worn under a bearskin overcoat, lined with more blanket material, complete with a high fur collar that would cover their faces against the blowing, biting north wind.

Also, they both had a pair of snow-goggles to protect their eyes from snow-blindness in the sun. On their heads, they donned wool army hats trimmed with fur mufflers and the same fur-lined army-edition gloves for their hands as frostbite was every bit as treacherous an enemy as would be a standoff with a Comanche war party. However, after wearing all this protective clothing, the invasive wind still managed to find its way inside to chill your bones, no matter what breed of man you were.

Jesse let Tomas take the lead so he could do the tracking. There were a growing number of travois trails cutting the ground on both sides of the river as they rode. Under constant observation, Tomas kept eyeing the river for floating objects, relieved that he never saw anything as they passed. "No sign of a moccasin trail. I guess I taught her too well, eh my friend."

As the pair got deeper into wooded territory, they saw mirror flashes and smoke signals, reminding them of the danger of hostiles not that far away. *Probably Crow,* thought Tomas. *The Sioux aren't about to raid or steal horses in this kind of weather. They are sitting in a nice warm tepee after enjoying a hot meal of buffalo stew, as he should be.*

After traveling many miles in silence, Tomas dismounted and bent down, closely inspecting the ground. "Here, a small print! I think she went this way, taking the forked trail to the south."

Along the way, he also spotted recent campsites where she had lit a small fire. Jesse's patience was plainly growing thin and worry for Meadowlark's safety gnawed at his already raw nerves. As the light faded and the temperature dropped, the travelers had nothing to show for the many miles they had put behind them, only the aggravating wind pushing them along and the bitter cold penetrating into their bones. They made camp in a hollow, out of the wind.

After eating buffalo jerky and a can of cold beans, Tomas watched Jesse, who stared into space with eyes as dark as the sky. This scout was the only one who ever looked the captain directly in the eye when he spoke to him. "She is a smart woman. Even though there are many dangers lurking about, she will be careful out here. Sleep with peace, my friend."

Jesse huddled deeper in his sleeping bag. He was very cold. The wind keened around him, plucking at his face while it howled forlornly in his ears. A renegade flurry of fat snowflakes leaped and soared on every gust of wind, in no hurry to reach the ground. They were not the mean-spirited flakes but were the lacy ones that adorn Christmas cards, their playful beauty seeming less personal, less deadly.

But, in this isolated place, Mother Nature would not go quietly; she still possessed the power to erase a life as easily as she could erase the prints of Meadowlark's moccasins with just one of her *beautiful* snowfalls.

They awoke to a dismal day. The wind had turned much colder, shifting around to the north and the clouds were very low, dark-edged, and heavy. It felt like a Norther was on the way and the farther across the barren north they traveled, the harder and colder the wind whipped across it. The hooves of the two horses clicked sharply on the cold earth. Jesse reined his horse in and rubbed its freezing ears affectionately.

They kept pushing against the wind, through one of the most severe storms ever recorded. They spotted nothing moving, no coyotes slinking, no winter hares stirring, not even a crow flying in this deadly cold country.

At night, they crowded around their campfire but were still unable to stay warm. The horses were also brought closer to the fire so they wouldn't freeze; without them, life would be over. In spite of the −30-degree temperatures, the snow kept falling. "We will never pick up her trail now," shouted Jesse over the howl of the wind.

"It doesn't matter," Tomas answered. "I know where she is going."

Snow fell most of the night. The earth lay frozen, completely covered with its bridal gown of virgin white and the heavy fog was her veil. They dismounted, Tomas relentless in his search for tracks. "Here, these are fresh this morning," he yelled. "This way, through the brush!"

Then he saw the wolf tracks, huge paw prints stepping inside the small moccasin prints, following close behind. *Stalking* Meadowlark. He heard the growl; it wasn't the wind. Jesse barreled past Tomas and headed straight for the vast thicket of needle-sharp brush. He felt the whip and insult of the sharp thorns tearing at his clothes, ripping the skin on his frozen face.

Tomas, following close behind, stopped midway through to catch his breath; his lungs felt like they were going to collapse from the rush of cold air pushed into them. He was utterly spent. He wondered where Jesse found the energy to keep going.

Suddenly, Jesse came to a grinding halt, extending his arm out to also stop Tomas. The tracks had abruptly ended! Nothing ahead but tops of trees, until he looked downwards directly in front of him. The earth had suddenly dropped off. A gully lay below, maybe fifty feet down. They both searched below them but couldn't see anything until Jesse spotted a red object partially covered by the snow.

"Over there! We can go down that way," he shouted.

The cliff decline was more gradual, but it was all brush. Both of them catapulted to the bottom, assaulted by sharp needles from the whipping branches on the way down. Jesse vaulted toward Meadowlark first, Tomas not far behind. She lay deathly quiet, her body partially covered by the fallen snowfall. Too late. He knew that even before his eyes fully grasped the grave situation before him.

"Meadowlark!" he cried. He pulled off his glove and felt her flesh; it felt cold and clammy, already starting to turn blue. He lifted her in his arms and cradled her stiffening body.

"Why? Why did you leave me?" But he knew why, feeling the noose of accusation tightening around his neck. This was all his fault; if he hadn't spoken so harshly to her, she wouldn't have left. And telling her that he didn't want the baby, his offspring! He should have told her why. He regretted not telling her and if he could have reeled in the words after he threw them at her that night, he would have done so. The howl of a wolf quickly brought him back, *reminding him.*

Tomas, meanwhile, was tending to another *urgent* matter. Meadowlark's baby was being born. Tomas threw off his gloves and pulled the baby from the birth channel; it couldn't do the job on its own. The tiny infant slid out onto the snow; it was still alive.

Tomas put his fingers in its mouth to clear the airways and it let out a wee cry and suddenly became more frantic. With his experience from working in the stables when he was younger and also fathering four babies of his own, he clumsily tied off the umbilical cord connecting the baby to its mother and by using the snow, he washed all the blood off the new arrival. He then wrapped the baby in his mother's red scarf and handed it to Jesse, who was standing over them, watching in awe.

"Here! This is your *little son.*"

For the longest time, Jesse gazed down at the tiny infant cradled in his arms. He was so soft, so small. And so helpless! It was a miracle that the baby had even survived.

Love for the newborn child showed on Jesse's face and his eyes suddenly grew moist. Tomas watched as tears slipped down his friend's face. But the tender moment was brief and when the baby squirmed and started to whimper, Jesse awkwardly handed the bundle back to Tomas. He abruptly turned around, straightened his back, and walked away. He headed back up the hill and Tomas heard his excuse as he muttered, "I'm going where it is a lot quieter."

He quickly regained his composure by busying himself tending to the horses still tethered to the trees.

Tomas held the crying baby to try and comfort him, disappointed with Jesse's reaction to fatherhood, and especially since it was a *healthy* baby after surviving such a traumatic journey and a fall that had tragically ended for his mother. When the baby kept crying, Tomas gently placed him at his mother's breast and led the little, searching mouth to suckle on the cold flesh.

Jesse returned, leading the two horses. His mood was dark as night. He angrily pulled the white wolf-hide out from under his horse's saddle and threw it at Tomas. "When the kid is done eating, wrap it up in this and load it down with a few rocks and toss it into the river. I will bury Meadowlark's body under a stone grave where this big boulder overhangs the others."

Tomas stood up defiantly. "Jesse, I won't do that!" he shouted.

"Corporal, I gave you an order!" retorted Jesse angrily, pulling rank.

"I still won't drown this baby."

"Why is *this* baby any different from the others, Corporal?" asked the captain. His harsh, professional tone relayed to Tomas that he wanted the order followed so he would be done with this whole situation.

"*This* baby is my blood also! Meadowlark was my *niece*. The Lakota woman killed in that Comanche raid ten years ago was my *sister*. I am Tomas Good Shield, son of Chief Kicking Horse of the Oglala tribe. I am a brave Lakota warrior, a shirt-wearer who fights *to protect his people*. And I will *not kill* this baby!" Tomas shouted as he defiantly wiped at the tears now flowing freely down his face.

"You are also *my* Corporal, and that's an order! And disobeying an order is punishable by hanging until you are dead. Do you understand, *Corporal* Good Shield?"

"Yes, Captain, I understand!"

Nothing more was said regarding the order. Tomas picked up the sleeping baby and snuggly wrapped him inside the white saddle 'blanket' that Captain Burns had thrown at him and he securely tied it with the red scarf that had been around his mother's neck when they found her. The Corporal's anger was evident when he mounted his horse while holding onto the precious, sleeping bundle cradled in the crook of his arm.

Before Tomas rode away, Jesse added, "When I finish here, I'm riding on back to the fort. I'll see you there, Corporal."

"Yes, *sir*!" Tomas Good Shield saluted and proceeded to ride toward the river.

It was nightfall when Captain Jesse Burns had returned to Fort Wilderness and twenty-four hours later, he was still sitting at his desk with an empty bottle of whiskey staring back at him, the laughing character on the outside of the bottle seemingly mocking his shit-faced condition. Tomas had returned that morning and immediately checked in with his captain.

"Did you complete the little task that I ordered you to do, Corporal Good Shield?"

"Yes, sir! I took care of it, *sir*." Tomas saluted and then left, slamming the office door shut behind him.

Jesse's head felt like it was going to explode from the loud noise. That's when the second bottle was brought forward and put on the desk beside the empty one, but nothing seemed to help. Nothing erased the memory of the past few days, much less all the other memories that he always carried with him.

Sitting there thinking, while drowning in his self-pity, he vowed that he would never again be *touched* by another human being as he had been with Meadowlark. Never again would he lose anyone he loved because he would never allow himself to love anything or anybody again. He uncapped the bottle and took a long swig; the golden liquid dribbled down his unshaven chin, staining his uniform. But nothing erased Meadowlark's beautiful face from his mind. Or the wrinkled face of his newborn son lying so content in the circle of his arms. So perfect! So warm! So *protected!*

And then he had given the order to Tomas, the order to destroy yet another loved one! Was it the battle of the two souls that lived inside him making him so callous? So hard-hearted? Was it the evil of the wolf making him feel so cold, so heartless? He felt like the wolf was winning the battle, making all the decisions. Giving him orders! Now he understood how Tomas felt all those times when he was given an antagonistic order to carry out. Jesse was no different than the evil wolf trapped inside his body.

Jesse took another swig of whiskey and set the bottle on the desk beside the gun. For a long time, he stared at the service revolver that he always kept inside his desk drawer. Countless times before, he had sat the gun on the desktop in front of him, tempted by his thoughts. Threatening to erase the memories!

Once again, he picked up the piece of cold steel and held it in the palm of his hand, the same strong hand that knew the shape and feel of a gun that could kill and destroy; the same warm hand that gently and lovingly caressed his woman.

Once again, his thumb tripped back the hammer; he pointed the gun to his head. His only thought at that moment was not only to erase the haunting memories that plagued him every day but to end them. And each time he'd tell himself that he meant to do it. But each time, he never did it and he would ease the hammer back in place and he would put the gun back into the drawer. Till the next time!

"What do you want from me? Haven't I suffered enough pain?" Jesse shouted at the walls. "Someday *I* am going to win and I *will* pull that trigger!"

From outside, Jesse heard the 5:00 a.m. bugle call; it was time to start another day. Captain Jesse Burns, trapped inside the crumbling shell of a man, had lived through another night. Without sleep! And now, he faced another long, painful day. Without feeling!

Part Three

In Blue Creek Camp, the Lakota village that Tomas Good Shield called home, Standing Buffalo awaited a vision on Sacred Hill, located at the top of a distant slope nearby. The great warrior, Tomas' blood brother, was soon to become a father, as his wife was having birthing pains at the women's lodge at that moment.

For Standing Buffalo, this was not the first time he had awaited a child's coming into the light; three times before, Red Leaf had walked heavily on the earth, and on one of those times she gave him a healthy daughter. But twice since, a small sickly thing had emerged each time, only to close its eyes in a silent death. He found it hard to understand why *Wakan Tanka*, the Great Spirit, gave life, only to take it away again. And why did he do this to such a great warrior as himself?

Each time, he had undertaken *Inipi*, the purification rite, as required. He was always generous to the needy; he hunted so his people could grow strong, and he never neglected to pray and smoke the pipe to give thanks to the spirit world. A warrior, so named after *Wakan Tanka*, the great buffalo who always runs first into battle, had been a shirt-wearer for six winters now and during that time, he had always put the needs of his people ahead of his own, always chanted the required prayers.

Giving him a son tonight would bring hope back to his people from the depths of winter's death. And winter is not a good time for a baby to be brought into the world. It is the time when things *die*; leaves wither away and fall to the ground, the naked trees left to tremble in the cold. Grass shrivels, then turns brown, only to poke out of the snow like stubble from a man's unshaven chin.

Birds fly south and the small animals burrow deep into the warm ground below. Even the big bear seeks out a cave to sleep in during the cold months. *He is the only smart one*, thought Standing Buffalo as he shivered in the cool night air.

In spite of the cold, Standing Buffalo stripped off all his clothes and stood naked on top of the sacred hill. He drew his knife from its sheath and cut the flesh on his chest four times. Blood seeped from the wounds and spurted across his scarred torso, making trails down smooth brown skin to muscular thighs, dripping down over a pair of powerful legs where the naked man stood in pools of red at his feet.

He threw back his head to gaze at the Northern Star sparkling in the sky above him and he prayed, "*Wakan Tanka*, grant me a *son*. Send to me a brave heart that can endure whatever will come to the Lakota people. One who will lead the others. One who has the wisdom that flows from your world and holds the power to see dangers ahead. Bless us with a child that stands strong against the white man, one that *stands out* from the rest of my people."

As blood continued to drip from his wounds, Standing Buffalo performed the ritual of chanting and dancing until his strength ebbed and he sank to his knees, eventually passing into the peace of dreaming:

There was a herd of buffalo and they were stampeding through the village. In the center of the herd, a little white wolf was running with them. The others around him fell behind, and he became their leader. He was fast and strong and wise; he showed them the way, driving the herd safely out of the village. He was from two worlds, speaking with two tongues. Others were jealous so he had to be careful as he was alone. His road was hard and as he grew, someone older and wiser showed him another, easier way. Guiding him to manhood.

There came a sudden roar from the marching of storm clouds forming above Standing Buffalo's head while he stayed inside the silent, hollow darkness of the spirit world where he had seen many things.

Thunderbird flapped his giant wings and yellow daggers from dragon tongues danced across the heavens causing mother earth to tremble. In spite of the blowing wind, a loud wolf's howl resonated in the distance. The awakening of the spirit world didn't rouse Standing Buffalo while he soundlessly slept through all the rejoicing as it continued for more than three hours.

The grandfather, Five Horns, had stayed out of sight among the trees during the birthing ritual. And while his grandson slept, the medicine man of great power had also rejoiced, dancing and chanting on the sacred hill, wildly shaking a rattlesnake charm in one hand while clutching the sacred medicine bag in the other, until he collapsed from exhaustion.

Earlier, *he* also had a vision telling him that there was a death in the wind as a mother hurries a child into the world. But right afterward, he had yet another vision, one that predicted a great warrior would be born and he would lead the Lakota people.

After resting, the old man applied a yellow salve to his grandson's wounds. Standing Buffalo finally awoke to his grandfather joyously shaking him. "Hurry and get dressed! Red Leaf has given you a *son.*"

Standing Buffalo raised his voice in a howl of thanksgiving and uttered a short prayer to the Great Spirit. They quickly descended the hill and returned to the camp, heading straight to the women's lodge. Two Faces in the Wind, the grandmother, greeted them while proudly unwrapping the white wolf-hide blanket; she showed the infant son to his father for the first time. "His name is to be 'Little Wolf'."

"Cinks? (my son?)" asked Standing Buffalo as he dropped his head in disappointment. "He hasn't the look of a *buffalo.*"

"But he has the look of a white wolf," defended Two Faces (It was the privilege given to the grandmother to name her grandchildren).

Standing Buffalo's frown did not linger as he gazed upon his son lovingly, a father's pride swelling within him. He hesitantly touched the infant's tiny, whitish hands and stroked the blonde curls framing his pale-colored face. Then he gently rubbed the baby boy on the forehead and silently pledged all the devotion a father could offer.

"You will be proud to walk the sacred path with me, little one; you will be proud to be the son of a shirt-wearer. And maybe someday, Little Wolf, you will make *me* proud if you become a shirt-wearer too."

Little Wolf learned early the lessons of being a Lakota child. When the urge to cry came, his nose was pinched and his mouth was covered until his lungs burned with the need for air and eventually, he learned the futility of wailing for attention.

For three months, Red Leaf and the baby stayed in the women's lodge. She carried the baby around in her arms all day; he was wrapped in the wolf blanket to keep him warm because he was so frail. Many babies died in the cold winds from the north and she did not want her son's spirit to be taken away. She held him close to her chest so he could hear her heartbeat with all the love she felt for him and he could drink from her breasts whenever he was hungry.

Standing Buffalo visited the lodge often, to see his wife and child. And each time, he would question the color of his son's liquid blue eyes and the paleness of his skin. And his hair! It seemed to grow lighter in the sunlight. Even though he was a bit disappointed because his son didn't look like the other babies, he loved him anyway.

When Red Leaf gained her strength back, she moved back home, into the family lodge. She strapped Little Wolf to a cradleboard on her back while she did her work, stretching and kneading the buckskin with deft brown fingers to soften it up, while all the time, thinking it would someday make a fine shirt for her son when he became a strong, brave warrior like his father.

And as the weather warmed up, Red Leaf let him crawl around the lodges but because he was so quiet and fast with such strong spindly legs bent under him like a young rabbit hopping along, he kept his mother running after him all day. The grandmother, Two Faces, presented the toddler with a special red scarf so it would make it easier for his mother to find her son when he chose to wander off.

Little Wolf loved animals but whenever he crawled near the dogs, they growled and snarled at him, sensing a feral smell that only dogs seemed to pick up with their sensitive noses. The baby's mother always stayed close by to protect her precious child. One day, the toddler crawled around the fire where the elders were seated and started to play with Five Horns' medicine pouch.

"Look, the little one wants to join in on our meeting," teased his grandfather. "This one is going to be a great warrior when he grows up, I have visions of him already."

But the others laughed, making jokes about the toddler's small frame. Five Horns retaliated, "Don't let his size fool you! He will grow to be *bigger* than all of us, you will see."

At that moment, Red Leaf ran to the boy and picked him up, scolding him for crawling off, and for bothering the elders while they were having an important meeting. But Little Wolf enjoyed his wanderings and the next time he crawled near the elders holding a meeting, Five Horns presented him with his own, smaller medicine bundle. The elders howled their approval as the boy clutched the sacred horn from within the pouch. The proud grandfather smiled.

"See! He is already the man of power that I foresee; as an infant, he already knows the sacred ways of *Wakan Tanka*. The young one will learn quickly if we leave the anxious mind to explore." The others laughed at him but they took a new interest in the restless, inquisitive child.

The other children always played tricks on Little Wolf, hiding behind trees, then jumping out at him to surprise him. He laughed with such an infectious laugh that they too, would roll in the grass beside him and laugh too. All the children except one; Spotted Dog was jealous of the youngster's attention given to him by the others. He was always tormenting Little Wolf and was sometimes mean with the younger child.

Soon after, Little Wolf took his first steps when he had the notion to walk. He spoke as he heard the words. Then came all the questions; they were answered when it wasn't inconvenient, and understanding began to supplement his impulses. But he was always inquisitive.

One day, when the boy was with his grandmother, the questions spewed out of his mouth. "Why does grandfather make funny noises when he sleeps? Why do the older people smoke a big pipe? Why am I a different color than the rest of the boys? Why are my eyes blue, while all the other boys' eyes are brown? Why is my hair like the silk at the end of a corncob? Why do they call you 'Two Faces'? Well! Where did all those come from? You must have stayed awake all night thinking about all these questions." Two Faces bent down and picked the child up in her arms. Lovingly, she told him, "Someday, I will answer all those questions for you. I promise!"

By the time Little Wolf reached his sixth summer, he knew much about the traditions of the Lakota people, how to recognize the garb of his Oglala cousins as opposed to the dress of the Pawnees or the Crows, their enemies. He sensed that his father, Standing Buffalo, was a great man among the elders as they often came to him, seeking advice. He learned to take care of his small horse, riding as if the horse and his body were one. He shot smaller, blunt-pointed arrows with the other boys, but they teased him because of his size.

"Take care, no hawk swoops down and takes off with you, little one," they called out as he hunted."

"No, hawks see good," replied Spotted Dog.

"He is too little to make a meal out of; even a Pawnee or Crow would not waste an arrow on *him*."

Overhearing the jeering by the older boys, Five Horns assured Little Wolf that, someday, he will be a man of power, and those other boys will hunt and live and die, but they will *follow* the small boy in time.

"It is good that a man who will lead the people should face hardships. You must make a prayer of thanks to *Wakan Tanka,* who sends you this struggle to make you stronger than the rest."

Little Wolf was grateful for his grandfather's words of reassurance but it was hard to feel glad when the sharp words of the older boys stung his six-year-old heart. Even his older sister teased him about his slow growth.

Little Wolf might have endured all the teasing more easily if it wasn't for the sun-bleached whiteness of his hair, his big blue eyes, and the light pigment of his skin. Even with the help from the hot rays of the sun, the pale-skinned boy became only slightly tanned compared to the other boys whose flesh was dark brown. When wagons of the white people passed along the road, the people often spoke to him in their strange tongues, thinking he was one of them.

"They want to know if you have a white mother or father," one of the traders' sons translated for him. That's how Little Wolf met Louis Dupont, a dark-skinned boy about the same age as himself. The traders' son wore glasses and Little Wolf nicknamed him 'Spectacles'. They became best friends.

Spectacles was also quite small for his age, but he had jet-black hair and brown eyes like the other boys that Little Wolf knew. And he was very affluent in the Oglala tongue because of his Lakota grandmother; within months, he taught Little Wolf the white man's language. It helped that the pale-skinned boy was a very smart child and learned quickly.

The two boys hung out together and they soon formed a friendship with another small, shunned boy in their age group, a Lakota boy named Chalk Face. He was also teased by the others because of his size and the large scar on one side of his face. The burn scar left the skin white underneath, so he was called 'Chalk Face'.

Three small misfits among their people, one with a white scar down the side of his face, one who had the reflection of four eyes from his spectacles supported on the bridge of his nose, and the other, a pale-skinned, blonde-haired, blue-eyed boy who always wore a red scarf wherever he went.

However, when Little Wolf was mingling among the white traders, his skin appeared not so pale and the color of his eyes and hair didn't seem to stand out in the crowd. He fit in with *them* more than his friend 'Spectacles' did. And he had to keep repeating that he was Lakota, not white. "I am Little Wolf, the son of the great warrior called Standing Buffalo," he would shout at them.

During the whole summer, the threesome spent many days swimming in the rivers, wrestling on the sandy banks, and racing through the trees of the Lakota camp while trying to avoid the unwanted company of Little Wolf's sister, Willow Legs, and her best friend, Yellow Bird. Many times, the boys hid from the two bothersome, giggly girls, hoping they would go away and play somewhere else. But they always seemed to come back, wanting to hang out with them.

One day, when the three small boys were playing a game of hide and seek, they were approached by the older boys, led by Spotted Dog. "Can we play too?" asked Banded Otter, the smallest of the older group, who had also been subject to many teasing jokes from the others in the past.

"We don't want to play with those *little babies*!" jeered Spotted Dog.

"Yes, we do! It will be fun," chorused the others, much to Spotted Dogs dislike.

"Come play with us!" shouted Little Wolf excitedly. He was so pleased to have the others finally join in on their games. "Banded Otter, you can be first to hide your eyes."

When Banded Otter covered his eyes, the others ran in all directions in search of a good hiding place. Little Wolf hid behind a tree and waited. Eventually, all the boys were found by Banded Otter. Everyone except Little Wolf, who managed to stay hidden behind his small tree as Banded Otter walked right past it many times, still searching. Finally, he found Little Wolf and asked, "How did you manage to hide behind such a small tree without me seeing you there?"

"I used my secret weapon. I turned sideways and became invisible because I am so small," answered Little Wolf laughingly. And all the boys laughed with him, except Spotted Dog, who stormed off angrily while the others stayed behind and continued to play the game.

When the Season of Falling Leaves came to an end, the traders bid farewell and Little Wolf had to say goodbye to Spectacles, giving him a parting gift of a fine buffalo hide coat that he had painstakingly worked on with his mother. "White men make poor coats," he said.

In return, Spectacles gave his friend a steel bowie knife with a polished bone handle encased in its own hand-sewn leather sheath. It was such a fine gift that Little Wolf rode his horse back home, feeling taller and prouder now that he possessed such a large hunting knife hanging from his belt. But he was very sad too; he had never parted with a good friend before.

Good fortune had smiled on the Lakota people during the hunt for buffalo. After the warriors returned, the camp was alive with the aroma of smoking meat and sizzling buffalo ribs while grandmothers were busy pounding chokeberries into thin strips to make *wasna*, the dried meat that would prevent winter starvation among the people.

Bellies were full and songs of thanks rose to *Wakan Tanka* throughout the Lakota camp. The well-stocked food supply and the many warm blankets promised a better winter for the people during the next six months, initiating the big celebration.

Little Wolf was too young to understand the need for rejoicing, also too young to go on any of the hunts but his father, sensing the boy's displacement, gave him a new bow; this act of kindness made him feel included. And it was an innovative bow, cut from the sacred wood of the ash and carved with great affection for a treasured son by a loving father; the grip was wrapped in buffalo hide with strips of beadwork on each side. He was also given a quill of fine new arrows that were much sharper and larger than the small ones he was used to.

"Your old arrows would never pierce the tough hide of an elk but these will," Standing Buffalo informed him. However, his arms were so small and thin, he couldn't pull back the bowstring to notch one of the new arrows.

"When you can pull the bowstring, then we will go hunting for deer or elk, maybe even the buffalo," his father told him proudly.

"Will that be soon?" Little Wolf asked expectantly.

"Many whole moons will pass and many will be chewed at until you have the arm strong enough to pull this string. Until then, your heart will pull it. *Hau!* Remember, as your arm grows larger and stronger, so does your heart. Others may pull it before you, but none will have the true aim that lies in your eye. Until then, keep practicing, my son."

Such praise from his father made Little Wolf glow inside. "And someday you will become a strong, brave warrior," his father continued. "Always remember, my son, a true warrior fights, not because he hates the ones in front of him, but because he loves those behind him."

Little Wolf still hunted with his small bow and arrow, shooting at quail and rabbit, and one day, he proudly came home with a plump porcupine that his mother gladly accepted. "The quills will be used to decorate a fine warrior shirt for you, my son."

In Little Wolf's seventh summer, the camp was invaded by the white soldiers. They were in search of a group of renegade braves that had been stealing army horses while they were corralled inside the post at night. Such unauthorized raids were bad business and the soldiers became angry. The soldiers rode through the Lakota camp, kicking up dust and knocking over racks of drying meat.

"Quickly, take your sister and run into the trees and hide with the other women and children," shouted his father as he picked up his bow and arrows to fight the *wasicun* (white men). "I am a shirt-wearer and I must look out for the rest of my people. Go, my son!" As his father rode away, Little Wolf heard his father shout again, "It is a good day to die!"

Little Wolf did as he was told; his sister often stumbled and fought to keep pace as he pulled her along toward the forest. He left her with the others, then rushed back to the battle-torn camp with his little bow and arrows. He heard a voice of a warning whisper in his ear, "Boy, you can't withstand the storm."

The small warrior lifted his chin and puffed out his bony chest and shouted to the trees, "*I am* the storm!"

But as he ran, he tripped and fell, slashing his arm. He stopped to wrap his arm in the red scarf and to wipe some blood on his face and bare chest, just like he saw his father do with the war-paint whenever he left for a battle.

"*Hau, Wakan Tanka*! It is a good day to die," he shouted again as he raced bare-foot and nearly naked past the soldiers, chanting and waving his weapon. But the soldiers had no eyes to see the little boy with his miniature bow and arrows; he posed no threat to the fighting soldiers on horseback. He notched an arrow and shot; it bounced off one of the soldier's legs. The soldier rode toward him and swooped him up with one strong arm.

"Put the boy down!" shouted their leader, a blonde-haired man who had the deepest blue eyes. He had been watching the little, pale-skinned warrior during the entire battle.

"Yes, sir, Captain Burns!" The soldier unceremoniously dropped the boy to the ground. Little Wolf quickly recovered from the fall and stood as tall as his small frame would allow, bravely facing their enemy's leader. He stared back at the *wasicun* leader with fire in his eyes. Defiant! Ready to fight! But it was hard for Little Wolf to be brave while facing such a big, intimidating man and his bleeding arm hurting him so much; he wouldn't show the pain it caused him. And he wouldn't back down!

In Lakota words, the small boy shouted, "Leave my people alone!"

Tomas Good Shield, who sat on his horse to the right of his captain, translated the boy's message.

Captain Burns saw a very young, bleeding warrior trying to defend his people. A brave boy, small in stature, who greatly reminded him of himself when he was about that age. Hell, he even looked like him! He gazed down at the blood-stained red scarf that was wrapped around the boy's bony arm. There was something *familiar* about that red scarf. The Sergeant, to the left of his captain, raised his rifle, aiming it at the boy.

Captain Burns immediately grabbed the gun from the Sergeant's hand and barked, "Leave him be! He's just a little *savage*."

He glanced over at his scout, Tomas Good Shield, for a brief minute, then looked away. "Sergeant, give the order for the men to move out. We're done here!"

All the soldiers rode out of camp in the same swirl of dust as when they had arrived less than one hour ago. The battle was over. And today, except for one *wounded* boy, there had been no casualties.

News of Little Wolf's bravery quickly spread throughout the camp. That evening, the elders called a meeting about the boy. Five Horns (the boy's grandfather), Crooked Finger, Red Hat (the boy's uncle), Four Toes, Twisted Heart, and Tomas Good Shield were among the great warriors who joined Chief Kicking Horse in his lodge that evening. Standing Buffalo, the boy's father, was also asked to be present.

After the pipe was passed around, Chief Kicking Horse spoke, "The spirits have given to the Lakota people, a gift sent from the great man in the sky, a fine leader in the form of a small, white child. I have been watching this child and I believe he is our *weapon*, an ally who will stand up to the white man and will fight for the rights of our people. One who is not afraid and who will not back down from them."

"I saw this today and I have seen it many times before in my dreams ever since his birth. My visions also tell me that the people have troubled times ahead. More wars, more powerful weaponry used by the armies, greater numbers of white people flooding our lands like dominating, evasive ants, and also, the senseless killing of our sacred buffalo, our most valuable gift sent to us to combat the mean Winter Man."

"We need to stand and fight to save our families. Our heritage! Our land! We must protect this uncommon child, this precious gift so graciously given to us, and help the young boy by teaching him all that we know so he can better lead our people through the hard times that are coming to us. Little Wolf has the *heart* of the spirits inside him; he will be our great leader. The range of his powers is yet to be seen; I foresee. Standing Buffalo, you prayed for a son, a great leader."

"Someone who would stand out from the rest! Well, the spirit world heard your prayer! We are here now, to discuss the little one's future."

Little Wolf knew he was different from the rest of the boys; he had always stood a little apart from them. At first, this caused him much unhappiness, as the choice to distance had not been his to make. He often looked out from the shadows of his father's tepee and watched the other boys playing their games without him. It hurt him to see the dark eyes of the women as they looked upon him as their enemy, a white boy. Even the dogs in the camp wouldn't come near him.

Time had passed so slowly as he waited for that growth spurt that his mother kept promising would someday happen. When he finally accepted his size, his skin pigment, and his light-colored hair and distinct blue eyes, his life began to take on meaning. After all, he was *Lakota*! And someday he *would* grow bigger and become a brave shirt-wearer, just like his father. Or perhaps a famous medicine man like his grandfather. But for now, he had to deal with his eccentricities and he learned ways to use his *smallness* as a secret weapon as he grew older and wiser.

Little Wolf *was* a gifted child; he learned his lessons well, his mind absorbing everything like a dry sponge. His father had already taught him, at an early age, to ride a horse bareback while retaining perfect balance and now that he was older, he had to ride hanging from the side of his horse while holding on to its mane.

He taught him how to handle a rope, making a loop and throwing it to catch his horse and then pulling up the slack. Then he had to do it all over again but this time, the horse was running. Standing Buffalo also showed him the art of tracking, distinguishing between porcupine and skunk prints in the snow, wolf and cougar, bear and moose; he also took him deer hunting on many occasions until Little Wolf could finally pull the bowstring on his new bow by himself.

His grandfather, Five Horns, taught him the arts of healing, and the medicinal use of tree bark, herbs, and other plants that grow wild in the ground. He learned how to set a broken bone, stop excessive bleeding, clean and dress an infectious wound, mend a tooth cavity with dried mushrooms and camphor oil, and make a mustard plaster to relieve a persistent cough.

Even his grandmother, Two Faces in the Wind, taught him lessons, about cooking, making *wasna (winter meat)* out of buffalo strips, working the hides, making a fine beaded bracelet, sewing a fancy shirt, and doing the laundry, the job that he despised the most.

As Little Wolf could also speak and read the white man's language, he acquired a love for books, some books that he borrowed and some that were given to him as a gift. When he wasn't *learning* from his family and relatives, he could be found reading down by the river or curled up in a corner of the tepee, his face buried in his favorite book, *Moby Dick.*

During his tenth summer, Little Wolf was allowed to go on his first buffalo hunt, but only to remain back with the women and watch. That morning, he was so excited that when he ran to jump on his horse, Two Faces raced after him, waving his red scarf.

"Here! This will bring you luck." She knew that her grandson left as a little boy but he would return as a young *man.*

Yesterday, from the top of a high cliff, two Lakota scouts watched as a small herd of massive black dots grazed on a lush pasture of grassland. And days prior, they followed the trampled, hard-packed ground where a path as broad and bare as a main roadway was left behind from pounding hooves. Hundreds of huge, greenish-black blobs of hard buffalo dung were scattered about, already drying and quickly losing moisture and turning white in the hot sun. About five to six hundred buffalo were slowly moving toward the north, soon to be gone until the fall. It was time for the hunt.

About thirty warriors carrying lances, bows, and arrows left the camp the next morning and were soon lost under the bowl of the rising sun after it sent up pink streamers as a warning from below the distant horizon. Even though the sun kissed the boy's shoulders and warmed his fragile bones as he proudly rode behind the hunting party in search of the buffalo herd, Little Wolf shivered from excitement.

"No further!" warned his father as Little Wolf and his pony remained near the butchering party while the warriors silently rode nearer to the grazing herd about a hundred yards away. The burning sun had finally reached its highest point in the blue, cloudless sky and the seasonal wind was blowing from the south as the buffalo mingled about and ate contentedly. The over-heated, malodorous beasts moved very slowly, calmly keeping their heads facing the same direction as the wind, as it carried no message of alarm to the animals.

"Buffalo travels a main path, always with their faces into the wind and if the wind changes direction, so does the buffalo," informed Standing Buffalo to his inquisitive son.

"You mean they always travel the same route every year?" Little Wolf asked his father.

"No, not the *same* route. In spring, they travel south and west. And in summer, they head south and east. When the winds come over the mountains in the fall, they move westward and then north for the winter. Be careful, my son! Always heed the direction of the wind."

Little Wolf drank in the sight before him. He was mesmerized by the massive older bulls that weighed well over a ton and the younger spike bulls nudging one another playfully. He studied the cows, especially the ones that he thought would yield the best meat; fat brown calves romping around in spite of the hammering blaze of the sun. How eternal it all seemed, the mighty herds peacefully grazing under the big sky. How *changeless!* So u*ndisturbed!*

Little Wolf was conscious of, but not interested in, the constant singing of a meadowlark in the tall, untouched grasses on the side of the buffalo trail beside him. He saw but did not bother with, the circling hawk gliding overhead. And he never noticed the warning howl of the blowing wind. He could only hear the snorts and bellows of the massive animals with the thick black tongues as they chewed their cud after grabbing the sweet grasses on the gently rolling hillside.

He could only smell the fetid breath of the massive beasts, the matted fur, and the constant plops of fresh droppings. And he could also feel the rapidly pounding heartbeats hammering inside his bony chest. He watched as thirty or more straggling cows, lagging at the back of the herd, suddenly fall to the ground with arrows protruding from behind their shoulders, precisely targeted to fatally puncture the animal's heart or a lung.

The slower buffaloes, except the ones that were wide and heavy with unborn calves, were shot by either Standing Buffalo or by one of the other warriors who had stealthily bordered around the outskirts of the herd from the rear while the other beasts continued to graze, unaware of the attack. The hunters rode bareback, holding on with just their knees while taking aim and accurately shooting their targets with bows and arrows at the same time, a feat mastered by *every* buffalo hunter in the Lakota tribe.

The buffalo were very stupid, as always, slowed by the grueling heat from the white-hot sun beating down on their heavy coats. Their weak eyes could not see the hunters. They continued to calmly graze as the hunters moved up, silently killing. Until they were almost side by side with the unsuspecting herd.

Awaiting at the top of a cliff, Little Wolf obediently sat on his pony and watched in awe while directly behind him, the butchering party, composed of the tribe's women and older children, were also waiting for the signal from Standing Buffalo to begin their work on the slain animals.

But something went wrong! Unexpectantly, the wind had changed. A vagrant cross-breeze gusting past, that carried the man-scent to one of the cow's nostrils, caused her to turn just as a lance-point touched her side. Instead of the needle-sharp tip slipping easily through spongy lungs, then piercing into the heart (the beast's most vulnerable point that is known to inflict a fatal blow), the cow's unpredicted movement caused the weapon to slightly veer off, missing her heart but striking her between the ribs.

The arrow tip protruded from her other side, stabbing her crosswise through the body. The cow continuously bellowed in pain as she repeatedly turned around in circles, lunging wildly while tossing her head as hard hooves and razor-sharp horns inflicted others around her; she remained very much alive and crazed by the wound. None of the warriors could get near her to put her out of her misery.

Yellow dust clouded the area while the horrific bellowing cries echoed through the hills, heard above the swooshing wind as it continued to change direction. At first, the rest of the herd immediately scented their danger, milling restlessly from the strong smell of blood carried by the wind. Then they heard the suffering cows' blats as she still tried to throw off the arrow that was lodged inside her body.

The bulls made a sluggish attempt to form a barrier, protecting the cows and calves, but they were too late. They bellowed and pawed the hot earth and tossed their sharp white horns in anger. Restless, they started to move. The frantic beasts turned, colliding with the others and creating confusion. Plunging forward through the crowded herd, gouging and hooking with razor-sharp horns as they thundered over the land.

The massive animals had succeeded in changing direction, facing the wind once more; but they were now thundering onto a new path, bolting toward the butchering party and Little Wolf where they were waiting and watching in horror near the edge of a steep cliff. They had nowhere to go to avoid the oncoming herd.

The warriors, sensing the sudden movement of the herd, charged into the hot wind, now whooping and hollering in an attempt to turn the herd again. Horses' hooves drummed on the baked earth while their riders still killed the buffalo, one by one. The panicky herd moved faster, stampeding toward the women and children. And toward the cliff where Little Wolf still waited.

"No further!" His father's words resonated in his mind. He was taught to always obey his father. But if he stayed there, he would be trampled, and so would the women and children. "I hope my father will forgive me for disobeying his orders today."

The air was heavily clouded with drifting yellow dust, becoming thicker as the moving buffalo gained momentum. Little Wolf moved his pony closer to the herd, creating a distance between him and the butchering party. He dug his heels into the animal's flanks; the pony responded with a burst of speed, stretching his sturdy legs into a wild gallop, closing the gap on the stampeding buffalo as they raced directly toward him.

Pony and rider suddenly stopped, now facing the approaching black, unbroken line of dust. The little boy attempted to turn the herd by whooping and hollering and frantically waving his arms. He knew he was in harm's way but he bravely stood there as the herd got closer and closer, the gritty dust choking him. The senselessly, thundering buffaloes were heading straight for him, their bobbing black heads bent in earnest as they ran.

In the swirls of dust clouds, Little Wolf could now make out each buffalo as individuals. When they got dangerously closer, he could hear the deafening blatting; he could see their long black tongues flapping from gaping mouths as they panted in the heat, now gasping for air.

He was close enough to see molting shaggy coats that covered the muscular shoulders as huge humps flopped from side to side with each stride that the powerful legs took. White billows of steam, similar to that of a locomotive train, puffed from their black rubbery nostrils and wild fear emanated from their rolling black eyes.

Little Wolf was going to be trampled; there was no place for the boy to go. He started to chant his death-song. That's when he saw two shining blue lights through the clouds of yellow dust, an unmistakable pair of distinct blue eyes belonging to a white *blur*, running in the front of the herd. Six huge, brown beasts flew past Little Wolf, falling to their death as they toppled over the cliff. The rest of the buffalo surprisingly swerved away from the precipice where the smell of fresh blood and broken bodies was wafting over the rim.

Little Wolf's pony, flanks heaving and legs trembling, also panicked from the smell. And as this was the young pony's first buffalo hunt as well, he was inexperienced when he was confronted with such aggressively massive beasts. The pony reared up and knocked his rider to the trembling ground as the buffalo stampeded all around them.

Little Wolf fell hard, his head grazing a horn as he sailed downward into the midst of the herd that was wildly reacting from terror spread by the wounded cow only minutes before. Little Wolf sat on the ground, waiting to be trampled as he continued with his death-song. At that moment, the white buffalo was beside him, forcing the runaway herd to pass on either side. Little Wolf understood the message transmitted to him from those eyes! He knew what he had to do. Little Wolf quickly grabbed onto the albino's underbelly and hung on for the ride of his life.

The yellow dust clouds settled slowly as the backsides of the herd eventually disappeared from sight. The butchering party, glad to have survived the stampede, were already falling beside the slain buffaloes to start the serious work of providing sustenance for their tribe for the long winter months ahead. In the shadow of the trees, green eyes of the wolves and yellow eyes of the coyotes waited for their share; they always got their share at every hunt. While high in the sky, scavengers circled in anguish, also waiting to cash in on the food chain.

Life continued, as usual, for the hunters when the killing ended. The air reeked of spilled blood. Death was everywhere. The warriors dismounted from their sweaty, hard-working ponies, to finally rest. But not Standing Buffalo! He rode the trampled field, his eyes franticly searching. He had watched in horror when his son fell from his pony during the stampede. There was nothing he could do to save him. However, he still searched; he didn't know why.

In the mind of a Lakota warrior, death was a part of life. To be accepted just as the sun warms the earth during the day, or the light of the stars that guides the way at night. 'It's a good day to die' is chanted by every warrior before he goes into battle, knowing that today could be his last. But a hope and a prayer were all that Standing Buffalo had left. The *hope* that made him still search! The *prayer* that might have gotten answered!

Maybe it was the white *blur* that he had seen just after his son had fallen. He had never seen a white buffalo before. But it was there! The dust was very thick and the distance was very great, but there was no doubt in his mind that he had just seen one of the rarest and most valued of all the animals never seen before by any man on this earth. An albino buffalo!

Far off in the distance, Standing Buffalo suddenly saw a red cloth waving at him from a hilltop. Little Wolf's red scarf! His son was alive! The boy ran as fast as his little legs would carry him, into his father's arms.

"Father, I used my secret weapon again. And because I'm so small, no one knew I was hanging under the belly of a big white buffalo during the stampede. He sent me a message with his shiny blue eyes as he ran toward me. That's what he told me to do!" shouted Little Wolf excitedly. Standing Buffalo was crying as he gazed at his son and knew he was telling him the truth.

Everywhere the people looked, large brown corpses covered the field. About seventy in all. The trampled ground was scattered with rancid buffalo droppings, the voiding falling in long streaks as the lucky ones ran for their lives. Trembling the earth until the calming herd finally stopped running some twenty miles away where they continued to feed on the long sweet grasses again. Life for the hunted buffalo returned back to normal, at least for the time being.

It took the butchering party most of the day to do their work in the field and after the meat was wrapped inside the hides, the heavy bundles were dragged aside, each bundle waiting to be loaded onto a travois or onto one of the many pack horses. Today had been quite a profitable day for the Lakota tribe and a memorable one for a special young boy. And a very *lucky* one for Little Wolf.

The stars began to choke the velvet sky, filling the world with a special glow. The gentle night winds were cool and came alive with a much cleaner, sharper air, erasing the blood-spattered smells of slain buffalo that had hovered over the steamy ground previously.

Surely, this was a land of changing relevance with a scorching sun and racing shadows hurrying through shimmering waves of heat by day, and then as it cooled down, the land transformed the world into a steady light of wonder by night. Unlike the buffalo being transported back to the camp, Little Wolf knew that it could have been him lying on one of those travoises. He shouted to the trees, "It was a good day to be alive!"

Rumors of Little Wolf's bravery quickly circulated throughout the camp after the hunt. He was a hero in the people's eyes once more, this time by saving the lives of the butchering party when he miraculously turned the stampeding buffalo in a different direction. The elders were impressed by the little boy's actions and spoke proudly about the small boy named Little Wolf, who had once again proven that he possessed prodigious powers and would grow to be a great leader; his was the true heart of their people.

After every hunt, Standing Buffalo had visions of the future. The visions were always the same:

Thousands of bleached skeletons of buffalo, rising like ghostly monuments out of the waving grasses, scattered all over these same fields like ground pepper sprinkled from a wooden pepper-shaker. Their bones lay in silent witness to the fact that the white man had been hunting here also, leaving the precious buffalo carcasses to rot on the ground. And the wind carried the last words of the buffalo, "I am no more!" Eventually disappearing forever!

Without the buffalo, the people were starving, often harried, and on the move, as their land was always taken away from them. They were no longer hunters but became the hunted, only to rot like the buffalo on the reservations. Doing what they were told! Eating what they were given! And living the white man's way! Like ants swarming a hill. There became more white men than Indians.

His people fell into long silences, staring at nothing. Old men died, women no longer laughed, and the children grew sick with swollen bellies and white man's diseases. The once-proud warriors never hunted anymore or protected their families anymore. Instead, they drank from the burning cup and reminisced about 'the good ole' days until they too, became the old men. And the land that once belonged to the Indians eventually disappeared with the buffalo.

Standing Buffalo went to seek out advice from Chief Kicking Horse. He spoke of his reoccurring vision and about the white buffalo, he had seen that day. For many minutes, the chief thought about the meaning of the vision, but he was more *fascinated* by the news of the white buffalo.

"You are sure of this thing?" he asked in amazement.

"*Aie!* Among the herd, I saw a white one! The boy saw it too, he told me so," answered Standing Buffalo solemnly.

"I have heard many stories about the great white buffalo. To my knowledge, no Lakota warrior living has ever seen such an animal. He only survives in the spirit world, not here on this earth. It has been told that a white buffalo possesses great powers! But it seems that his power that day was lost. There was a *greater* power standing before him in front of the stampeding herd, that of the boy's. You did not follow the herd with the white one in it?" asked Chief Kicking Horse.

"No! The white buffalo had suddenly disappeared and I never saw it again during the stampede. My horse was too winded to chase the running herd. And besides, I only wanted to find my son's trampled body."

"Was the white one leading the herd when you saw it?" The anxiety hadn't left the chief's voice. The people believed that a white buffalo had led all the buffalo out of a hole in the earth shortly after time began and that someday, another white buffalo would come along to take up the lead again.

"It was when I first saw it! But I lost sight of it in the dust," answered Standing Buffalo. "The white one was *not* in the lead when I later saw it. It was among the others." Nervously, he added, "*My son* was in the lead when I saw him last. That is why I thought he was trampled by the others behind him."

The old man rubbed his weathered face with a bony hand. "That is what I thought you would tell me." Chief Kicking Horse struggled to rise up from the sitting position, his bones creaking from the strain. "About your vision, I foresee a lengthy battle with the white man. Maybe we can avoid this from happening by wisely using the gift we were given by *Wakan Tanka* to fight them."

"The boy given to us has a big impact on the white man who leads the soldiers and he can help our people. For ten years now, I have had many visits with *my* older son, Tomas Good Shield, regarding the boy. Although the boy's skin is white like that of the albino buffalo, his *mind* is Lakota and he has been given great powers by the spirit world as I truly believe this to be true. Both are rare creatures. One, a giant and the other, very small! But soon the small one will grow."

"So, we must prepare him to *fight* in other ways, by using his mind. When the little one reaches his eleventh summer, I will call a meeting with the elders and afterward, we will have a big feast to celebrate. It will be time for Little Wolf to have the honor of carrying the sacred arrows for his people. And he will have the right to choose who will ride with him in battle, to carry the sacred buffalo hat."

Chief Kicking Horse did call the meeting with the elders on Little Wolf's eleventh birthday, and he told them about his decision regarding the sacred arrows. "Also, there are many fine horses near a Crow camp, not far from the river. Scouts counted over two hundred and only thirty Crows were guarding them. We will keep track of these horses and when we are ready, Little Wolf will carry the sacred arrows to give us good medicine when we capture the horses from our enemies, the Crows."

The night before the feast, Standing Buffalo lay beside his wife, Red Leaf, inside their lodge. Thoughts about their son kept them from sleeping. "Soon, our son is going to battle and he is so young, so small," she stated in a concerned voice. "My little boy! He will never return to me," she sobbed.

Her husband reached out for her and gave her a comforting hug. "Little Wolf *will* return, but he will return from battle as a *man*. A boy's eyes no more, but a man's, full of the light that shines in a warrior's heart. A light fiercer than that of the sun and more dazzling than the winter moon." He leaned toward her and placed a kiss on her forehead. "Try not to worry! I will be there to watch over him. Besides, he has the spirit of the wolf inside him. He will also be watching over our son. Now, woman of mine, get some sleep."

At the celebration, all the boys gathered around the huge firepit like swarms of night moths. Everyone was present, waiting for Chief Kicking Horse to speak to the crowd. "I ask that two young boys carry the medicine arrows and the sacred buffalo hat into battle. I will look them over; they must be strong, brave boys."

The older boys, including Spotted Dog, pushed and shoved the smaller ones to the back while trying to get the attention of the chief as he searched the crowd. Little Wolf stood off to the side with Chalk Face, his legs quivering with excitement and his stomach tied in knots even though he knew they would not be picked because of their size.

Spotted Dog's father joined his son, standing moccasin to moccasin with him as the other boys crowded around. Little Wolf suddenly felt like a chewed, dead stump left from a gnawing beaver as the rest of the log floated down the river. Then he glanced over and met his father's warm, reassuring eyes.

"You there! Come out where I can see you, boy!" the chief said sharply. "Why are you standing over there, away from the rest? Are you not Standing Buffalo's son?"

The boy nodded, struck mute by the sudden attention. His face grew hot and turned red, like the scarf that he wore; he waited for the blood that had rushed to his head to blow out of his burning ears.

"Step closer, boy! Don't shy back like a young colt." The crowd laughed, everyone except Spotted Dog, who glared at Little Wolf with hatred in his eyes. Little Wolf stepped forward on trembling legs while Chief Kicking Horse looked him over.

"He's not very big," said a warrior.

"He is as thin as a reed," shouted another.

"But he has the legs of a young antelope. And his hair is yellow, so no Crow will want his scalp," shouted yet another warrior, in the boy's defense.

"Can you run fast, boy? Are you strong and brave? Are you afraid of the People of the Raven, our enemies that the white people call the Crows?" The chief stood in front of the boy, waiting for answers.

"Yes! Yes! And, ah, I don't know," stammered the boy as he looked around him.

There was no laughter now, only stern, stolid faces that floated out of focus before his eyes. Only his father with a look of encouragement on his somber face clearly appeared before the nervous boy, and he drew courage from that quick glance and suddenly lifted his chin defiantly and stated, "Little Wolf is not afraid to die for his people."

There was a silence that fell within the circle as the other boys shifted their feet and lowered their eyes, but made no signs or spoke no words.

"This one will carry the sacred arrows," said Chief Kicking Horse. "And he will choose the boy who will bear the sacred buffalo hat. Who will you choose, Little Wolf?"

Looking at the faces of the others crowding around him, the boy knew that each one of them was eager to have the honor. But Little Wolf quickly made his choice.

Pointing at his friend, he said, "I choose Chalk Face."

"This is good, you have a good heart. Let it be done!" agreed the chief with a broad grin. "They are both small, so let us hope they will be invisible to our enemies when we steal many Crow horses. Now the elders and the two boys will come with me to my lodge and listen to the blessing of the sacred arrows and the buffalo hat before they are handed over to them."

Spotted Dog glanced over at Little Wolf, jealousy and bitterness written all over his face.

Standing Buffalo approached the two boys, who were excitedly jumping up and down as if they were trying to hold their water.

"Be little men and remain silent in the lodge. It is a great honor to be chosen and the spirits will be contacted by Chief Kicking Horse, asking them to watch over you both. I have to go and prepare for the buffalo hunt when the sun wakes in the morning but I will see you when I return. And someday soon, when we go together to seize more horses from the Crows, I will watch my son become a man, as well as you, Chalk Face."

The boys patiently sat through the long ritual and silently watched while the elders smoked the pipe and talked. The air was thick and hazy with the smell of the yellowish-colored smoke inside Chief Kicking Horse's lodge. "My stomach is full of buzzing bees," whispered Chalk Face.

"So is mine! Do you see the medicine hat lying beside the sacred arrows?" asked Little Wolf.

The medicine hat was a thick bonnet made from the skin of a buffalo cow's head. The glistening horns were shaved down and polished to a high sheen, flattened, and hand-painted with sacred colors and designs. There were rawhide straps on each side of the hat that tied under the wearer's chin to hold it in place.

Besides the buffalo hat, four arrows were neatly laid out on a piece of elk skin hide, each one containing sacred markings and had long and delicate fringes attached. The polished tips, made with the stone points found only in the ancient days, were shiny with no trace of blood on them. They looked like they were pulsing with life, almost magical to Little Wolf; he could almost feel their power burning inside him, scorching his skin. Searing his eyes!

It was probably the heat from the fire pit located in the center of the room, or maybe it was the smoke that made his eyes suddenly tear up and drip water down his face, he thought.

Chief Kicking Horse stood up and cleared his throat; he began to speak to all those gathered around him. A hush fell over the group. "Now I will begin the ceremony of handing over these sacred items that hold the power to protect our people. These gifts give us strength, health, and a long life; they give us victory over our enemies in war. My father gave these sacred gifts to me, and his father gave them to him. They are very old and have been restored many times in the past."

He held them in his hands as if they were the proudest, most important possessions that he owned. "I give these gifts to the two boys who have been chosen to carry them into battle. I ask the spirits to protect these two young boys from danger so they will walk through life unharmed, as long as the sacred gifts remain in their possession. So, guard them well! Do not let them fall in the hands of the enemy. If they are lost to you, then their great power is broken and harm will come to us."

The chief began to dance around the outside of the group while the others chanted, using gravel-throated sounds that echoed off the walls of the stale-smelling lodge jampacked with over twelve perspiring bodies. This was the *finale* of the ceremony and when the singing finally stopped, the elders talked among themselves in hushed voices because the two young boys had curled up together inside one of the buffalo robes and had fallen fast asleep in the chief's lodge.

The next morning as they were leaving the lodge, Spotted Dog stopped them. "Little Wolf, come with me! I have picked out a fast pony for you to ride tomorrow."

"Are you coming, Chalk Face?" asked Little Wolf when he noticed that his friend lagged slowly behind.

Chalk Face hesitated and said, "No, I am going home, I'm still tired."

He went on his way, feeling left out.

Little Wolf, surprised at Spotted Dog's sudden generosity, followed the older boy to the pasture where the ponies were kept. He did not trust Spotted Dog, but the promise of a fast pony interested him. He trotted after the tall boy as he quickly walked toward the slope where the ponies grazed on the long grasses. They left behind the circle of tepees with the lazy curls of smoke that rose from their smoke holes, the sound of laughter from the children playing games outside, and the steady yapping of the dogs; all this seemed so far away now.

Instead, his ears filled with the sounds of the hills. He heard the flutter of small insects buzzing around his head, the faint trilling of a meadowlark lurking in the long grass and he heard the low murmur of the wind, voices that sounded like spirits roaming through the trees. He smelled the scent of the ponies as they drew nearer and his excitement rose to a new level.

Spotted Dog suddenly stopped, turned to face the young boy with narrow, hate-filled eyes. "I hate you! You get all the attention! You wear that stupid red scarf all the time! *And* you look funny!"

He charged at the younger boy, slamming his body into the side of the unsuspecting youngster, knocking him to the ground. The breath in his lungs blew out in a sudden rush, leaving Little Wolf gasping for air. Strong arms clutched him, rolled him over on his back while fists punched his thin, bony body.

Tears welled up in his eyes as he stared at the evil smile on Spotted Dog's face. Dark spots danced in his brain as white sparks flashed within the darkness. Spotted Dog pulled at the light-colored hair while straddling the youth pinned to the ground.

Little Wolf struggled, attempted to unseat the heavier boy by grabbing him by his legs; he rolled, his quick movement catching the bigger boy off guard. He crawled out from under Spotted Dog and scrambled to his feet. He watched as Spotted Dog stood up, surprised by Little Wolf's quick recoil and he bent his head like a bull to charge at the youngster once more.

But this time, Little Wolf was waiting for him. He used his secret weapon and turned sideways, sidestepping just as Spotted Dog charged at him. Spotted Dog flew past the boy with his head bent down and slammed right into a rock, stunning him. Angered, he whirled around, staggered, and stumbled for a few steps, then collapsed on the grass, face up.

"Why do you hate me so, you big bully?" asked Little Wolf as he sat on top of his opponent.

"I should have been chosen to carry the sacred arrows. Not you! I hate you!" gasped Spotted Dog. He tried to get up and strike at the young boy again.

Little Wolf hit the older boy in the face, giving him a bloody nose. He then clenched his fist and drew back his arm as far as he could (just like he did when he successfully notched his new bow for the first time) and he let his fist fly into Spotted Dog's face again, striking him with all his might. Spotted Dog's head fell backward, the swelling already rising in his left eye. The boy on the ground briefly sat up and blood dripped from his nose.

"Stop! Stop! Can't you see I'm bleeding and I'm going to be sick," wailed Spotted Dog as he rolled on his side and emptied his stomach. He laid on the ground, curled in a ball like a small child with a stomachache, crying.

Little Wolf stood over Spotted Dog, suddenly feeling remorse toward the older boy. "Just because I look different doesn't mean I am less Lakota than you!" He spit on the defeated boy and walked away, his moccasins barely touching the ground. He felt taller when he entered the camp, victorious for the first time in his life. *It was a good day to be alive!* he thought.

Inside the lodge, he shook for no reason at all. He knew that Spotted Dog would seek him out again; he would want retribution. His mother looked at him oddly. "There is blood on your hands," she said softly.

"I must have cut myself," answered Little Wolf as he looked at his scraped knuckles. It wasn't really a lie! Well, kind of!

"Go to the river and get cleaned up before we eat." Hiding a smile, she shooed him outside. After Little Wolf had left with Spotted Dog earlier in the day, Chalk Face went straight to Standing Bull and told him about the suspicious encounter. Both parents were anxiously awaiting their son's return, knowing that Spotted Dog was up to no good.

Little Wolf ran to the river and jumped in, the cool water quickly calming him. He didn't see Spotted Dog for the rest of the day. He wanted to boast and tell the other boys about their fight, but after thinking about it, he felt it was better to keep this good secret to himself for a while. Besides, he knew that the older boy would not speak with a straight tongue; he would talk from the side of his mouth in order to save face.

Diving deeper, he opened his eyes to visualize another world full of shimmering wonders and bright glitters that changed color from the ribbons of sunlight streaming down through the clear water from the surface above.

Suddenly, in the depths of the river, there appeared before him the face of a woman he had never seen before. She was beautiful! She smiled at him and in an angelic voice, she said, "I love you, my son!"

Frightened, the boy swam upwards and surfaced, gasping for breath. His body floated on the water as he tried to clear his head of the vision he just saw.

All night, he tried to forget about the face of the beautiful woman he envisioned under the water, but he kept seeing it whenever he closed his eyes. "Who was she?" he asked himself over and over. "And why did she refer to him as 'her son'?"

Earlier, he had mentioned the vision to his parents and he noticed the look that had quickly passed between them, but nothing more was said about the incident at the river.

The next day, Five Horns and the boy went for a walk and stopped at the bottom of Sacred Hill. "Do you see this rock?" his grandfather asked.

"Yes, Grandfather!"

"I want you to come here every day and try to roll this rock up the hill. When you can do this, then I will look upon you as a man. And if you succeed in getting this boulder to the top, you can place it near the medicine wheel, where other 'tokens' were scattered to represent strength and honor among the many other brave warriors who have walked the path on Sacred Hill."

"The medicine wheel is a sacred symbol of courage and honor; it was discovered by the Lakota when they first moved into this country many, many years ago. Only a chosen few are permitted to walk this path to bring their tokens, a treasured *gift* for the Great Spirit. Your rock will be *your* token, Little Wolf."

"Couldn't you have chosen a *smaller* rock for me?" moaned the boy.

"The bigger the rock, the bigger the satisfaction you will have when you complete the task. I saw Spotted Dog today and he has a whopper of a black eye. Do you know anything about that, my grandson?" There was no comment from the young boy. The grandfather continued to speak, "He has two years on you and he is much bigger and stronger. He will seek revenge as others have been ribbing him about his black eye. He has a mean heart inside and he is not to be trusted."

"But the rock is so *big*, Grandfather. It is almost as big as me!" Little Wolf quickly sidetracked the conversation as he still felt guilty about the fight. He was hoping that someday him and Spotted Dog would have become friends. But now, he knew that was not going to happen.

"The rock will be smaller as you grow stronger."

"I will try to do as you ask, Grandfather."

The next morning, Little Wolf stood beside the huge rock, wondering if he would ever fulfill his grandfather's wish. He couldn't understand why his grandfather would give him such a mindless and seemingly unending, difficult task. It was enough to break his spirit.

The boulder *was* as big as the boy, egg-shaped, making it more difficult to roll and impossible to steady or balance even if he did manage to get it to roll. The rough and pitted exterior pricked the tender skin on his palms when he gently touched it. With his finger and some war-paint he had borrowed from his father, he drew a face on the flatter surface of the rock and when he was finished his artwork, he stood back and admired it.

"I will break *your* spirit, Mr. Rock!" he vowed to the face, smirking back at him.

It took weeks for Little Wolf to even *move* the big boulder. He had pushed and pushed with all his might, bracing his bony back against the cold, rough surface and pushing with his skinny legs, his moccasins digging a deeper hole into the dirt to gain more traction. The inch that it had moved wasn't noticeable as the smirking face still looked back at him from the same spot as before.

Chalk Face came to the bottom of Sacred Hill many times to keep his friend company while Little Wolf struggled with rolling the rock. He only stood and watched, feeling so helpless because he couldn't help him. "Did you draw the face on the rock?" asked Chalk Face.

"Yes! Why?" huffed Little Wolf as he pushed.

"Because it kinda' looks like me!" said Chalk Face.

"Nah! He is better looking," joked Little Wolf as he quit fighting with the rock and flopped down on the grass beside his friend. The boys wrestled and rolled on the grass, laughing and carrying on until they were interrupted by Willow Legs (Little Wolf's sister) and her friend, Yellow Bird. "Go away! Can't you see we are busy?"

"You don't look busy to me! What are you doing?" asked Willow Legs.

"Little Wolf is rolling this big rock," informed Chalk Face.

"It doesn't look like you rolled it too far. Can we help you?" asked Yellow Bird.

"No one can help him, not even me," answered Chalk Face.

"The face on the rock looks a bit like Spotted Dog," piped up Willow Legs.

"Why are you doing this?" asked Yellow Bird.

"Would you girls just go away. We have work to do!" spoke up Little Wolf agitatedly. He went back to the mindless task, thinking the same thing to himself. Why was he doing this?

As the days passed, Little Wolf pushed and shoved the rock, moving it inch by inch as sweat poured down his aching body. He faithfully went there every day and Chalk Face was always nearby, giving encouragement and offering advice to his friend. Also, not far away, was Five Horns who periodically checked on his grandson's progress as he remained hidden in the bushes.

Weeks faded into months and months turned into a year until the boy finally rolled the stubborn rock across the rough terrain, where it came to rest at the bottom of Sacred Hill. The gritty pitted surface of the rock left his hands chaffed and cut; blood trickled down both of his wrists when he held them up, inspecting the puffy blisters that had quickly formed over his raw palms. Five Horns watched from his hiding place as Little Wolf sank to his knees and lowered his head in dismay.

Maybe the task proved to be too much for the lad, thought Five Horns as the boy sat at the base of the rock. But, to the old man's surprise, Little Wolf pulled himself up and stood like a statue beside the rock, staring at the sneering face for at least five minutes; he was just contemplating about his next plan of action. *Now comes the hard part*, he thought; he had to roll the huge rock *uphill*.

He looked upwards and then looked back at the sneering face on the rock. He felt that the spirit of the rock was fighting with him. "You will *not* break me!" yelled Little Wolf. "I *will* get you to the top of this hill and I *will* get to see the great medicine wheel, finally! Not today. Maybe *not* tomorrow. But *someday*, you will see!"

Each day, Little Wolf tried to muscle the rock up the hill and after hours of struggling and puffing and getting the rock about halfway from the top, the rock always rolled back down to the bottom for the thousandth time, coming to rest with the painted face sneering up at him again and again. *And again.* Discouragement showed on his weary face.

"Maybe it is time for you to step away from the rock and take a break, my friend," suggested Chalk Face. "Let's go down to the river and go for a swim."

The boys swam all that day and Little Wolf decided not to return to the rock. The rock had won. It had broken the boy's spirit, at least for now.

A month later, Little Wolf and Chalk Face celebrated their fourteenth birthday. The elders held a meeting. In the Moon of the Ripening Cherries, the raiding party prepared to go in search of more horses.

The next morning, a party of thirty warriors was ready to leave the Lakota camp. Little Wolf, wearing his red scarf, a breechclout, and moccasins, proudly carried the sacred bundle containing the four sacred arrows across his lap. Beside him, Chalk Face, who was also dressed in a breechclout and moccasins, wore the sacred buffalo hat on his head.

Little Wolf brought his fine ash bow and a full quiver of arrows and the new buffalo shield that his father had given him the day before in honor of his first raid. *It was a good day to be alive*, thought Little Wolf.

It was nightfall when the warriors finally arrived at the outskirts of the Crow camp. "We do not come here to kill Crows," reminded Five Horns as he addressed the party of warriors around him. "We will quietly take their horses and leave them to walk back to their women when they awake."

"These are good words! And these two brave boys will bring us good medicine tonight." Standing Buffalo stayed close to his son, not forgetting the promise he made to Red Leaf to take care of Little Wolf in case something went wrong during the raid.

"*Hau!*" the others cried wildly but quickly became silent again as they rode closer to the enemy's camp.

Among all the people, the Crows were most skilled at stealing *army* horses, as the army was known to breed only the best horses in the land, thus making the Crows 'prime targets' for their enemies to steal from them over and over again.

The Lakota had stolen Crow horses many times in the past, usually during a dark, moonless eve, just like tonight. The plan was the same as before, to quietly overtake the guards who watched over the herd while the others slept, steal their prized horses, and then get as far away as possible before the unsuspecting Crows awoke in the morning. The plot was good! But sometimes, things don't always go as planned.

On the ride there, a wolf howled, not once, but four times. To the Comanche, this was an omen, a *bad* omen. And if they were going on a raid, they would immediately turn around and go back home because this was a sign of death among their people. The Lakota warriors kept going, getting closer to the Crow camp. They could hear the horses not far away.

"I will scout ahead to see where the guards are," offered Swift Deer as he rode away, his braids flopping on his sweat-sleeked back. The others awaited his return.

One hour passed and Swift Deer was still not back. To Little Wolf's disappointment, Standing Buffalo decided to send the two young boys to the rear of the party so the older, slower warriors could watch over them. Even so, Little Wolf could feel the excitement within him. He looked over at Chalk Face and he looked afraid.

"We go to steal, not to do battle," reminded Five Horns quietly.

"But with the Crows, sometimes the two tomahawks get crossed," spoke up Black Cloud.

The band had gathered together in a wide grassy spot. "We shall meet back here in this clearing before we head home."

Five Horns had held the warriors in silence for a long time while they waited for Swift Deer to return. The sun was trying to hide in the hills to the west before it went to sleep and there were long shadows creeping along the ground.

Finally, Swift Deer appeared out of the bushes. Gone were his lance and his shield. His body was leaking sweat, smeared clots of dirt and scratches covered his face, his arms, and legs. And his eyes looked ferocious like that of a wild animal. "The Crows have made camp below a ridge near the river. Many horses! Many braves too! There are three scouts guarding the horses. They are just young kids, maybe Little Wolf's age," reported Swift Deer between gasps of breaths.

"Three of you go and take care of the guards," ordered Five Horns. "Be cautious! Just because they are young doesn't mean they aren't dangerous. The Crows are taught to be fierce warriors at a very early age. Wait five minutes! Then the rest of you can go to the herd and bring back your horses. When we have enough, we will go home."

Little Wolf watched the brown shadows slink through the trees like phantoms in the night after Five Horns made the advance sign with his hands. He looked over at Chalk Face, who tried to manage a sickly grin, who jumped at every faint sound. The soft footpads of the stalking warriors, the rustle of leaves in the wind, the rattle of an overturned stone.

Chalk Face was trembling all over and his blood had drained away into his neck; a short time later, Little Wolf heard his friend give up his food in the bushes. Little Wolf waited for his friend to return. He continued to watch in awe as the warriors slid over the bank of the dry creek, crouching. Moving closer toward the massed hulk of the pony herd.

A shadow cautiously moved down the streambed and bent toward another shadow from behind, like a spider embracing a fly; the man in front fell to the ground and laid there as if he was asleep. After receiving a hand signal, Lakota brothers disappeared into the herd like fish diving through clusters of minnows, disturbing the passive ponies.

This disruption created a nervous reaction, causing them to move about. They shoved and snorted at each other as they tried to spread out, fanning into smaller bunches of fifty or more which made it easier for the raiders to drop ropes around their necks and lead them away. One by one, the warriors passed by Little Wolf, each pulling strings of six to a dozen rope-haltered ponies to take back to their meeting place until finally, the convoy stopped.

While Little Wolf waited for Chalk Face, a rider rode up and stood beside him. "I'm going to make you sorry for what you did to me. I will seek revenge!" spat out Spotted Dog. "I should have been the chosen one to carry those sacred arrows. *Not* you!"

As the moon peeked out from behind the clouds, Little Wolf caught a glimpse of the infuriated face before the older boy rode off into the darkness. Spotted Dog was consumed with hate. His grandfather's warning flashed into his mind about the boy having a mean heart and was not to be trusted. A cold chill ran down his spine. Little Wolf suddenly felt fear around him. His hand went down and reassuringly touched the bundle of arrows.

He closed his eyes and listened; it was as if the whole world had suddenly stood still. It was so quiet, only time was moving in the emptiness. He had to strain to hear his own breathing, even though his heart was pounding in his chest. Still, he was suffocating, wrapped in an eerie darkness as it closed in all around him.

He felt so alone in a *hushed* world. He heard the soft whickers of ponies nearby, the short wail of a child that was quickly silenced, the break of a twig. He heard a *crunching* sound, like that of gristle and flesh being stabbed by a knife. And then another louder crunch, like the sound of breaking bone, coming from a man locked in a death grip, his neck suddenly twisted.

Little Wolf heard a grunt, like someone passing wind, then there were no more sounds.

An uneasiness engulfed Little Wolf; he sensed danger. *Something* was wrong! He quickly opened his eyes, expecting to see a Crow warrior waiting to club him with a tomahawk; no one was there. But he *did* see shadows, losing their shape and becoming dark blotches without form or substance. A crouching shadow, outlined against the black skyline, then another, and another. Advancing!

They were not Lakota! Where was Chalk Face? He never came out of the bushes. Now worried, Little Wolf still waited, but there was no sign of him. He couldn't call out to him for fear of alerting the enemy. He didn't know what to do.

Little Wolf, detecting movement coming toward him, jabbed moccasined heels into his pony's flanks and galloped toward the clearing, their meeting place. But horse and rider were caught in the middle of a herd of runaway ponies. Little Wolf hung on to the rope strung around the pony's neck with both hands.

For fear of being trampled, he steered the terrified pony into the trees in order to get out of the way. The pony broke away from the stampeding animals but left his rider with the task of ducking at tree branches as they unexpectantly whipped at him out of the darkness like grasping hands and pinching fingers, raking his skin, and pulling at his hair. He rode through dust, tasting grit between his teeth. Cries from the Lakota pierced the night, their voices floating through the trees like ghostly echoes fading in and out. His crazed pony finally slowed and came to a stop near the clearing.

Most of the warriors were at the meeting place, holding lead ropes of captured ponies, about a dozen each. Little Wolf saw his father and his grandfather whispering to the others as he rode up. But he did not see Chalk Face in the crowd. Then he felt his lap, remembering about the sacred arrows. His fingers groped for the precious bundle, but it was not there. The bundle was gone!

He turned his pony around and rode back the same way he came; his father called out his name but he kept riding away, back to where he had been waiting before, with Chalk Face. He knew he had the bundle then. It must have fallen to the ground, lost *somewhere* in the darkness. He blinked back the stinging tears; no one must know that he had lost the arrows, the bundle so sacred to his people that had been entrusted to *him*. He choked back a sob, his heart pounding inside his chest. He was *chosen* to take care of the precious bundle. He must find it!

However, the darkness wasn't Little Wolf's only challenger. The Crow camp had been alerted and burst alive. And he was riding toward their camp; at any minute he could come face to face with angry Crow warriors. He must hurry and find that bundle! He kept riding, backtracking. Searching the ground, even though it was too dark to see anything. The arrows could have gotten trampled during the stampede, broken into pieces.

He frantically searched, relying on his night vision but it wasn't very good. Not far away, he suddenly heard a wolf howl and about forty feet in front of him, he saw two shining blue lights, the eyes of a large white wolf, staring at him. When the frightened boy got closer, the animal disappeared. Little Wolf stopped his pony and looked at the ground where it had stood just minutes before. There, in its tracks, was the bundle of arrows.

Little Wolf bent down and grabbed the precious bundle and securely planted it back on his lap. He looked all around him, but because of the darkness, he saw nothing but the trees surrounding him. He quickly turned his pony around and galloped back to the meeting place again, this time keeping one hand over the bundle as he rode.

When Little Wolf dismounted, he tied his pony to a small tree and heaved a deep sigh of relief for a safe return. He clutched the bundle of arrows close to his chest, not wanting to let them out of his sight. Strangely, the temporary camp seemed very subdued, whereas the warriors should have been elated with such a large number of fine ponies they had captured. His father approached him.

"Our medicine was strong today," said Little Wolf as his eyes roamed over the herd. "I still have the sacred arrows; I did not—lose them." There was no reply from Standing Buffalo. Little Wolf continued, "I am anxious to speak with Chalk Face. Where is he?" He heard his father draw in his breath, but he couldn't see his face as he had lowered his head.

"Father?"

"Show me the arrows, Son." Standing Buffalo pulled the arrows out of the bundle and inspected each one. "There is one that is broken!"

Little Wolf saw that one of the arrows *was* broken. "I did not break it, Father!"

"One broken arrow, one death," said his father sadly.

"What do you mean, Father?" asked Little Wolf, confused by his words.

"Chalk Face is dead!"

Little Wolf's throat tightened; he could not swallow and he suddenly felt light-headed. "No, this cannot be! The last time I saw him, he went into the bushes to vomit; he said he suddenly felt sick. I waited, but he never returned."

"Five Horns found him; he spoke a few words before he gave up his spirit in your grandfather's arms. He was stabbed twice in the back and his neck was broken."

Little Wolf still wouldn't believe the news. But when he looked over and saw Chalk Face's father crying, he realized it was true. A sob escaped from deep within the boy's body and his eyes misted over; his father's face swam before him like a reflection in a stream. He felt his father's consoling hand pat his shoulder. "We have one broken arrow and the buffalo hat is gone. Do not lose the sacred bundle, my son! That could mean death for us all now." His father walked away.

"No," said the boy, his lips quivering. He wondered now if Chalk Face had died while the arrows were lost. Or was that crunching noise he had heard when he had his eyes closed, coming from the bushes where Chalk Face was killed. Was his killer *that* close to him? Could he have saved him?

He blamed himself for his friend's death and also for the loss of the buffalo hat. "Father, wait! I have something to tell you." But his father couldn't hear him.

Just as he went to go after him, a shadow appeared and a hand gripped his arm above the elbow. He saw Spotted Dog's sneering face. "Here! You can have this back." He threw the buffalo hat at him. "I have taken my revenge! But this is not the end of it. There will be more deaths and each one will be on your head because I *hate* you!" he spat at Little Wolf before he stalked away.

Minutes later, Five Horns and Spotted Dog were having a heated conversation. Five Horns was saying strong words while shaking his fist into the older boy's face as he spoke. As their voices got louder, the others gathered around and stood beside Little Wolf, wondering what the trouble was about. The charged air was emitting sparks of anger from the old man, directed toward the older boy. If the boy had raised his eyes and looked at Five Horns at any time, he would have been killed on the spot; that is how outraged the old man was.

Five Horns continued to shame him by insulting and provoking while not once mentioning his warrior name. "This coward squats to pee like a woman! This coward does not fight like a man! This coward steals from his people! This coward doesn't fight with men! Instead, he fights with a young boy whose voice is still high and who will never see his fifteenth summer. This coward killed Chalk Face! He has the Evil Spirit inside him and he must be punished."

Little Wolf watched as Spotted Dog's face grew dark with anger and then a vein in his neck started to quiver and pulse as he began to shake with fear like the quivering chest of a frightened bird suddenly caught in an eagle's claw. As Five Horns stepped closer, Spotted Dog snatched the old man's lance out of his hand, and with a swift sweep, he struck Five Horns in the head, knocking him to the ground. A loud, collective *'hooouuu'* tore from the bystanders like a gust of wind ripping through the trees. Five Horns staggered to his feet, holding up his hand to stop the angry, advancing warriors.

Meanwhile, Spotted Dog ran through the crowd, swinging the lance in one hand and jabbing at his brothers with the knife held in his other hand. Warriors fell away from him as he slashed and struck like a wild man. He reached his pony and quickly mounted, then before he galloped away, he turned and shook the stolen lance at his people in defiance. Five of his friends ran to their ponies and also mounted up, following close behind him.

"We should chase them. Spotted Dog should be punished!" shouted one of the warriors.

"No! He *will* be punished!" Five Horns looked straight at his grandson, who fumed with anger. "But *not* at this time! Do you hear me, Little Wolf?"

"Yes, Grandfather. I hear you!"

"If we chase after them, we could lose all of our ponies. No!" Five Horns repeated. "We will take the ponies home. And the wounded. We will return to our people. We will tell Chief Kicking Horse what has happened here. Come! We must leave this place before the Crows find us. And," he paused, "we will take Chalk Face home too."

Little Wolf was disappointed. He wanted to go after Spotted Dog, to punish him. He wanted to make him suffer, then kill him just like he killed Chalk Face. Just like he hurt his grandfather and all the rest of his Lakota brothers. But he would wait. And when he got bigger and stronger, he *would* kill Spotted Dog, even if it took him years.

After losing the sacred bundle and then finding out that one arrow had somehow gotten broken, he wondered if all of his hate was just more bad medicine for the Lakota people. Did these things cause Chalk Face's death? Spotted Dog's angry outburst? And what else was going to happen after today?

His heart cried out and shouted, but his voice was silent. He wanted to ask his father, confide in him, about losing the sacred bundle. But Standing Buffalo had turned away from him when he tried to talk to him. Little Wolf had never felt so alone.

When the sky was the color of skinned salmon, the warriors started out for home, herding over one hundred fine ponies with them. They traveled all day and throughout the night, putting much ground between them and the Crows. There was no sign of anyone following, as they kept a steady pace. All the way home, Little Wolf brooded, his thoughts as dark as a moonless sky at night. Thoughts of Chalk Face and how he died occupied his mind. Was he to blame?

He knew that guilt rode with him and he wanted to gallop far, far away; feel the wind blow through his hair and infiltrate into his mind until it eliminated this horrible feeling. Eventually ridding his body of the numbness that was eating away at him from within. But he knew he could not outrun the wind. No more than he could turn back time to change what had happened to his friend back there.

Thin clouds of powdery dust rose from the horses' hooves and the sunlight bounced off the bobbing rumps of the loping herd in front of Little Wolf as he strained to hear every word spoken by the men around him. But he didn't understand what they were talking about even though he thought he heard his name mentioned a few times, and their voices grew softer when they realized that he was listening.

He looked at the fine ponies and grew proud that there was so much wealth for his people; their medicine was not *all* bad. He thought of Chalk Face and how proud he was to wear the buffalo hat. It was hard to imagine his friend not being there with him, *never* being there to swim or play with him again. Even just to talk to him! He wondered where his spirit was if he could hear his thoughts.

"Can you *hear* me, my friend? Can you *see* these things in my heart? Do you *know* how much my heart hurts?" he asked silently. A big gust of wind suddenly blew up and he saw Chalk Face's image in the swirl of dust that rose up directly in front of him.

As the image disappeared, Little Wolf suddenly felt his *presence* close by. *Imagined* him sitting behind him, riding on the pony with him. He felt the *caress* of warm breath on his neck like a feather tickling his skin. Something Chalk Face would have done whenever they played jokes on each other.

"Your spirit is with me now, and maybe it will be with me always," said Little Wolf silently. "Maybe your spirit will help me live, just as the meat from an animal nourishes me." His people strongly believed that whenever they killed an animal and took it for food, it was a gift and they must thank that animal for giving up his life to save the people. This way, they become one. These thoughts made him feel not so alone. But the emptiness was still there.

A week had passed after the raid and Little Wolf felt that he needed to talk to someone, so he went to see Chief Kicking Horse. "I see you have grown, young man. Soon you will see your fifteenth summer," greeted the chief in Lakota. "You have a reason for coming to see me, finally?"

Little Wolf shamefacedly confessed about losing the bundle of arrows and he told him about the wolf with the shining blue eyes that showed him where he had dropped them. He told him about the threat

Spotted Dog had made to him, telling him that there would be more deaths as he still sought revenge. He admitted that his body was filled with an enormous amount of hate for Spotted Dog and how he wished bad things would happen to him.

They talked about the death of Chalk Face and the vision he had seen on the ride home. And he had many questions about death. "Where do the dead go?" he asked.

"The spirits of the deceased will find the road that leads to where the footprints all point the same way. They will follow the trail that leads to the stars and will meet all their ancestors and friends who live there," Chief Kicking Horse answered.

"Is that where Chalk Face is now?"

"I do not know. Maybe his spirit is still on the road," replied the chief.

"What is it like there?" asked the boy.

"Well, that is the great mystery. I do not know because I have never been there. I have heard of others, though, who have been sick or wounded, small children with fever who have closed their eyes and went to this country in the sky, but they were sent back. They have seen the camp of the dead, even spoke to the people there. When they try to enter, they are turned away and return to life. Afterward, they do not speak about this place very much."

"Will the bad people like Spotted Dog go there, too?"

"I believe that people are equal after death. There is no punishment there, nor are there any rewards for virtue. Spotted Dog's spirit will travel on the 'Delayed Road'; it is a wider, longer path that is more difficult to navigate."

"You are very old! Aren't you afraid of dying?" asked the boy.

Chief Kicking Horse chuckled. "Yes, I am *old*! But life is only temporary." The wise old man hesitated and took a deep breath. "And in every lifetime, there is no losing, only learning, and pain is part of growing. Every little struggle is a step forward; as a Lakota warrior, your scars are a symbol of your strength."

Another hesitation and deep breath. "Unfortunately, as we age, there is more pain. Cold weather brings more pain to my old body; my fingers swell and my legs are bent from too many battle wounds, and my bones have become brittle. Winter is coming again, and it is a time for things to die. Death will soon be knocking at *my* door. Until then, I am not afraid. Besides, why should I fear something that I have not seen?"

"I feel so much better now that I have talked to you," blurted out Little Wolf. "Soon, you will take up the lance and you will fight battles also. Be not afraid to die. A Lakota warrior would rather die for his people in a battlefield than waste away in a square, wooden house, eating store-bought food and travel the white man's road until he dies."

"Chalk Face will never get to experience this. But he will experience life through you! His spirit walks with you every day. His scaffold has already been prepared. So, go and mourn with his family tomorrow on Sacred Hill. He would like you to be present at his funeral." The meeting with Chief Kicking Horse had come to an end.

Chalk Face's small body was wrapped in a robe and was placed on a travois. The funeral procession moved slowly toward Sacred Hill; women wept as they followed alongside and the warriors on horseback carried their bows and arrows and lances as if they were heading to battle. The children lagged behind, for fear of being snatched up by the ghosts of the deceased.

They came to the bottom of Sacred Hill, walking past Little Wolf's big rock, and climbed the steep hill until they came to the empty land where the dead were always taken. A loud keening arose from the women when they saw the old scaffolds with tattered pieces of hide clothing flapping in the wind. Chalk Face's pony was killed earlier and laid to rest near where his scaffold was erected.

This was done with the horse of every warrior that had died in the past. Little Wolf went over to his friend's weeping family as they huddled together under the empty scaffold and he stayed with them. Atop the wooden construction, was all the young boy's possessions.

There wasn't much inside the small bundle. Placed on top of the bundle by Chief Kicking Horse, was the sacred buffalo hat.

The funeral didn't last very long and everyone made their way back to camp. Everyone except Little Wolf! He stopped at the bottom of Sacred Hill and stared at the big rock with the painted face. It stared back at him. "I will not give in to you. You will not win this fight!" he vowed.

He had made up his mind to finish the task that he had started more than two years ago, a mindless task whereas Chalk Face faithfully stood by him day after day, hour after hour, and had relentlessly cheered him on. Encouraging him, until the rock finally broke the boy's spirit. Now that he was older and smarter, he was confident that he could get this rock on top of Sacred Hill. And he would do it for Chalk Face. He owed his loyal friend that much, at least.

For weeks, Little Wolf pushed the rock. Not only was the boy's spirit unbroken, he seemingly gained strength and more confidence from the task. The more the rock resisted, the harder the boy pushed and when it inevitably rolled back down the hill, he showed no disappointment and would start all over again.

Five Horns, watching from his usual seat in the bushes, noticed the firm, defined muscles forming on the boy's body; his legs and arms grew stronger and sturdier, his shoulders widened and he developed sizable pectorals on his chest. *The boy is becoming a man. We will have to change his name because he is not little anymore*, thought his grandfather.

Little Wolf's mother had commented just the other day about her son getting taller and his body was outgrowing all of his clothes lately. Even the girls, especially Yellow Bird, were stealing second looks of admiration whenever he was passing by. She would sometimes sit nearby while Little Wolf struggled with the rock, offering him encouragement also. It was as if Chalk Face had sent her to take his place. And, instead of shooing her away like he used to do, he actually liked her company.

In fact, he seemed to show off and try to push harder whenever she was around. As the word spread, more spectators from the village came to watch. They sometimes brought food and water and offered some to Little Wolf as he persistently struggled with the rock.

A month went by, then two, and on an especially powerful eve, because it was going to be the shortest night of the year, the summer solstice it was called, Little Wolf rolled the rock right to the top. But as usual, it was starting to slip back down. "Not this time, rock! Not this time!" He turned his back to the boulder and braced it with his legs. Blinking back tears, he shouted to the wind, "I am not giving up!"

He heard the howl of a wolf nearby. He looked all around, then above him, while still fighting with the rock; he saw the huge white wolf again, waiting at the top of Sacred Hill. It had great power because its presence seemed to gladden Little Wolf's heart, giving him more strength and encouragement. Temporarily forgetting about his visitor, he reached behind him and grasped a smaller rock within reach, and jammed it beneath the surface of the boulder to keep it from rolling back down the hill.

He then cautiously turned around to face the rock once more and gave it one last shove, realizing that before today, he had never experienced such strength. He felt the spirit of the rock relent as it suddenly rolled easily over the lip of the ridge, and it kept rolling for a few more yards before it finally came to rest beside the sacred medicine wheel.

Little Wolf stared at the painted face as it looked back at him; when the rock had finally gone over the ridge, smaller stones had scraped the surface and disfigured it, drawing a distinct line down the left side of the painted face, like a white scar. And instead of a sneer, there was a definite smile. Now it really did look like Chalk Face looking back, congratulating him for finally completing the difficult task that his grandfather had given him so long ago.

"We did it, my friend! We did it *together*." Thoughts of Chalk Face immediately filled his heart with sadness; he sank to his knees and sobbed until he couldn't cry anymore.

The sun silently slipped into the western horizon. It was nearly twilight and stars were beginning to appear in the clear sky. The night of the solstice! Little Wolf got up and walked around the plateau. Beyond the two-hundred-foot clearing, were acres of rolling land divided by flowing waterfalls that intertwined as they descended down the steeper hills. Falling, until the water came to rest at the base of a big valley, tons of fresh, foaming water dumping into a large stream that seemed to get bigger over the years.

On almost every hillside, sacred headstone markers representing Lakota ancestors dotted the land. He walked back to the medicine wheel that was placed so reverently in the center of the grassy plateau where few visitors were allowed to tread, except to leave their tokens. There were massive buffalo skulls flanked with eagle feathers fluttering in the wind; each skull was painted with power symbols like the sun, the moon, stars and bolts of lightning, and even the buffalo itself.

There were other 'tokens' scattered around the wheel also, medicine pouches filled with secret things, skeleton bones of human fingers from famous holy men, chiefs and medicine men, and brave warriors. But the 'token' that surprised him the most was a beautifully painted tomb that was inscribed in gold lettering on the outside. The name inscribed was 'Meadowlark'. Draped over the tomb was a white wolf-hide, protecting it. Guarding it!

Little Wolf suddenly remembered the white wolf who was still waiting at the top of the hill when he pushed the rock for the last time and the strength he had felt inside him at that moment. The power he possessed had come from that wolf. The *spirit* of the White Wolf was inside him. For the first time, he actually felt it!

Darkness fell and Little Wolf made his way down Sacred Hill. The wind suddenly picked up and above him, coming from the top of the hill, a piercing howl sliced the air. The sound gradually faded away.

Part Four

The Sweetheart's Dance was a big, yearly event put on by the *Hee-maneh* people; they were special people, half men-half women, who usually stayed to themselves and were seldom seen but were revered by the tribe whenever they walked in procession beyond their circle or domain. Everyone loved these men who had taken up the ways of women and the smaller, nastier boys often made fun of them, only to be severely punished by their elders afterwards.

Thus, they only mingled with the others on very rare occasions, like a wedding or a special feast. This was the only event that they organized and it was always a success among the younger group that were coming of age to enter into matrimony, like sixteen-year-old Little Wolf and Yellow Bird. The dance was created by their ancestors for the sole purpose of matching up couples and helping them to get to know one another better.

In following with tradition, before the last dance of the night, a gift chosen from the heart was to be presented to the lady by her suitor or suitors, whichever the case may be; if she accepted the gift as she bobbed and stooped and twirled around that suitor, then that was her chosen partner. However, the courtship wasn't to really begin until the father of the future bride gave his blessing to the couple. And sometimes, that blessing *never* came from the over-possessive dad.

Little Wolf was joyfully matched with Yellow Bird at the dance more than four months ago, after giving her a beaded bracelet that he had made especially for her. She had looked at him in *that* way and batted her long black eyelashes and his heart soared like a hawk.

After that night, whenever he got a chance to see her, his stomach felt like it was filled with fluttering butterflies and when she smiled at him, his insides melted like fire held under beeswax. He saw her face in every twinkling star and the tangled rush of emotions that always overcame him when he tried to sleep were like scattered leaves in a fall windstorm.

He became clumsy whenever she was near, stumbling over his own moccasins and then quickly recovering, always hoping she never noticed. If she had noticed, she would just smile, and the butterflies would come back to invade his stomach again. The fact that Yellow Bird had become more beautiful than all the other maidens didn't help the matter, leaving Little Wolf more smitten than before. And Black Elk, Yellow Bird's father, was still skeptical about allowing the relationship to continue.

"Maybe you should have sent a more respected messenger with a more valued endowment to my father. Your messenger made my father angry by offering four *dogs* instead of four fine horses," retorted Yellow Bird.

"Standing Colt is my *friend*! And I don't have four fine *horses* to give to your father!" answered Little Wolf angrily.

"Oh, Little Wolf! Do you really want to be my husband? Sometimes your mind is like stone! Your eyes are like blue granite! My heart beats fast for you, but you wait and wait until sometimes, I think you have changed your mind about me."

"Do not say that, woman! You are so fickle! I will send a good messenger this time, and I will get four fine *horses* so we can get married."

"*Good!*" she snapped and stalked away in a huff.

The next day, Little Wolf's grandmother, Two Faces in the Wind, tied six fine horses in front of Black Elk's lodge and waited for him to come outside. "My grandson wishes to have your daughter, Yellow Bird, for his wife," the old woman bluntly stated.

Black Elk hummed and hawed as he walked around the horses, inspecting them before he spoke. "They are a fine breed you have offered. I am pleased. But before the marriage ceremony takes place, Little Wolf has to accomplish the hunting ritual to prove his ability to provide for my daughter. He must go by himself and bring back a large buck for their wedding feast. When he does this, then I will give them my blessing."

The next day, Little Wolf, pulling a travois behind him, left the camp to go on a hunting trip. On the first day, he only saw a rabbit. He shot it with an arrow and cooked it for his dinner that night but the meat was stringy, tough. The second day, he became irritated as he waited in vain. Waiting had never been easy for the young man. Little Wolf could see the well-worn path leading to the creek's edge where deer came to drink. He knew they were there; he just had to be patient.

As he waited, the clouds rolled in and darkened the sky. It was a cold rain which added to his misery. He spent a long night discouraged and shivering and wondering if maybe he should rethink his plans. Was all this really worth the effort of taking a wife? Already, she was telling him what to do and they weren't even married yet. *Hei!*

As the sun warmed his skin the next morning, things seemed a lot brighter, and his determination to please Black Elk returned. He expanded his chest and yelled to the trees, "I am Little Wolf! I am the son of a brave warrior, Standing Buffalo, and like my father, I will someday be a shirt-wearer who hunts for his people."

With his bow held firmly in his right hand and an arrow with a sharp iron point nocked to the gut-string, Little Wolf squatted in the long grass and waited downwind, amidst the morning mists. His breath made little clouds and the cold seeped through open seams in his buckskin shirt. There was the taste of coming snow in the air, even though the rising sun was trying to draw the coolness out of the earth.

Little Wolf shivered from excitement as well as from the cold. He massaged the backs of his hands and made fists to warm his fingers, trying to keep the warm blood flowing so that he could shoot true when the time came. The slight breeze blew against him from the north so he had to remember to take into consideration the wind velocity when he took his shot. Little Wolf *waited*.

Yesterday, he had seen fresh droppings along the game trail. He had also spotted fresh rubs, a scrape that gave off the musk of a buck deer in the rut. Saplings had been driven into the ground by the buck's antlers, the earth gouged where he pawed with his hooves and dug with his sharp tines. Little Wolf guessed him to be a ten-pointer for sure.

Hours passed slowly, and he *waited*. The sun had dropped in the west and dusk was falling around him. Shadows of tree branches reached out to hug his cold body. Once again, the unsureness closed in on him as he laid in the dewy grass, teeth chattering from the cold wind that had arisen from the north. His patience was wearing thin.

When suddenly, something crashed in the brush on the other side of the creek. Little Wolf brought his bow up slowly, ready to pull back on the arrow. He heard a buck snort. A few minutes later, two do nonchalantly walk to the edge of the water, the white of their under-tail flicking in the wind. Not far behind, a young buck playfully romped, flipping *his* black-tipped tail. The yearling, wanting to mate with one of the does, was half blind with the lust-heat of the rut. Little Wolf chuckled to himself; he knew exactly what that young buck was going through.

He always felt the same way whenever he was around Yellow Bird.

Then Little Wolf saw him! Emerging from the tree line, a big mule buck showed himself. Closer and closer he came, rubbery nostrils twitching, his ears perked. He was also lust-driven, chasing the smaller buck away from the does. He came back to the water's edge and lowered his magnificent head to nibble from the rippling creek bed while never taking his eyes off the lustful does.

Little Wolf was reluctant to kill such a magnificent creature but then Yellow Bird's face flashed before him, reminding him of why he was here. His long hours of waiting had finally come to an end. He took careful aim, steadying his shooting hand against his cheek. He sighted down the shaft, released his fingers while the horny buck was still preoccupied.

The arrow whispered through the air, cutting a straight path toward the big buck. The point thudded into the buck's side, penetrating his lung. The animal reared back, fell on its side. It quickly got up again, glaze-eyed and wobbly on his feet. He flicked the massive rack of antlers from side to side, trying to dislodge the arrow. But it was sunk too deep into his flesh. Finally, the magnificent animal gave up the struggle.

Little Wolf ran as fast as he could go until he reached the edge of the creek. He crossed at the shallowest point, carefully stepping onto the big flat stones wedged in the muck. When he reached the buck, *two* arrows protruded from the deer's side. And another arrow had also dropped the yearling nearby. Its forelegs were doubled under his body and frothy blood bubbled from its open mouth. The yearling kicked out one knobby leg for the last time and let out a long, raspy wheeze, emptying the air from its lungs.

At this point, Little Wolf, kneeling beside the big buck with his bowie knife in his hand, was about to cut off the scent glands so the meat wouldn't get spoiled; he looked up into a painted face. The warrior was also brandishing a knife. A savage war-cry rose up out of the warrior's throat as he lunged at Little Wolf. They rolled over each other, down the hillside, and came to rest in the creek. Both of them were dripping wet and they still lunged forward with their knives.

Little Wolf struck the warrior in the crotch, missing his privates by only inches. Then the attacker plunged forward, also missing Little Wolf's crotch by inches. Little Wolf saw his chance and grabbed the attacker by the wrist, dislodging the slippery knife handle from his hand where it fell into the water and floated downstream. The two young braves still stood in the water, facing each other. Glaring!

The attacker spoke in Lakota. "That was my deer! My arrow is in his flesh."

"No, I shot that deer! My arrow is also in his flesh," argued Little Wolf. The two braves stood in the freezing water, arguing about whose deer it belonged to, until finally, they both started to laugh.

"We will share it!" suggested the attacker.

"No, I need that deer!" pleaded Little Wolf. He then told him why he needed this particular deer. "Without it, I cannot marry Yellow Bird."

"OK, you can have it. But I will take the little one," relented the brave. "Now, can we get out of this freezing water? I am cold."

The two young Lakota warriors formed a truce between them and helped each other load their bucks onto their travois'. Before parting, they exchanged names. Little Wolf told him his name and the other warrior volunteered his name. "I am Fast Walker."

At long last, Little Wolf returned to the camp with the large ten-point buck strapped to his travois. *Now, I can marry Yellow Bird and we can have many children together*, he thought excitedly.

A storm was brewing from the north-west and the cool wind howled, heeding a warning of everything blocking its path. As Little Wolf got closer to the camp, he could smell *bad* smoke, the sickly-sweet scent of burned flesh. He dropped the travois and took off in a gallop.

When he got to the camp, he sat atop his horse and stared in disbelief. All was quiet, except for the haunting wind whistling through smoldering, skeletal lodge poles that hovered over cold ashes. The blood-stained ground was littered with dead bodies, pierced bodies of elderly brave warriors, and the mutilated bodies of many women and children; all were still dressed in their bedclothes, surprised by a middle-of-the-night ambush.

An arrow protruded from the chest of a small child nearby; his mother, also dead beside him, an empty cradleboard still attached to her back. *Comanche!* thought Little Wolf at first. But no! They were *Lakota* arrows! Little Wolf slid off his horse and emptied his stomach. These were his people. His *family*. He knew all of them; he had played with the little boy not that long ago.

Inside his father's scorched lodge, he found the mutilated bodies of his mother and his sister. Both had been scalped between their legs. Nearby lay his father, Standing Buffalo, also dead and scalped. The firepit in the center of the room still contained amber coals casting long eerie shadows across the charred tepee walls. A little, terrified dog suddenly ran under what was left of the singed canvas flap, yipping at him, and when he realized who it was, he leaned against Little Wolf's leg; he could feel the small dog's fear as it shuddered and shook.

His grandmother's dog, Bones, was the only dog that had ever allowed Little Wolf to get close to him without growling. Suddenly, he heard his grandmother calling his name, her voice coming from outside, behind the tepee. Little Wolf ran to her. She was alive!

Two Faces in the Wind was propped up against the trunk of a large tree, her face and hair were blackened from the smoke. Little Wolf saw dried trails of tears that had run down her face earlier. Her dress was pulled up, exposing her private parts. She had a *penis*! And *testicles*! His grandmother was a *Hee-man-eh*, a half man-half woman. And Little Wolf never knew! He quickly looked away to hide his shock. But deep-down, he really didn't care what she was. He loved her anyway!

"The only reason that I am still alive is because I would have brought them bad luck if they killed someone like me," she choked out.

"Grandmother, where is Yellow Bird?"

"Over there!" She pointed her finger. She would never forget the dread in her grandson's eyes before he turned away. He was crying as he walked among the bodies strewn on the ground, frantically searching. He saw an outstretched arm with a beaded bracelet on it. He couldn't recognize the woman's mutilated face but he knew who she was. That was the bracelet that he had made for his future wife. His beautiful Yellow Bird!

Who would do this to a human body? Someone evil! Someone sick! he thought. The broken warrior cradled the young girl's body in his arms and sobbed. In that moment, Little Wolf was holding his whole life in his arms!

He went back to his grandmother. "They came in the night when we were sleeping," she said. "The soldiers came the next day. They are with Chief Kicking Horse right now, talking to him in his lodge. He is hurt pretty bad. I heard them say that everyone else is dead."

"Who did this, Grandmother?"

"Some renegades! Maybe nine or ten! They were led by Spotted Dog!"

The rage inside Little Wolf exploded inside his body. "I will *kill* him! I will *find* him, and I will make him pay for murdering my family, my people! I will *look* until I find him! As *Wakan Tanka* is my witness, *I promise you!* But first, I will see that my family receives a proper burial."

Just as Little Wolf was about to make scaffolds for the dead bodies, the soldiers came up behind him. The Sergeant jumped off his horse and tackled the young brave, thinking he might be one of the warriors responsible for this massacre. The leader with the yellow hair like his own barked at the soldier, "Leave him be, Sergeant! Can't you see he is just taking care of his family?" To Little Wolf, he said, "*So,* we meet again! Only now, the little *savage* has become a man."

Captain Burns noticed that the kid's skin had slightly darkened to a golden color from the sun and his body had developed into a mass of rippling, hard muscle. He also noticed that the young brave had on the same red scarf that he had worn on the day they had met when the boy was just a small child.

Captain Burns would have recognized that scarf anywhere; he had purchased it in Paris when he went on vacation with his wife. It had cost him a small fortune at the time because it was spun with pure silk and fringed with hand-sewn, colorful beading. It was the same scarf that he had given to Meadowlark on her birthday. It was the *same* red scarf that she had worn on the day she died.

Little Wolf ignored the captain, letting him think that he didn't understand his words.

"Corporal Good Shield, this man is in need of our assistance. Choose ten good men to stay with you to assist with the burial procedures. Sergeant Collins, take four men to attend to the chief and to the old lady, so they can be transported to Fort Wilderness hospital as soon as possible. And don't forget to take along her yappy dog!" To the rest of the soldiers, he shouted, "Let's move out! There's nothing more we can do here." Captain Burns took one last look at Little Wolf and quietly said, "I'm terribly sorry for your loss, son. Until we meet again!"

"I am *not* a *savage*! And I am *not* your *son!*" spat out Little Wolf angrily, speaking with an English tongue. "*My* father is *dead*!"

Captain Burns saw the hate in the young man's eyes; they were so blue, so defiant. So much like his own! He had called the boy a 'savage' years ago; the kid had never forgotten. After the angry outburst, the captain tipped his hat, turned his mount around, and left with the rest of the soldiers who trailed behind him in perfect formation all the way back to Fort Wilderness.

With the help from the white soldiers, seven makeshift scaffolds were erected from tree branches and lodgepoles that were still left standing from the burned tepees, to accommodate Little Wolf's family. The young man gathered a few personal belongings for each of the deceased family members to be placed on their scaffolds. The rest of the bodies, about two dozen women and children, were set on fire to be cremated so animals would not feed off them.

Most of the warriors had left to go hunting for their winter meat a few days prior and Little Wolf knew that by the time they returned if the bodies were just left, there would be nothing left after the coyotes, wolves, and other scavengers finished with them. Unlike the other hunters, Little Wolf had been in a rush to get home in anticipation of starting the preparations for his wedding day.

Little Wolf remained with his family for the rest of the week, mourning over his loss. Six members of his family—his mother and his father, his sister and grandfather, and two aunts. And Yellow Bird!

Every minute of the day, hate and revenge built up inside him and ate at his soul. He knew what he had to do!

He just wished he had done it sooner. Then maybe his family would still be alive. And also, Yellow Bird, the love of his life.

"I will make you pay, Spotted Dog! Do you *hear* me? I will find you and I will make you pay!" he tearfully shouted to the trees. He made a promise to his family. And a Lakota always keeps his promise!

The ride to Fort Wilderness was a long, gloomy one, as revengeful thoughts plagued Little Wolf's mind. Faces flashed before him, innocent faces of children, his family, and Yellow Bird. He was going after Spotted Dog and the nine other renegades that had killed his family, his people, and Yellow Bird. And the sooner he left on this mission, the sooner it would be done with.

He had always hated violence and tried to avoid it. When he had the fight with Spotted Dog when he was just a small kid, it had bothered him for years later. He never regretted having the fight with him, but he never approved of it either. He had hoped they might have solved their differences in a more peaceful way. Spotted Dog's pride was hurt more than anything else and now, a lot of people have paid the price with their lives.

"How much is his *pride* really worth?" asked Little Wolf to the trees as he rode. "I guess he will soon find out when I find him!"

Revenge kept driving him forward. Hate overflowed from his soul. He would find Spotted Dog and his band of renegades and he would kill every one of them, even if it took him the rest of his life.

"This promise I will keep, even if I die doing it!" Little Wolf shouted to the trees and a wolf howl echoed down from the hills just above him.

The irritable wind suddenly arose, fiercely pushing at his rigid back as he rode. Before, he was a bent, broken man who had lost everything. Now, he must begin his trek, fulfill his promise to his people, to his family. And to Yellow Bird!

When Little Wolf finally arrived at Fort Wilderness, he purchased enough rations to last him a month and loaded them onto a mule that he had acquired the same day. When suddenly, a voice from his past called his name; at first, he never recognized it. But as soon as he turned around, he knew who it belonged to. "Spectacles!"

The two friends hugged; it had been over ten years since they had last seen one another. The little boy with the big eyeglasses that always slipped down onto the bridge of his nose had grown into a dapper-looking gentleman, a big city lawyer by profession. He was dressed in a gray, pin-striped suit, white ruffled shirt, and a fancy blue cravat and he wore a gray derby hat that covered his well-groomed haircut.

"I'm very sorry for your loss, Little Wolf! Is that where you are going now, to look for them?" Little Wolf never answered his friend.

"I'm going with you!"

"No!" stated Little Wolf firmly.

"There are nine of them, ten counting Spotted Dog. I can help you."

"*No!*" Little Wolf repeated. "I have to do this on my own. If I don't come back, will you see that my grandmother and Chief Kicking Horse get proper care for me? Promise me, my friend!"

"*I promise*! I will take care of them while you are gone," swore Spectacles. The two young men shook hands, sealing the promise made between Little Wolf and Louis Dupont, his closest friend.

"I will go over to the hospital and see them both before I leave. To say goodbye!" He gave Spectacles one last hug and added, "Maybe we can go hunting for deer when I return, just like we used to; I would like that, my friend."

"That sounds like a great plan. You stay safe and always watch your back. Spotted Dog is a *mean* son-of-a bitch," warned Louis Dupont, or better known as 'Spectacles' to Little Wolf.

A soldier approached Little Wolf and gave him a message. "Captain Burns requests a meeting with you in his office. He is waiting for you right now. Follow me!" Little Wolf hesitated but followed the soldier because he was curious to hear what the captain had to say, hoping he had information about Spotted Dog's whereabouts.

Captain Jesse Burns stood at the window and watched his son reluctantly walk toward the office door. The boy had grown into a man, with ax-handle shoulders and rippling muscles. But Jesse only saw the same young boy who still carried the weight of an anvil on those shoulders; the captain could see it with every stride the boy took.

The boy also wore an invisible metal suit of armor, allowing no infiltration of his feelings whatsoever. *How am I going to penetrate that shield?* he thought. "What must I do to keep him safe? If he goes to the Badlands of the North looking for Spotted Dog, he will surely get killed. I know what that country is like! I have been there and I barely made it out alive."

The captain had filled his pipe with tobacco earlier and finally, he lit it after nervously chewing on the pipe stem worrying about the fate of his headstrong son.

Even from this distance, he saw the defiance cross over the boy's face, the dark scowl suddenly running furrows across his forehead. Even his son's gait matched his own when he walked, so filled with determination and arrogance with every step he took. How can someone so close to him be so far away? Always so much hate clouding those deep blue eyes. *My eyes*!

Even before he spotted the red scarf, he would have known that Little Wolf was his son because of the mirrored image staring back at him. He could also see Meadowlark in the boy's features, the way she used to question his actions, argue about his decisions. Her emotions, even the same scowl, all showed up on her beautiful face. A face that, over the years, continually surfaced whenever he closed his eyes, her memory burning like a forever flame within his heart.

"Now, our love-child is filled with such *hate*! And there is nothing I can say or do that will ever take those bad feelings away."

Regrets? Sure! He had regrets! Especially when he watched the boy hold his Lakota father in his arms and weep, so much love pouring from him. *I really envied that moment of tenderness!* Jesse thought to himself sadly.

Captain Burn's walked back to his desk as the boy entered, motioning for him to have a seat across from him. "I hear you are going after the renegades that killed your family. Is that true?" Little Wolf did not answer. "I have sent my men out to apprehend them, as we speak. They will be tried in a court of law and if found guilty, they will be punished. If you take the law into your own hands and kill them, then you become a criminal also and I will have to bring you in to stand trial for murder. Don't make me do this!"

Little Wolf stood up, clenched his fists, and leaned toward the white leader behind the desk. "Spotted Dog is *smart. You* will not catch him. *But I will.* I will find all of them and they *will* die. They will pay for what they did to my family."

Just as Little Wolf turned his back to walk out of the door, Captain Burns added, "My scouts have been tracking them. They are headed further north, toward Forbidden Valley. Be careful! It is not a friendly place. Strange creatures that live inside the caves have been sighted in and around the area. Men, on the run from the law, have often hidden out in Forbidden Valley because they know that no posse in their right minds will venture that far north, but none of them have ever come back."

"Winter comes earlier in the mountains; temperatures can suddenly drop as low as −40 degrees Fahrenheit overnight. If the cold doesn't kill you, then the cannibalistic cave dwellers will. In the past, everyone who has risked going that far north, strangely disappears. Except for ole' Silver Fox; for years now, he goes trapping there for the elusive silver fox and nobody seems to ever bother with him or his mule because they think he's tetched in the head, a trait believed to bring bad luck to the Indians."

"He winters in a cabin up there until he gets his quota, then he heads for home before the snowdrifts get too deep. He knows the area like the back of his hand. And just so you know, he's not as crazy as he lets on. Maybe he can help you."

Captain Burns handed Little Wolf a piece of paper with a hand-drawn map etched on it. "Until then, here's a map that will help guide you through that rough territory. Be careful!" he warned again just as the door slammed shut before Jesse could say another word. Jesse knew that this could possibly be the last time that he would ever see his son alive. But he had to let him go.

Louis Dupont, or better known to Little Wolf as 'Spectacles', watched his friend stomp out of the building and head toward the fort's hospital where his grandmother was recovering. *I wonder what riled him up?* thought Louis.

Before Little Wolf went to see his grandmother, he visited with Chief Kicking Horse. He was informed that the chief was not doing well. A Lakota arrow had been removed from his chest when he was brought into the hospital; the doctor hadn't expected him to last this long. The arrowhead had penetrated deep enough to score the lungs and, as a result, his breathing became shallower each day. He kept asking about Little Wolf, said it was imperative that he speak with the boy before he died.

When the young man's shadow finally darkened the doorway of his room, the old man tried to sit up but found the task too difficult so he lowered himself back down, exhausted and gasping for breath. He opened his eyes wider to get a better look but his eyes watered with pain.

He coughed; a bright red, foamy string trickled from the corner of his mouth when he tried to speak. His voice was raspy and Little Wolf had to lean closer in order to hear him. He could see the fist-sized wound packed with mud and medicinal leaves after the arrow had been removed. Chief Kicking Horse looked very frail; the young man could smell *death* in the darkened room.

"There is something I must tell you before I am taken away! Listen carefully to my words!" The old man tried once again to sit up but to no avail. "All your growing years, you have been my pupil, my protégé. I wanted you to learn the Lakota way and see that you had the best teachers. I was always so proud of you. But you weren't just my protégé, you are also *my grandson*."

"Your birth mother was my youngest daughter, Meadowlark. She died giving birth to you during a snowstorm. Her brother, Tomas Good Shield, was there with her; he saved your life by bringing you to our village and leaving you with Two Faces in the Wind at the birthing lodge the same night you were born. She took the baby boy from Tomas' arms; you were wrapped in a red scarf, the same red scarf that you are wearing right now. It belonged to your mother, Meadowlark. My daughter!"

"A white wolf's hide was covering your small body to keep out the cold; that was how you got to be called 'Little Wolf'. Two Faces then placed you beside Red Leaf, who had just given birth to yet another baby boy who never opened his eyes to our world. She became your new mother and Standing Buffalo became your new father. They never knew any different; they always thought you were their real child. This secret remained with only three people for the longest time, Tomas, Two Faces, and myself. And now, your real father also knows; all this time, he thought you were dead."

The old man's eyes rolled back in his head until just the whites showed and Little Wolf thought he had died. But he seemed to gain a sudden spurt of energy, even though he was in such a weakened state; his eyes focused once again and he continued to speak.

"I waited for the right moment to tell you myself but now that the spirits are calling my name, I wanted you to know the truth. We thought that you were a *gift* sent to us from the Great Spirit. You were special to us and in my visions, I saw you as a great leader to the Lakota people; as you grew older, we groomed you to be that leader. On numerous occasions, we noticed that you possessed great powers; you have the spirit of the White Wolf inside your body. He goes with you. And he will always protect you!"

Little Wolf watched as the old man grew weaker, starting to fade away. "Don't go, Grandfather! There is so much I want to say to you. So much I want to know!"

"Talk to Two Faces, she will tell you more." The old man's voice suddenly faded to a mere whisper. "Your birth father is—"

Little Wolf waited with bated breath. But it was too late. "Wait!" Little Wolf shouted. "Who is my *real* father?" But Chief Kicking Horse never heard him. He had drawn his last breath.

Little Wolf remained sitting at his grandfather's bedside, tightly clutching onto the limp, cool hand as tears streamed down his face; he bowed his head in prayer. He was alone in the small room but he suddenly felt a *presence*. He raised his head and saw her as she bent over the body.

It was the same beautiful woman that he envisioned when he was swimming in the river, the one who had called him 'son'. His *real mother*? Was this really *her* father lying here? Was she an *angel* sent to take him back home, on the road that leads to where the footprints all point the same way? Suddenly, all the visions of the beautiful woman he had been seeing were visions of his real mother. Her Spirit watching over her child!

When the door opened, the ghost woman disappeared just as the doctor entered the room.

Closing the door behind him, Little Wolf quietly left; there was nothing more he could do for Chief Kicking Horse now. He knew that his grandfather's body was to be taken to the cemetery on Sacred Hill, where it would be placed on a scaffold so that his people could come and mourn his death.

The saddened young man went down the hall to Two Faces' room; he had a lot of questions to ask his grandmother. Two Faces was peacefully sleeping so he planted a kiss on her forehead and left. As much as he wanted to know the answers, he felt that they could wait for a few more days; her state of health was of the utmost importance right now.

As Little Wolf stood by her bedside and looked down on her battered face, hate for Spotted Dog once again overcame him. How many more were going to die? "I promise you, Grandmother! I will seek retribution."

He knew that the sooner he left, the sooner he would find them. And hopefully, return to take care of his grandmother and her beloved dog and hopefully get all his questions answered.

During the next three days on the trail leading to the Badlands of the North, Little Wolf thought long and hard about Chief Kicking Horse and their last conversation they had before he died. A conversation that had left so many unanswered questions! He wondered *who* his real father was. What was he like? Does he live nearby? Was he a white man? Why did his father think his son was dead? And why does he keep having visions of this ghost woman, supposedly his real mother? All he knew about her was she was very young and very pretty. He so needed that talk with his grandmother when he returned.

As he rode, he chuckled to himself as he fondly remembered all the questions he had fired at his grandmother when he was a very curious, little kid. They came flooding back and of all the questions he had asked, the only question that *did* get answered was why his grandmother was called 'Two Faces in the Wind'. Now he knew why! But it didn't make any difference to him that she had worn two pairs of pants; he would always love her. She was the one who had taught him so much about life. And about love!

"Life is not always as easy as it seems," she often told him. "You are a mere boy and you have big shoes to fill and when you grow to be a man, you will be stronger and smarter than all the other boys who tease you." And whenever Little Wolf failed to complete one of the more difficult tasks given to him, her words of encouragement seemed to make him try harder. Because of her, he never quit. She will always remain a true *hero* in his eyes.

As Little Wolf traveled past the low rolling hills studded with taller sentinel pines and occasional cedars, a lone eagle circled above him. The sky was clear and cloudless; the land was awesome, so *untamable*. Occasionally, huge mountains erupted out of the ground, casting dark shadows across the natural trail. The earth seemed to temporarily fall away when their perpendicular granite walls rose up on both sides of the lonesome rider. Little Wolf let out a holler, testing the echo, and quickly began to sing:

"Heavy-hipped woman, where were you last night?

The nights are cold and I need your warmth.

Heavy-hipped woman, where will you be tonight?

Come to my campsite and we will make love under the stars."

Then the singer began to yodel, Indian-style, at the top of his lungs. The form of entertainment displeased the big black horse. And he was not impressed by the yodeling attempt; his ears went back and he tried to drown out the off-key yodeling with his loud whinnies.

"OK! OK! I will stop." Little Wolf reached down and patted the horse's neck. They continued their journey in silence.

The mountains backed away from the trail, sprawling closer to the western skyline. There was snow in the gashes of the peaks where the sun never reached. The wind was now cold on the rider's back as the late orange-hued sunlight dipped behind the mammoth mountains.

According to the map given to him by Captain Burns, there was a small settlement not too far ahead, where a man could get food for himself and grain for his horse as long as he had the money to pay for it. It was supposed to be just past the forest that loomed straight ahead of them. The nights had been cold; there was a taste of ice on his tongue when the wind blew in small snowflakes from the north last night.

Little Wolf took one last look at the darkening mountains before he moved on. Notches in the highest peaks showed the brilliance of red-gold colors from the dying sun ribboning down the mountain faces. The spectacular display wouldn't last much longer. There was a raw, primitive beauty to the mountains, a grandeur that surrounds a man, making him feel very small amidst such timeless beauty. *It still doesn't explain why anyone would want to live in such a cold, isolated place!* thought Little Wolf.

Before entering the pine forest, Little Wolf looked first to the east, then to the west; he studied the trail behind him and also ahead of him. Carefully scanning for a splash of color or reflection where it didn't belong! Searching for any movement! But he saw nothing out of the ordinary. He listened, hearing the wind whispering through the swaying pine branches above his head and the monotonous ripple of escaping water flowing from a black, silky river that snaked along the trail as he rode.

He halted, slid off the black horse, and stroked his nose. He was riding over tracks of ten unshod ponies and according to the dung droppings, they had passed this way either late yesterday or early this morning. Definitely Sioux ponies!

As a precaution, Little Wolf checked on his friends that served as his backup, removing the elk skin sheath from Big Spencer and laying his hand on Razor-sharp Bowie. His sixth sense had suddenly kicked in. He rode silently through the pines. The big black's hooves were also noiseless on the fallen needles. A howl, like the sound of a wolf, drifted past, creaking and swaying of the branches in warning.

Suddenly, a warrior rose up out of the brush and grabbed Little Wolf by the waist, pulling him off the black. The attacker fell backward from the weight of Little Wolf, who landed on top of him. They rolled over and over on the forest floor, each one evenly matched in size. On the third roll, Little Wolf landed on top, his bowie knife sticking into flesh at the attacker's throat, drawing blood. Ready to slice his artery with just a slight push from Little Wolf.

A trickle of red blood slid down the mirror-polished blade of the bowie knife.

"Kill me!" the warrior spat in the Sioux tongue.

"Let go of your knife!" shouted Little Wolf. The warrior released his grip on the knife and Little Wolf kicked it away. "Now, slowly get up."

"That is what I cannot do, long-haired one." The warrior turned on his side so Little Wolf could see the arrow shaft protruding from his leg.

"I will never be able to walk again. Just get it over with and kill me!" he pleaded again. "I would have killed *you* if I had the chance."

"You are hurt! What happened?" questioned Little Wolf. He reached down and took the warrior's hand to pull him up, noticing the great strength in his upper body, the powerful arm, a fighting man's arm.

"Ten Lakota braves attacked me and stole my horse. The one who shot the arrow into my leg was called Spotted Dog. He has a black heart. He tried to cripple me."

"Let me look at the wound." Little Wolf crouched to examine the warrior's right leg. "The arrow cannot be pulled out. But I can cut it out if you will let me. You will have much pain. You will have to trust me. Otherwise, the wound will become infected and you will die." The warrior suddenly looked awfully familiar to Little Wolf.

"I will endure this pain because I do not want to die. So, I will trust you, my friend. Besides, how can a person not trust someone who *sings* so terribly?"

Smiling, Little Wolf built a small campfire and when the coals became red hot, he placed the blade of his bowie knife in the midst and waited. "What is your name?" he asked.

"I am called 'Fast Walker'." The warrior chuckled at the irony in his answer. "I am Lakota also. My camp is about three hours away if you keep riding further north from here. I was returning home when those renegades attacked me."

"I remember *you!*" chuckled Little Wolf. "We killed a big buck together many moons ago. And we stood in a freezing creek, dripping wet and arguing."

"Did you get married?" asked Fast Walker.

Little Wolf pulled the knife from the coals and began to pry out the arrowhead from Fast Walker's flesh, thankful that the tough material of his buckskin pants had greatly reduced the penetration of the arrow.

"Why are you doing this for me? I was going to kill you, not once, but twice now," Fast Walker asked between wincing gasps of pain.

"You are a warrior. I am a warrior. And we are both *Lakota*, and we are like brothers now. We fight for the same cause and someday, we might find ourselves fighting on the same battlefield together." Little Wolf kept digging.

"What is your name, long hair? I have forgotten! I want to know so I can tell my children, and their children, about the yellow-haired warrior who saved my life. They will sing songs about your fame. Songs better than yours, my friend."

Little Wolf chuckled and said, "I am called 'Little Wolf'."

"Listen to my words, Little Wolf! My life is yours if you ever need it. I live because of you and I shall never forget it."

After much prodding, the arrowhead was extracted but not before Fast Walker went unconscious. Little Wolf dressed his wound the best he could, packing it with mud to slow down the bleeding, then tearing a strip of cloth from his shirt to act as a temporary bandage. The task of getting him on a horse seemed endless but with a little assistance from the groggy warrior, they finally rode out of the pines together.

It was chilly, dark, and moonless when they rode into Fast Walker's camp three hours later. Still speaking in the Sioux tongue, Little Wolf explained to the warrior's family what had happened to him and they immediately took control of the situation. After receiving a fulfilling meal of antelope, a good night's sleep, and many heartfelt thanks, Little Wolf continued on his journey. Fast Walker remained unconscious and never got to say goodbye to his new friend.

"I hope he is going to make it," worried Little Wolf as he kept riding in a northerly direction. As the morning passed, all thoughts of Fast Walker faded to the back of his mind as *Hate* reclaimed the predominant space, taking priority over everything else once again.

However, too much hate can cloud an ordinary man's mind; it has the ability to deflect or alter the truth, which could quickly escalate into a life-threatening situation. A situation that might have otherwise been avoided! But not so for Little Wolf; he was no ordinary man.

As he traveled deeper into nomad's land, his instincts honed in and he became *more* alert. He saw things that no one else would ordinarily notice; he listened for any movement, straining to hear sounds that did not belong. He had the instincts of a wolf, one hundred percent sharper than any other man. His friends often told him that he was different, that he had something deep inside him that was powerful, seemed even magical at times. He often predicted things before they happened.

Was it instinct? Or was it a *magical power*?

A dead silence fell like a heavy blanket over Little Wolf. Cloaking both him and his horse in it! Not even the wind acknowledged its presence. Nothing disturbed the primitive wilderness. There was no smoke rising to meet the dark clouds, no sign of man-made structures. No sign that anything on two legs had ever crossed this broad and savage land.

Little Wolf was truly alone in the middle of nowhere. But strangely, there had been times in the past when he *felt* alone and he wasn't. His body seemed to be a little bit further *away* from everything, and everybody, even when it was actually quite close. An 'out of mind, out of body' magical moment?

He paused not once, but twice along the trail, crouching in the shadow of a big rock to check his back trail. Numerous times, he stopped and dismounted, placing his ear against the hard earth. There was no one following him. The silence still bothered him, though. He was taught by his elders that silence and patience could differentiate between life and death; a noisy man broadcasts his whereabouts and an impatient man is reckless. And Little Wolf's lack of patience had landed him in trouble before.

As the lone rider traveled deeper into an encrusted world of rocks and pines, he became more cautious. The bleak trail shrunk, becoming just a narrow, stony path covered in shale and rubble. He led Shadow, the big black, off to the side of the trail, weaving through the tall ranks of trees, making for a much quieter ride on the sodden pine needles underfoot as he moved slowly through the wooded area.

With icy blue eyes always watching, scanning the perimeter, Little Wolf remained cautious. He knew there was a lot of danger lurking in this country as they got closer to the Forbidden Valley.

Little Wolf glanced upwards again, noticing how darker the skies had become as he continued to ride higher into the hills. Further ahead, he saw the rise and fall of snow-covered peaks beyond the bountiful, picturesque timberline; while all around him, cedars and spruce grew contorted and twisted and the pines were flagged with bare branches on the northerly side from the constant assault of the powerful seasonal winds. The same winds whipping against his back today, reminding him of just how powerful they could become!

Little Wolf tugged his hat down to protect his face and the big black tossed its head and blew air from its nostrils as another commanding gust pushed them along, overriding the shelter provided by the dense trees. Little Wolf patted the horse's sleek neck in reassurance and said, "Looks like it's just you and me, Shadow."

They continued to plunge forward through the eerie, slanted forest. About a mile later, as they rode even higher, the snap and whip of the keening wind was relentless. The trail had become rough and broken, now covered in shale and rubble. It gradually faded and eventually vanished, leaving them to contend with just a winding rocky pathway that kept climbing skyward.

As Little Wolf looked ahead, the pathway converted into a narrow ledge. They cautiously continued on, his leg dragging against the rising cliff face to the left while on his right side, both horse and rider tilted perilously over the uneven path as the side dropped off to about three hundred feet straight down where a massive gorge awaited. Higher up, the air grew colder and a light, icy drizzle splattered both horse and rider.

Within minutes, the angry clouds opened up and the mild rainfall suddenly became a mix of sleet and snow falling like a thundering waterfall, making the rocky path slippery and dangerous. Even though their vision was badly distorted, horse and rider still lurched forward in the downpour; to stop now would mean certain death for both of them.

Hoping to quickly find a safer, sheltered place up ahead, they came to a spot where the ledge widened, branching out into a small, grassy clearing.

On the cliffside, an overhang of rock sheltered a hollow cave about two horses in width; a perfect spot for the two drenched travelers to camp for the night. Little Wolf pulled back on the reins, stopping the big black. The horse thankfully looked back at its master with big soulful eyes, its backside coated with sheets of ice.

Little Wolf unsaddled Shadow and rubbed him down with a blanket, lit a small fire, and attempted to boil a pot of water for coffee. He then rolled up in his blankets and fell asleep to the sound of the blowing cold winds. The strange and haunting growl of the wind in the canyons continued throughout the night as a large, white wolf protectively watched over them.

At dawn, Little Wolf awoke, shivering from the cold. The temperature had plummeted during the night and snow covered the ground. With freezing fingers, he built up the smoldering ashes in the firepit as the rock-faces around him were stained orange and rose from the dawn's early light. When Little Wolf saddled the horse, he told Shadow that this place was not fit for man nor beast and anyone had to be crazy to travel here. The horse turned his head and looked at him with big woeful eyes as if to say, "Are you crazy! Really?"

The lone rider continued. He picked up a trail again and the ride was less perilous. It widened out into more tall timbers and there was less climbing for them. Even the wind seemed to cooperate, making travel almost pleasant.

Muffled hooves whispered through the trees; only a blue jay squawked as horse and rider approached a smokeless campsite where an old trapper was seated; he was busy skinning a silver fox hide beside the low-burning firepit while puffing on a corncob pipe clenched between the gap in his mouth where four or five decayed teeth used to live. The trapper was wearing soiled buckskins, knee-high fringed moccasins, and a floppy-rimmed hat that successfully shielded his crusted eyes from the weather.

No wonder he didn't see anyone approaching! thought Little Wolf as he came closer. Holding up his hand in a friendly greeting, Little Wolf spoke to the old man using his English tongue. "I am a friend! I come in peace."

The trapper jumped up; a big skinning knife held firmly in front of him as his weapon of defense, ready to strike. "You should be more careful, ole' man. The time it took you to reach for that knife, an Indian could have snuck up on you and taken your scalp," warned Little Wolf.

"I guess when a man gets up in years, his ears'll betray him. I never heard a damned thing!" admitted the trapper.

"It's because you got too much hair around them. It's a wonder you still have all that hair. And especially with all that chin scalp you're wearing also, why you'd be givin' him a two-for-one deal when collecting coup. Just think about the stories he'd tell to his kids around their winter campfires, braggin' about his luck. What's your name, ole' man?"

"Name's Jean-Luc Fox, better known as 'Silver Fox' in these hills. What's your handle, Indian?"

"I am called Little Wolf, better known as 'Little Wolf' in these parts," he answered with a chuckle.

A loud, horrible noise bellowed from the shade of the trees not far from where Silver Fox was sitting. "What the hell was that?" asked Little Wolf. "I've never heard anything like that before."

"That, my friend, is 'Poke', my mule and my best pal. That's his way of always lettin' me know when I have company. Guess he was sleepin' on his watch! Or maybe you were just so damned quiet that he got snuck up on too, just like you done to me."

Little Wolf liked the trapper straight away. He was a singular man, always traveled alone with just his mule for company. He was the last of a dying breed, a man with the wiles of a French-speaking Micmac Indian warrior and the instincts of a stalking wolf; both the old man *and* the mule knew a new *hunter* was in the area because they had been watching him for a long time.

They both knew that he was friendly and meant *them* no harm. Little Wolf also learned that the trapper was a master mountaineer with the sharpest shooting eye of anyone in this unforsaken country. At any given moment, the old man could have shot him from any one of the mountaintops with his big Spencer long-range rifle.

So, the crazy-looking, floppy hat covering the old trapper's eyes fooled Little Wolf at first, but not for long. Even though the man looked 'simple' and 'grizzled', he was very *smart* and confident, a reverent man not to be reckoned with.

He was spry, not as old as he pretended to be. His six-foot, cleverly disguised frame was sturdy, rippled with rope-like muscles that could take down a grizzly using only brute strength and his bare hands. He could hunt buffalo or venison just as good, or better, than any of Little Wolf's friends. He had often lived in the 'raw' during the entire winter here, surviving on whatever the land provided when others could not.

"All I got with me is my trustworthy rifle, my Colt revolver tucked in my belt, a long-bladed bowie knife, lots of ammo, and my own two hands. That's my survival kit."

He had built his own log cabin with those big, calloused hands and he made many a bow and arrow for hunting when he ran out of ammo. He knew his way through the mountains and he also knew the whereabouts of every ravine and river surrounding them. Over the past twenty years, he's had to find his way through many blinding snow storms when waiting too long to get out of the mountains. But ever since he turned fifty over three years ago, he makes it a point to head back home before the snows get too deep.

"In winter, the cold is too hard on my old bones," he complains. "And one of these days, my reoccurring nightmare, which is my biggest fear of this place, might come true. In this dream, it always takes place in the spring after Mother Nature finally decides to warm the earth. A big alpha wolf has dug me out of a snowdrift from an avalanche that careened down the mountainside many weeks prior. The hungry wolf just sits and patiently waits, refusing to eat me because I'm still a frozen chunk of ice. That's when I always wake up."

Yes, Little Wolf really liked Silver Fox. And wow! He sure could cook.

The best food he ever tasted. "Where'd you learn to cook like that?"

"My mother taught me. The Micmacs have their own style of preparing food, similar to the way French people cook. My family lives back on Prince Edward Island, beautiful place. Ever heard of it, boy?"

"No! Is it far away?" asked Little Wolf.

"Well, it's past Quebec, traveling by way of the St. Lawrence River for many, many days. Prince Edward Island is mostly surrounded by the Gulf of St. Lawrence; it's like a big, beautiful island surrounded by water." The trapper spoke more about his Micmac family and their ways and told Little Wolf how he had earned his reputation of being the best trapper of one of the most eluded and valued animals in all of North America, the silver fox. He also spoke of his Sioux wife, Ilkcaw.

Little Wolf listened to the trapper, immensely enjoying his company. He felt at ease, more relaxed than he had felt in a long time. He divulged to the trapper about his mission and the reasons why he wanted to kill Spotted Dog and his men. He asked if he had seen them on his travels.

"As a matter of a fact, I have. Headin' into Forbidden Valley about a week ago. Probably all dead by now!"

"Why do you say that?"

"Nobody comes out of there alive. I'm not that crazy to go there again, *no siree*! The place is crawlin' with the cave dwellers. They're big and strong and *ugly*! And those bastards will eat you alive. They create their own set of rules when it comes to the 'survival of the fittest' on the food chain ladder."

Silver Fox kept shaking his head. "There is a *she-devil* that leads them and if any one of them crosses her, she butchers him up and feeds him to the others without even blinkin' an eye. I highly recommend that you steer clear of Forbidden Valley. The rivers have no bottoms and dead men's whispers can be heard in the night. I went to the valley once and my curiosity led me to the entrance of Dead Man's Cave."

"Inside the cave, it was dark and there was a crunching noise under my moccasins whenever I took a step. And as I walked further inside, my feet felt like they were moving on a conveyor belt, so I lit a torch and saw that I was standing on broken skeletal bones scattered among hundreds of crawling snakes that were trying to go up my pant legs. The snakes were also slithering among the piles of skeleton heads stacked along the walls, crawling through the eyeholes and any other opening they could find. I got the hell outa' there, pronto."

"After I scrambled down the mountain, I came within twenty feet of the *ugliest, biggest, stinkiest* creature that I had ever seen. I jumped on ole' Poke and the two of us skedaddled out of there. I've never seen the legs of that mule run so fast as they did on that day. He never slowed down until he reached the cabin some two hours later. I thought he was going to drop dead in his tracks from exhaustion. Let me tell you, I've seen a lot of weird things and I have been in a lot of scary situations in my lifetime but that was the worst. I never want to go back."

"Where did these cave dwellers come from?" asked Little Wolf. He knew that he would hear the truth from Silver Fox, as he was not one to exaggerate when telling the story.

"I've heard stories about these savage beasts, mostly from the Sioux and the Cheyenne. Apparently, they first came to earth from over the moon, at the time of the dark ice age. At the time of endless winter. That is why they live here in Northern Canada, where the temperatures are cold and the days are shorter; they are terrorized by any form of heat and by the light of day. These oversized creatures, more animal than man, remain in their caves during the day and emerge when the moon rides across the sky to look for food."

"The few brave men who *did* return to civilization after venturing this far north, told stories about spotting these big, hairy, bare-footed beasts that resembled gorillas, lumbering through the trees and valleys at night. Huge, webbed footprints over twenty-five inches long sunk into the ground wherever they walked, documented by the survivors. Massive, horned hands attached to long powerful arms hung down to their knees, and muscular legs were bowed as they shuffled from side to side."

"Eventually, these creatures will become extinct because they eat their young, the weak, and most of the female babies being born. Now, there are about thirty males left and only six older females left that can reproduce. When the females become too old and weak, they will be eaten also, thus reproduction will stop. They are too stupid to figure this out."

"The story is told that when the Sioux and the Cheyenne came upon the earth, these creatures were driven back into their caves. But the price of war was heavy as these 'pillars of enormous strength' were savage beyond belief, savage enough to scare the hell out of the most hardened and bravest warriors, some of which had been captured, their ashes of smashed bones left in piles inside the dark, massive caves. The primitive drawings on their walls depicted the many battles fought between them."

"As time passed, the Indians thought they had finally driven these creatures to the ends of the earth. As the legend goes, the caves were left alone, forgotten. It is said that even the *evil spirits* shake in their boots when venturing inside those dark caves. The territory was believed to be evil, the mountains twisted, *cursed*. And rightfully named 'Forbidden Valley', the badlands of the Canadian North."

"Never again shall any Sioux or Cheyenne venture into this land to hunt. Mountain men avoid it because of the strange sightings reported by the few that have been lucky enough to return. In this world, we suffer with snakes, scorpions, coyote, wolf and bear; they are here for a reason. And it is not up to us to kill every last one of them. We should leave them be. In time, they will die out on their own."

Little Wolf had been informed that Spotted Dog and his men had gone to Forbidden Valley, knowing that no posse would go that far north to capture them. He felt that Spotted Dog was more of a dangerous predator than these cave dwellers. *They* kill to eat; Spotted Dog kills for his own pleasure.

"*Go home!*" advised Silver Fox, knowing that the half-breed wasn't going to heed his warning. "That's where *I'm* going! I got two more traps to check on first thing in the morning before I head back to my Ilkcaw. I miss her! The snow is coming in tonight, lots of it; I feel it in my bones."

And the trapper was right; it did snow! When Little Wolf awoke in the morning, the trapper was gone and there *was* two feet of the white stuff on the ground. With much more still to come. Silver Fox was right. The air had quickly cooled down in the night, engulfing them in an early winter blizzard. Little Wolf stayed put inside the warm cabin, worrying about the trapper as he watched the weather getting worse, hoping Silver Fox had the sense to go home like he said he would.

It snowed for five days and four nights before it finally let up a bit. Little Wolf mounted the big black and decided to go for a ride toward Forbidden Valley. He carried his bedroll, his slicker, and buffalo coat, and in an elk skin pouch stored behind him, he packed some jerky and canned goods. He kept his rifle close at hand across his lap in front of him. It was slow going as the trail had disappeared under three-foot drifts of fluffy snow.

The river water shimmered like black silk beside him while above, the mountains rose dark and sullen against the horizon. The wind was cold, the sky gray and listless. The empty blanketed land passed beneath his horse's hooves. Suddenly, the black's ears picked up and twitched. His rider fondly patted the long neck.

"Yes, I see it too, Shadow." There was a thin rooster-tail of snow dust rising from the trail behind him, just one horse, one rider following far enough back to remain out of gunshot range.

Little Wolf kept watching his back trail but the rider disappeared inside the tunnels of snow from the gusty wind that suddenly seemed to be pushing him *backward*. Whispering his name. Warning him of a cold predictable death up ahead.

He rode further north into unknown territory, going deeper and deeper into a dark abyss between skyscraping rock walls. Leaving behind the land of the Sioux and the Cheyenne. Leaving behind the land of civilization where *any man,* whether Indian or White, was an interloper, an enemy. Approaching a forbidden stone valley where even the wind seemed reluctant to go. The land that fell away at *the end of the world*!

Little Wolf stumbled upon an old, abandoned campsite near a fast-flowing ravine where a collection of rusting tools was left propped against a tree, a pick, a shovel, an axe, and a sledgehammer. He led his horse to the edge of the water. If a person didn't take good care of his horse, he'd be soon dead out here; he was more valuable than anything.

As the horse drank, Little Wolf noticed the large web-footed prints in the mud, prints larger than any man or beast that he had ever seen before. A haunting wind shook the branches of the trees all around the circle of the camp. He glanced upwards, seeing the red-faced cliffs through the parting clouds as the sun lowered in the west.

He could smell a musty, definable odor of meat that had rotted away, desiccated on the bone. The black could smell it too; he lifted his head and looked to the left of the campsite and then looked back at his master, droplets of water glistened golden orange from his mouth and bridle. Flecks of gold fell back in the water, making it ripple with shimmering gold waves.

"All right, we'll stop here for the night. I'll build us a fire while you fill your belly some more."

Little Wolf walked to the trees to the left and proceeded to gather some dry branches under the fallen snow, attempting to build a smokeless fire like the old trapper had taught him. He dug in the snow until his hand touched cold flesh, at least what was left of it. The bones of a man lay under the pile of snow; most of the flesh was eaten or pulled off weeks ago. Little Wolf jumped back and tripped over a saddle and bridle and the remains of a dead horse; the flesh also removed. Now exposed, the smell of death was very strong in the air. The wind hadn't lied.

That was when Little Wolf first saw her. She was across the river, riding bareback atop a white horse, watching him. Gusts of wind tussled her long black hair, lifting it off her shoulders and whipping it across her face. He couldn't see her face and he wasn't looking at it, anyway; he openly stared at her beautiful breasts; the cold temperature had a visible, protruding effect on her large bare nipples.

She was naked from the waist up and below her waist, she only wore a breechclout and a pair of knee-high, fringed moccasins; he immediately recognized the familiar craftmanship of his people, the Sioux. Being temporarily preoccupied, Little Wolf never realized that she had nocked an arrow and shot it through the hat he was wearing. He somehow knew that she could have aimed lower and shot him in the head if she wanted to. Definitely a warning shot!

She suddenly turned her horse and rode away, disappearing into the darkness of the surrounding forest. He didn't think she would return. She had the chance to kill him but she didn't. Little Wolf managed to get a campfire lit and, with one eye open all night, he spent the night. His sixth sense told him that Spotted Dog and his renegade friends were not that far away.

Little Wolf saw the Sioux woman for the second time. She was mounted on her horse across the river again, only this time she was closer than before. He still couldn't see her face because of her long dark hair. She never spoke but used sign language to tell him that she liked his horse. Little Wolf answered her back, also by signing in the Sioux language, "He is not just my horse; he is also my friend!"

She signed once again and said, "There are no friends in this country." She turned her horse around and rode back into the darkness of the trees, her long hair flying in the wind.

Before dawn, Little Wolf loosely tethered his horse to a tree. "If I don't come back for you, you will be able to break loose," he told the black sadly.

He set out on foot, following the tracks in the snow by the light of the moon. He was following the river until he came to a waterfall cascading about fifty feet down to where he stood. He waded across the cold, stony floor and started to climb up, finally reaching the summit. He picked up tracks again at the top and kept following them. He was horrified at the sight when he came to a hidden clearing flanked by caves on all three sides. He remained deathly quiet, hidden in the bushes, and waited to make sure no one was around.

A sudden flash of lightning revealed twelve ten-foot poles erected in a circular formation and at the top of nine of them, skulls were placed. They were all facing eastward; the moaning wind whistled through the empty eye sockets. The skulls were all stripped to the bone, no flesh remaining. Except one!

The naked body of Blue Otter, one of Spotted Dog's renegades, hung limply on the tenth pole, and he was still alive, crying from pain while red ants and other flying insects fed off his putrid body. His skin was partially peeled down from his head to his toes. Fresh blood dripped off his raw flesh and mingled with the rest of the dried blood around the bottom of the other poles. No one was around so Little Wolf snuck up to the bloody pole, letting Blue Otter know that he was there.

Blue Otter's voice was just a whisper when he spoke, "These are all Spotted Dog's men. My *friends!* Spotted Dog got away yesterday." His bloodshot eyes rolled toward the cave openings. "They are asleep inside the caves. They hate the light. When they awake at dusk, they will eat me too. I'm so thirsty! Can you get me a drink of water, Little Wolf?"

Little Wolf tried to pour some water into Blue Otter's mouth from his canteen but only a few drops came out; he must have spilled the canteen when he climbed the rocks. "I'll go to the river and fill it for you, Blue Otter. I will return as soon as I can."

He quietly ran to the river and dipped his canteen into the water and filled it. When the canteen emerged, it was covered in flecks of gold. "That explains the body and all the tools from the campsite he had seen earlier. The dead man was a panhandler, mining for gold, and by the looks of it, there was plenty here."

Little Wolf stood up to go back to Blue Otter and that's when he saw the she-devil once again. She was riding toward him, and now he got a good look at her face. She must have been beautiful at one time. But now, her face was scarred; she was missing a nose. It had been cut from her face, making her ugly and disfigured.

Little Wolf had heard about a primitive Indian custom that if a married woman cheated on her husband, she had her nose cut off for all to see. She lived in shame and was banished from the tribe for the rest of her life. That is probably why she lived here in this godforsaken place where no one could see her. Or would judge her!

The she-devil firmly held a severed head in the crook of her arm. She smiled a wicked smile revealing jagged, rotten teeth and reached into the bleeding mouth of the head she held and pulled out Blue Otter's tongue, throwing it onto Little Wolf's lap. He was stunned by the 'gift' and didn't see the real danger lurking behind the she-devil until it was too late.

An army of bare-naked, hairy creatures had emerged from the darkness of the trees and were shuffling from side to side like giant, ten-foot-tall gorillas, heading toward Little Wolf. Creatures, with their mouths hanging open to breathe as they shuffled but never spoke; they didn't seem to have any intelligence in their oversized heads. They were just as Silver Fox had described them, only uglier. *The cave dwellers!*

The first creature flew at him, knocking him down to the ground. Little Wolf was strong, skilled with a knife, but the creature on top of him was like no man he had ever tangled with. The oversized, thorny hands struck like hooves of a horse thudding down, the weight and strength behind them were incredible.

Its arms were massive; its stark black eyes empty of emotion. Its mouth hung open, revealing broken, fang-like teeth and the breath that fanned Little Wolf's face smelled of rotten meat. He thought he was going to throw up all over the hairy chest pressing against him. The creature was an inexperienced fighter, grappling and pawing at Little Wolf's body with its huge hands. Hands that could squeeze the breath out of a man's neck in seconds if choked.

Little Wolf fumbled for his bowie knife and prayed to Wakan Tanka, thanking him for the help in guiding his hand. The knife cut through flesh in the abdomen and Little Wolf drove it upward into the creature's heart. The creature let out a guttural, bloodcurdling noise that sounded a lot like Ole' Poke's when he had first met the mule and his master some five weeks before. The creature rolled over and drew its last breath.

Lightning flashed, revealing another creature hurling itself at Little Wolf. But the *boom* of a gunshot, combined with the loud crack of thunder, stopped the cave dweller in midair; the powerful rifle had exploded with a blinding flash from a mountaintop far off in the distance. The shooter, possessing accurate sniper skills, had slid his Hawken from its quilled elk skin sheath just in time.

He lifted the heavy octagon-barreled rifle and aimed without dismounting from his paint pony, blowing off the creature's face and the top of its head. The shooter felt the jolt from the rifle go deep into his shoulder. He waited, watching the thing take the bullet; he was making sure it was dead. He quickly poured another round of powder down the barrel, drove the patch and ball down with the rod; he was ready for his next shot.

But he saw Little Wolf run, escaping into the biosphere of rocks when the rest of the ugly creatures temporarily backed away, startled by the sudden flashes of light, the ear-splitting sound of the shot, followed by the loud clap of thunder. The shooter kept following while maintaining his distance as Little Wolf climbed higher. He watched, ready to release another shot if it meant saving his friend's life.

Little Wolf had seen his chance, that moment of hesitant fear from the cave dwellers when he ran, the thunder of his pursuers advancing closer behind him. But as he climbed higher on the rocks, he realized he was trapped; he had no place to go. The cave dwellers were still following close behind him, and as big and unintelligent as they were, they appeared to be quite agile with climbing skills and were gaining on him.

His chance of escape grew smaller with every foothold he took as the cave dwellers' putrid breath fanned his ankles. He looked down; his eyes evading the ugly, sneering faces staring up at him. He shifted to the left and spotted his only distant promise of survival, a loose stone and a fast-flowing river thirty feet below him, the latter a route that he didn't want to undertake. He grabbed at the loose stone while holding on with his other hand; then he grabbed at another. And another.

The smaller stones dislodged bigger ones, creating a small avalanche. But the rolling stone didn't stop the creatures, only slowed them down. When he reached a ledge, he spotted another larger boulder and he gave it a shove; it didn't move. Little Wolf, having experience in moving a big boulder, he turned and put his back to it and, using his weight and his feet, he pushed. And he pushed until the boulder finally gave up and moved.

It rolled off the lip of the ledge and knocked down the ugly pursuers, sometimes three at a time. The boulder created a larger avalanche of rocks and shower of stones, clearing the path all the way back down as guttural screams echoed off the mountainside. However, three creatures still remained, climbing closer to where Little Wolf stood on the narrow ledge. Below, the thin, narrow thread of hope awaited, rapidly flowing with black, foamy water.

Little Wolf dove off the eighteen-foot ledge into the river below. The water was ice cold but he swam for his life, staying under the surface as long as his lungs would allow. He rode the swift current down the river while trying to conserve his energy. A violent storm burst from the clouds overhead. Ice pellets stabbed his face and plummeted to the glassy surface of the river.

The wind suddenly whipped up, making the black water choppy, bending the trees over the banks until their branches dipped into the churning waters, creating a camouflaged tunnel for his body to float, undetected, down the river. But the cold finally soaked through his buckskins, searing his flesh. Then it didn't. Icy fingers crept up his body, then a foray of soothing numbness; he could no longer feel his feet, his legs, his arms weightlessly floating above his head.

His heart quit beating, starved; no longer a frenetic drumbeat pounding in a deaf world. He had lost essential body temperature; his brain was shutting down. No more! His body was weightless, still floating downward. He sank deeper and deeper! There was no bottom to stop his fall.

Suddenly, there was a bright white light within the liquid sky. A hand reached out to him, a woman's hand. The same woman that he saw underwater before, the one with the voice of an angel. The one who called him *son!* His mother, Meadowlark! She was pulling him up through the light, through the black water, pulling him until he surfaced.

He felt weightless, like a feather treading water. Underneath a waterfall! Dragging him to shore! Little Wolf coughed, sputtered water from his mouth, his ears, his nose. When he opened his eyes, Shadow was nudging his back. The soaked warrior patted the horse's nose, so grateful to see him. So grateful to still be alive! It wasn't a good day to die.

As Little Wolf slept, all thoughts of Spotted Dog, who was still lurking in the area, and a mystery sharpshooter, who was following threateningly close behind him, couldn't keep him awake.

Part Five

The walls of Fort Wilderness were chiseled against the unsettled sky, the hills beyond were snow-covered and cold. The temperature hovered at minus ten degrees Fahrenheit during the day. Captain Jesse Burns sat at his desk, pondering over the documents in front of him, his new assignment.

"Colonel, are you *fucking* kidding me?" fumed Jesse, his face flushed red with anger. "You want *me* to take a bunch of inexperienced greenhorns who are still wet behind the ears and march them into the *worst* country of the North, a dead man's trail. And in the middle of *winte*r! Have you *completely* lost your *fucking* mind?"

"Look, Jesse, the decision didn't come from my department. The orders were issued by the Secretary, himself. His strategy is to round up all the Indians and get them on government-run reservations, keep tabs on them."

"You mean *control* them? Make them live the *white* man's way!" interrupted Jesse angrily. "It is *bred* in them to hunt for their own food, make their own clothes. But we are killing off their sacred buffalo. And we are taking their land away, telling them *where* they have to live. These people are not much *different* than us, just more primitive in their ways. They don't want war; they don't want to live like you or me. They just want to be left alone, *in peace*."

Colonel James McEwan squirmed in his chair. "I understand where you are coming from, Jesse. We've known each other for over ten years now; I've supped at your table every Christmas. We're like family. Hell, Jesse! You know, my grandmother was Cheyenne. Yours was Sioux.

We could easily be two Indian warriors, two *brothers* talking to each other right now, smoking the peace pipe, instead of two *white* men sitting here, trying to figure out a way to change those poor bastards' lives. It only depended on how *we* were raised, that's all."

By the tone of his voice, the Colonel sounded like he had a bellyful of all the bureaucrats clogging the mechanisms of the military. During his distinguished career, he has had to constantly deal with civilian interference from higher classes of people who think they can overrule the smarter, experienced brains behind the military. Decisions coming from men who have never traveled outside their own front gates much less fought in battles, men who have never seen the aftermath of a bloody battlefield when it was all over. Men who have never held a dying child in their arms.

"Look, Jim!" sighed Jesse, "I'm not a youngster anymore; my blood has thinned, making it unbearable for me to take the damned cold nights, night after night, even though my skin is thick as rawhide. I am almost fifty years old, months away from retirement and I don't want to end my career buried in some cold snowbank or in some unmarked grave where the sun rarely shines in this forgotten frozen north. *Hell* might seem like a better place; at least it will be warm there."

"Whose ever idea this is, I don't know what they have for brains. This territory is unsettled, even uncivilized. The place is inhabited by creatures that are neither man nor beast, except maybe for the few hostiles escaping the law, if they are fortunate enough to remain alive. This is not an assignment; it is a written invitation to slaughter or to be slaughtered. The unlucky soldiers chosen to accompany me have no idea what they are in for. Hell, most of them probably have never even seen an Indian up close, much less ever heard of a *cave dweller*."

"I will send the best I have right now, Jesse. I have half of my forces in the field at the moment, chasing or being chased by these renegades. You are the best man there is to lead a troop of soldiers there, to teach them the ropes. To bring them back alive! Here is a list of names that are to be brought in, dead or alive. Good luck, Jesse." Colonel McEwan shook Jesse's hand and walked toward the door. "Tell your lovely wife to save me a dance at your retirement party."

Jesse stared at the closed door for a long time. He had just been assigned to a fool's mission. He glanced at the document containing the list of names he was to apprehend and he knew that most of them would never be taken alive. Spotted Dog was on the top, his renegade friends underneath.

Spotted Dog was a man without a soul, a madman who walked the earth killing because that was his only pleasure in life, a life filled with revenge, dirt and blood. He had a grudge against the world. Stories were written in newspapers about him and his men; they had a reputation of rape, torture, and killing of the white settlers, even the small, defenseless children and many women during their raids. There was a reason why he was at the top of the list and he would go on killing until someone finally stops him.

Jesse scanned further down the list and suddenly froze for a minute. He opened the desk drawer and pulled out a glass and an unopened bottle of whiskey; uncorking it, he downed half the bottle before he put it away. He leaned back in the chair, his eyes pools of liquid blue. Little Wolf's name was also on that list.

The captain had his orders and was to leave in three days, to kill his own son because he knew that the kid would rather die than be captured. He rose out of his chair and walked to the door and flung it open wide. The cool wind greeted him, slapping his face; its sardonic way of laughing at him. *Fool!* The echoed hammering of the blacksmith rang out from the shed beside the front gate.

Across the parade ground, a company of soldiers drilled, quite possibly his new greenhorns; they looked like a bunch of awkward school boys, fledglings that had just enlisted. He snipped off the end of a cigar with his teeth and lit it; he stood in the doorway and angrily smoked. "*Fuck me,* are they in for a treat!"

On the night before Jesse was to leave for his assignment, he locked up his office and made his way back to his house. The half-chewed moon hung over the rolling hills to the north. His footsteps crunched on the frozen grass, glazed silver with frost. The familiar howl could be heard, piercing the clear, crisp air.

It was late! He went straight to the bedroom he now shared with Abigail. He could hear her soft breathing, see the profusion of mousy-brown hair across her pillow, stared at her overripe lips. She was no longer young, but her body under the cotton sheet was firm with a lushness that comes with maturity. He climbed in bed beside her and gently cupped her breast, stroking it with his one hand while the other one followed the curve of her hip, traveling sensually across her stomach and moved lower, until his fingers felt the moist cleft between her legs.

She licked her lips hungrily and rolled to him, lifting her trembling leg over his erection. Jesse leaned over her to kiss her on the mouth. Her eyes were wide with excitement; she waited. Suddenly, he stopped, backed away from her; his face went ashen, like he had just seen a ghost. He rolled over to the far side of the bed and whispered, "I'm tired, Abigail."

Hours later, he finally fell into a troubled sleep.

The old dream came again, as it always did. *He was standing in the snow at the bottom of the cliff. Waving blood-red poppies were growing in a perfect row, popping out of the snow. Meadowlark was holding the baby boy in her arms; she was wearing the red scarf that he had given her on her birthday. The baby started to cry. He backed away and fell into the river. He was drowning; he saw her in the water and when she reached out, he grabbed her hand but her arm fell off and the river swept her away.*

The water suddenly drained from the river, leaving him rolling on the ground with a Sioux warrior straddling over him. The angry warrior was holding a knife at his throat; he was going to kill him. His face was the image of himself with long, saffron hair and cold, blue eyes. The warrior suddenly turned into a large white wolf, staring back at him.

Then there were two white wolves. Two babies! Two of his sons staring into his eyes!

Jesse awoke, sweat creased his brow. He rolled to the far side of the bed and shivered from the predawn cold that had filled the room. A sliver of gray leaking through the window fell across Abigail's shadowed body. How peaceful she slept every night! He got up and broke the film of ice from the washbasin; he splashed cold water onto his face. Peering into the mirror in front of him, he briefly saw the image of a white wolf with the same familiar pair of deep blue eyes, the reflection staring back at him in the darkened room. The strange image disappeared.

Abigail rose sleepily from their bed and walked over to Jesse, interrupting his shaving. She leaned into him and he put his free arm around her waist while kissing the tip of her nose. He gently kissed her mouth, searching for the spark that he could never find. Without saying a word, he finished shaving and got dressed to leave.

Long underwear made of merino wool went on first, followed by the lamb's wool, knee-high socks. He then put on a double-breasted blouse and the rest of his standard army-issued uniform, including a pair of high shiny boots. And over the boots he wore outer moccasins, also knee-high and lined with buffalo fur for warmth and durability. He adjusted his beaded gun belt containing the Colt revolver, the butt handle positioned forward on his right side as he was left-handed; also attached to the belt, a sheathed razor-sharp, stag-handled bowie knife weighted down the other side.

He grabbed the bearskin overcoat with the high fur collar, his army-issued wool hat with the muskrat-lined fur earflaps, and a pair of wool army gloves. The mittens that went over the gloves, he stuffed into the coat pockets. He knew from experience that during the next four to six weeks, frostbite could become a bigger enemy than the dangerous warriors they were stalking.

Abigail watched with moistened eyes as he bent down and kissed her goodbye. He grabbed his Spencer rifle, leaning against the wall near the door, and left. There was something cold and final in that kiss, just like the gusty wind that blew about her blanketed body. A *last* kiss! She stood at the open doorway, watching Jesse walk away from her.

A ghost always walks with him, she thought as the tall man in the striking army uniform, his back straight, strode toward the parade grounds where his soldiers awaited. The only thing left behind were his spade-shaped footprints in the frosty grass. The walls of the fort chiseled against the sky, seemed different now, stark and barren. And *Cold!* Abigail, shivering from a sudden gust, wrapped the blanket more tightly around her nude body and returned inside, closing the door behind her.

Little Wolf slept most of the day and part of that night. Something had awoken him from a deep sleep. He laid on the ground and listened; the land had gone suddenly still around him, even the frogs from the river had quit croaking. Nothing moved.

He sat up then, wiping his long, blonde hair away from his face. He stole a quick glance over at Shadow tethered to a tree nearby; his ears were perked up, alert; he was staring into the willows to the right of his master. His whinny was muffled, meant only for Little Wolf's ears. But it was too late. The arrow came from within the willows, penetrating deep into his chest, a fatal wound that was meant to kill him.

He collapsed back to the ground, unable to catch his breath. His body was immoveable, his eyes trying to focus on his assailant racing toward him, brandishing a knife in his hand. Little Wolf reached down under the blanket for the big bowie and just as the assailant lunged at him, the bowie spoke with its metal blade as it sliced through flesh, right through the blanket.

Spotted Dog took a few steps backward while grabbing his stomach, his eyes were black with rage. Little Wolf got to his feet, quick like a panther; he was face to face with the devil, a madman who had only one thing on his mind, to kill. Little Wolf's cold, blue eyes stared at him, the loathing was deep and real, almost virulent also, awaiting his next move.

Ignoring the searing pain, the red-hot-branding-iron-inside-his-chest pain.

Through the foggy haze, the fuzziness, he heard the wind roar, and above it, the maddened howl. Then he heard the other sound, a growl that was low at first, building up to a savage rumble. The air filled with a strong, feral smell. There was a flash of a body; a close brush of immense heat suddenly circled Spotted Dog.

The animal was sizing him up with cold, bloodcurdling eyes. Eyes that became a pair of blue, shining lights illuminating the whole campsite. Spotted Dog's eyes opened wide with amazement and fear as the white wolf, half the size of a horse, was about to launch itself at his throat. Huge yellow teeth were barred. Another loud, deadly growl coming from the depths of the angry animal's stomach.

Any second now, Spotted Dog was going to die; he envisioned himself being savagely mauled and shaken like a dog shakes a rag. He glanced over at the blanket, hoping for some assistance from Little Wolf but no one was there. Spotted Dog simply dropped his knife and ran to the big black tethered to the tree nearby. With one leap, he jumped on the horse's bare back and rode off toward the darkness of the willows. The white wolf limped back to the blanket and laid down so he could lick his wounds.

Little Wolf didn't know how long he laid on the blanket in a foggy state of mind. He knew he was badly hurt by the immense pain he felt. Spotted Dog was gone, so was the big black. When he managed to open his eyes, snow was tumbling down from the frothy sky. He tried to sit up but pain enveloped him. The only indication that there had been a major scuffle here was the large, deeply imprinted wolf tracks circling the blanket and droplets of blood from the animal splattered in the snow.

He tried to organize his memories that swirled in his mind as to what had happened but to no avail. He recalled someone calling his name, the fuzzy face looking intent, very concerned. Strong arms lifted him on a travois and brought him down off the slope. Fast Walker led the way out of Forbidden Valley as Shadow pulled the travois close behind, away from the distant, dreaded mountains. Was he going home at last?

There were other memories as well. Memories that made no sense. He remembered the wind howling, the massive white body, red blood dripping from its chest. He also remembered the vision he had of the she-devil holding Spotted Dog's severed head in the crook of her arm; fresh blood trickling down her bronzed skin and landing on her beaded moccasin.

The woman with no nose who could not talk told him in sign language with her free hand that she had brought back his *friend*. She had Shadow on a leash and tethered him to the closest willow tree. She slightly raised up her arm, indicating the severed head and signed, "Now you can go home, Little Wolf!" She had remembered his name.

She turned and rode back into the darkness of the trees.

Fast Walker took his injured friend to his camp, to his people. To a small, peaceful village with about forty Oglala Indians, including women and children, a happy, contented tribe living independently on their own.

When Little Wolf finally awoke, feeling much better, he noticed his arm had been bandaged and his ribcage tightly wrapped. He heard laughter outside of the tepee, something he hadn't heard in a long time. Three small children were running around the trees, playing a game of tag that he used to play when he was approximately their age. Fast Walker sat beside the bed, watching him, smiling. In his Sioux tongue, he told him he was glad that he was finally awake.

"You have been sick for a very long time, ever since the big snowstorm. We made it home just before it hit."

"That was *you* who shot the cave dweller!" exclaimed Little Wolf, also speaking in the same language.

"Yes, you would have been their breakfast that day. I have been following you for a long time. Watching out for your safety. That is a bad country. You are lucky to still be alive," answered Fast Walker.

Little Wolf made the sign of 'thankyou' in Sioux.

"Now we are even, my friend. When you saved my life, I promised I would be there when you needed me also."

"I had a strange vision after the fight with Spotted Dog." He told Fast Walker about it, leaving out none of the details.

"That was no vision, my friend. It was real! That ugly she-devil brought back your horse while I was making the travois to bring you home. You tried to sit up when she spoke to you in sign language. Just looking at her frightened me, and I don't scare easily. That is going to be quite a story to tell to your grandchildren when you get old, my friend."

"I feel old *now!*" chuckled Little Wolf. He remained at his friend's village for many days, where he was treated with much hospitality and he enjoyed their company. They were a peaceful tribe, wanting to be just left alone on their land, to raise their families and hunt when they needed food for the winter.

"Ride with the wind at your back," said Fast Walker when Little Wolf rode away, heading for home.

The sky was clear, the sun was shining but more snow had fallen last night, making travel slower than usual. It was in the Moon of Being Snowblind; he had to shield his eyes from the sun's bright glare reflecting off the snow. The temperature had dropped considerably from the previous day, making for a frosty ride.

It was so quiet; nothing stirred as Shadow broke a fresh trail through the deep drifts. Little Wolf could almost *touch* the silence, *think* the quietness. But the moment didn't last long. He had not ridden very far when he suddenly heard someone call his name; the voice was muffled as if spoken underwater. He stopped; his hand quickly found the Spencer lying across his lap. The she-devil rode up alongside of him. "I need to ask you for a favor, I have no one else and I know you can help me."

"I'm listening!" returned Little Wolf cautiously. After all, she was still a person not to be reckoned with, a woman of circumstance. A ruthless killer!

"I want you to deliver a message to my mother. I haven't seen her for over five years and I just want her to know that I am all right. Would you do that for me?"

"Where does your mother live?" asked Little Wolf.

"On Beaker's Bluff, in an abandoned cabin that belonged to a friend of hers; she used to go there many times and visit him years ago. Her name is Ruby, Ruby Long Bottoms."

"Who shall I say the message is from?"

"My mother gave me the name of 'Pretty Flower'. Ironic, isn't it?" She attempted to smile. "Do you know where Beaker's Bluff is?"

"Yes, I know where it is. I will find your mother and give her your message. I promise, Pretty Flower!"

She signed him in the Sioux language saying 'thankyou' and before she left, she signed him again. "I *also* like your red scarf!"

"That was *my* mother's," returned Little Wolf. Pretty Flower gave him a look that said 'she understands' and rode back to Forbidden Valley. He never saw the noseless woman again.

Captain Jesse Burns looked over his men; Silent Hawk, the half-breed scout, was mounted off to the side of the thirty mounted soldiers who remained in formation, also waiting for their leader. The young Oglala scout was a man of few words but he was a good tracker.

"Where's Sergeant Donavon?" barked Jesse. He was the only experienced soldier in the whole group, other than himself and the scout. He needed him! But whiskey was his downfall.

Ten years ago, the captain rode with him into Forbidden Valley during one of the worst storms ever recorded. Coping with minus thirty-nine degrees Fahrenheit temperatures and forty feet of snow that had dropped that winter left them stranded for more than six weeks in the mountains. Their food supply ran dangerously low; they ate the mules and four of their horses to keep from starving.

Between battling with the hostile Indians, the cave dwellers, frostbite, and starvation, only sixteen men returned; the others didn't make it. The whiskey probably kept Donavon alive. Jesse vowed that he would never return to that godforsaken country. *Why does my last assignment have to take me back to that fucking valley?* he thought angrily. "Does anyone know where Donavon is?"

"Sergeant Donavon spent the night in jail for being drunk and disorderly at the saloon," offered one of the soldiers, sheepishly.

"We're ready to move out. Go get him!" ordered Captain Burns.

He rode around the three supply wagons, each pulled by a team of mules, his mule train. Inside these wagons contained supplies that meant the difference between life and death, coffee and food rations, including beef jerky and salt-pork for forty days, tents and blankets, and bags of grain for the stock. He knew the wagons were a necessity but if the terrain got too rough, the wagons could get left behind and they would have to depend on the mules and whatever they would be able to carry.

Looking at the *softness* of these green soldiers made him wonder if they would ever make the journey further north, much less last four weeks of it. As they march mile after mile, deeper into the northern badlands, the winds will howl and blow more cruelly, showing no sympathy for dying men. Mother Nature just didn't care!

While they waited, Captain Burns spoke to the soldiers. "Our assignment is to capture and apprehend as many of the hostile Indians who have not complied with government commands and return them to their designated reservations. They have opted to move further north where they think the army will not go, to set up new villages, turning their backs on the agencies."

"The ones we're tracking would rather starve than eat handouts, the white man's food; they would rather die in battle than die of starvation. A few of the young hotheads have already taken off and have been spotted in Forbidden Valley. The terrain is rough, hard going during the winter months and we could encounter Sioux and Cheyenne warriors on the way."

"Are the stories true about the beasts, the cannibals who eat people?" asked one of the soldiers.

"Yes, I'm afraid so! It is dangerous territory. We will have to be very vigilante and watch each other's back. However, frostbite scares me even more. You can't see *that* enemy coming until it's too late. Try to keep your skin covered at all times."

At that moment, Donavon showed up looking like he had been run over by a stampede of buffalo and he smelled even worse. "Sorry, Captain!"

The sudden shrill notes of the bugle rang through the cold, predawn air. "They are playing our song, boys. Let's move out!" yelled Captain Burns.

On the eighteenth day of November 1903, the army left Fort Wilderness as a light snowfall began to cover the trail leading northward with a promise that much, much more would accompany them.

The trail was snow-covered, hard to follow. But Little Wolf was making good time until he heard the most horrible wail. It sounded like a desperate cry echoing from some animal up ahead. The bellowing came from a mule and it was standing knee-deep in a freshly fallen snowdrift; its head hung in weariness as frost rose in a steamy wreath around pointed ears. An avalanche!

Little Wolf peered up through the glistening windows of ice crystals which, even now, hours later, still floated down in the crispy, mountainous air. The slide had spilled down a mountaintop of snow and now threatened to slide once again and this time, with an even faster momentum, it might not stop here. It could keep going, slipping further down into the icy, cold waters of the river below, and in the process, could possibly shake loose the frothy stuff below their feet, spewing them all into the freezing blackness of the river. Either way, they would be doomed.

The utter stillness hung like a hoarfrost shroud just above them while the avalanche threatened to dislodge another sprawling layer of heavy snow that would bury everything that got in its way. And nothing would stop it. Any sudden movement, even a trickle of a small stone, could erupt this cold tomb again. He momentarily held his breath, knowing that the mule, the black, and himself were in grave danger. The pack mule, elderly and mountain wise, stayed put, not even moving a muscle; it showed more sense than most men in such a dangerous situation.

"God help anybody who was up *there* earlier today!" muttered Little Wolf.

He had seen many avalanches but had never gotten this close to one before today. He glanced over at the mule, who stood motionless, anxiously waiting. "I remember you!" he said to the mule. "Where's your master, Poke? You two are always together."

The mule twitched his ears and rolled his oddly-colored eyes toward the deep snowdrift near the vicinity of where he was standing. That was when Little Wolf realized that Silver Fox was buried underneath. Little Wolf carefully started to move around the massive fan of whiteness, reaching down inside. Feeling for life, groping for anything in the depths of nothingness.

Eventually, his fingers brushed against a waxen object that raised the hairs on the back of his neck. The faint warmth of skin at the end of his fingertips told him that someone was still alive inside there. He frantically dug with his hands, moving armfuls of fluffy snow while keeping his eye on the cliff above him. He dug until he had exhumed Silver Fox's face, then the rest of his body. He was still alive! He sputtered out chunks of snow from his mouth and gasped for air.

"What did you do, ole' man, fall in an air pocket under there?" said Little Wolf, relieved that he had found him so fast.

The mule quietly shook his head in glee. Little Wolf cautiously got them away from the area and built a fire for warmth. It took two days for Silver Fox to recover enough so he could travel and they continued with their trip home, going first by way of the trapper's home where Little Wolf first met Ilkcaw Fox, his friend's lovely, *lonely* wife.

She was banished from the Sioux tribe when she had married a white man, a white trapper who was frequently away from home in search of the elusive silver fox. Large sums of money were paid for the beautiful fox hides; it was an expensive rarity to own a beautiful, silver fox coat.

Jean-Luc was making a fortune every time he went trapping. Ilkcaw always referred to him by his white man's name, Jean-Luc. The couple had tried for years to have children; Jean-Luc had always wanted to have a son to follow in his footsteps, to teach him how to hunt. But to no avail.

Jean-Luc *was* getting older and he accepted the fact that this was never going to happen as Ilkcaw remained childless. And Little Wolf wished great happiness for his friend, hoping that someday soon, Jean-Luc's dream would come true and he would finally get his son. Little Wolf remained with his friends at their cabin until the weather broke and then he rode in the direction of Beaker's Bluff. He had a message to deliver. A promise to keep! And Little Wolf always keeps his promises.

After marching for eight hours and the skies were darkening, Captain Burns halted the procession and announced they would make camp in the little sheltered, teacup valley. "We're in Indian country now so keep your eyes peeled, Sergeant Donavon. Hopefully, most of them will be inside their nice warm tepees, enjoying a buffalo stew instead of roaming around outside in this cold weather. I will post guards throughout the night from here on in."

Campfires were built and a mess hall was set up by the cooks for the evening meal; the horses were led to the nearby river to drink, unsaddled, and fed, settling them down for the night as their means of travel was most important in this unsettled wilderness.

During the night, a howling wolf kept the soldiers awake. "Where the hell is that coming from?" asked Corporal Drake. "It sounds like it is right here, in the camp."

The next morning, Jesse lumbered out of his bed; he had not slept well. It never ceased to amaze him that no matter how far he traveled in no-man's-land, the dream always managed to find him, always invaded his sleep. The temperature had dipped to −20 degrees Fahrenheit during the night and snow covered the ground in bridal white satin. As he moved about, trying to get circulation in his cold limbs, the soldiers were looking at all the huge wolf tracks passing through the campsite.

"See, I told you it sounded real close," spoke up Corporal Drake.

For two days, the army marched, breaking through new snow still falling on trails that few had traveled on, knowing that those same few had probably only pointed one way, never to return. Captain Burns pushed his men to their limit each day; they were weary and cold and the further north they traveled, the colder it got.

They complained when on the third day, he ordered them to keep going, not letting them stop for their lunch break. He told Donavon that more snow was on the way and, with the temperatures still dropping, they should keep moving. To stop now, the chance of getting frostbite was greater as the day wore on when the temperatures usually drop even lower.

As it was, when they finally stopped to make camp, one soldier's gloves were frozen to the horse's reins. They grumbled among themselves about their captain. "He has the devil lurking in his eyes!" stated one of them.

Their respect and trust were evaporating fast, just like their body temperatures. Jesse knew the soldiers were upset with him, but he was not there to win a popularity contest; he was there to save their lives. There were already too many nameless graves out here. Only Donovan and the half-breed understood.

It was so cold; the axles were freezing on the wagon wheels and had to be re-greased every hour. The coffee in the tin cups immediately grew cold in their hands before they got to drink it. And all the utensils had to be warmed in the ashes of the cook fires before anyone could use them. Otherwise, the frozen metal could rip the flesh from their tongues or the skin on the inside of their mouths.

Jesse went around, inspecting the soldiers for possible signs of frostbite, warning them once again to keep their skin covered.

"Put some of this salve on your cracked lips. Pass it around to the others." He tossed a blue jar at the youngest soldier, whose tears froze in his eyes even before they had a chance to fall on his cheeks. "And do *not* lick your lips anymore!" he voiced sternly.

Silent Hawk knew the secret ingredients inside the blue jar, most Indians did. They referred to it as the 'magic salve'; it healed everything *fast*. "Where you get this?" he asked in the white man's language.

To hear the quiet Oglala scout speak, much less speak in English, was a shock to Jesse. "It's an old Indian secret!" he chuckled.

When the jar was returned to him, he placed it back into his breast pocket. Jesse had been observing the half-breed who had purposely avoided the others. He chose to ignore their hurtful comments; the soldiers didn't think he understood their language but they had been wrong.

The pair of deep-set eyes, moving like restless, brown beads surrounded by turkey-track wrinkles, showed no emotion on the coffee-colored face. The scout just sat back on his paint horse and scrutinized, listened. The experienced scout *knew* the dangers they faced. Not just from the minus thirty-nine degrees recorded earlier that morning on a thermostat where the mercury inside the glass bulb had congealed into a solid ball of red molasses at the bottom, but also from the mirror signals flashing from the hilltops and the smoke signals curling like fingers, trying to reach up to the clouds with messages being sent.

With every mile they rode, the country grew rougher, much more *dangerous. These young soldiers will grow up fast after this assignment. The hard way, I'm afraid!* thought Silent Hawk.

When the army continued on the trail, they crossed an increasing number of travois tracks, accompanied by a large number of unshod pony hooves also imprinted in the fresh snow. They came across a deserted Sioux village, not one living soul. Just dead bodies scattered on the frozen, bloody ground. A severed arm of a child lay in the snow, torn from a body that was nowhere to be found.

Warriors, women, small children stripped off their nightclothes, then eaten. The meat stripped to the bones! Fast Walker, his woman, and their three small children were among the bodies. The tracks they had passed on the trail earlier were probably made by the survivors of the vicious attack on this peaceful village. The *cave dwellers*! And the she-devil had taken her revenge once again.

The horrifying scene in front of him only reassured Jesse that he had made the right decision; this was his last assignment! The soldiers stared wide-eyed; some threw up their food over the side of their mounts. "Welcome to the army, boys!" stated their captain.

Donovan, using the excuse of wanting to relieve himself, returned from the bushes wreaking of whiskey. Jesse shot a warning glance his way but didn't reprimand him. He probably needed that drink. They rode on in silence, watching the snowflakes flutter and eventually fall to the ground. Donovan licked his swollen lips, savoring the whiskey taste as long as he could, sucking on his tongue to draw on the memory.

"What you lookin' at, half-breed? You just do your job and keep your eyes straight ahead and I'll do mine. That way, we might not kill each other before the end of this expedition. You hear me, boy?"

"I'll give the orders here, Donovan!" Jesse spoke with authority in his voice. He realized the men were edgy, tired, and cold. And stopping was not going to happen just yet. He wanted to cover a few more miles before dusk settled on the land.

"Sorry, Cap'n!" apologized Sergeant Donovan. "It's just that I *hate* Indians and *half-breeds* even worse."

"I'd appreciate it if you would keep your opinion to yourself, Sergeant. The men are wound up enough! And lay off the whiskey!"

"Yes, Sir!" Donavon was hot under the collar for being called out, but he didn't say another word. He knew when to quit when he had pushed the captain to the limit.

The sun was setting in the west, giving the land an orange-gold glow. The scout signaled Jesse. There was a silhouette of a rider up ahead in the distance, seeming to be in no apparent hurry, then the silhouette suddenly disappeared as popcorn-sized snowflakes began to fall and visibility was restricted. And the temperature fell noticeably lower.

Twice, a soldier had dropped from his horse, so stiff from the brutalizing cold and lack of movement, sleeplessness, and overpowering fatigue, that he could no longer stay in his saddle. He hit the snow-covered ground and attempted to rise up, but his legs were so wobbly and unworkable and after the second fall, he had to be helped back onto his horse.

At that point, Jesse reluctantly decided to make camp for the night, making sure guards were posted in case the lone rider he saw earlier had friends traveling with him. An attack was the last thing he wanted to have happened, especially with the deteriorating condition his soldiers were displaying.

Winter's early twilight was crowding the light out of the sky. The wind picked up and Jesse pulled up his fur collar. The wind prowled among the higher peaks, whistling and howling, swinging down on him like guffaws of raw laughter. Making no attempt to hide, stalking him with a vengeance; icy pellets of hail struck Jesse in the face. The wind would temporarily die down to a whisper, muttering his name; and then it would start up again, hoping to catch him off guard, more hollow-boned and even more revengeful.

A white fog was rising out of a valley up ahead. Frozen crystals were emitting from the layers of paralyzingly cold frost, painfully stinging the reddened, raw skin on every man's face. The ethereal fog crept around them, blanketing them. Jesse looked over at his scout; all he could see were the roaming, glassy beads of his eyes carefully scrutinizing their surroundings, his gloved hand hovering on his rifle. Ready for anything in the ghostly whiteness!

In just two hours, the temperature had dropped even further, registering a record low of minus forty-three Fahrenheit. Once again, Jesse examined the soldiers for frostbite; with these temperatures, it wouldn't take long for Jack Frost to inflict the first signs of irreparable harm to one's body. Upon checking one of his soldiers, who was gripping his hand awkwardly, he asked, "Are you alright, soldier?"

"I think I've lost my hand, Sir. I can't feel it anymore." His skin was motley white, spotted, icy cold to the touch. His hand felt *foreign* to the rest of his body.

"Long ago, I got myself a hand just like that one you're holding, soldier," Jesse told him as he pulled off the mitten from his left hand. "Ole' Jack Frost has hit me twice before on this hand. Now, every time it gets real cold, this hand always gets frozen first. The same thing will happen to you. You have to watch out for that from now on."

"You mean I won't lose it then?" the young soldier anxiously asked.

"No, not as long as you do as I say. Come with me! We're going to save that hand." As Jesse passed Silent Hawk, he asked him to fetch him a piece of canvas cloth. "Watch the camp until I return. We're going to the river."

"Frostbite!" The scout knew without being told.

When Jesse and the soldier reached the frozen river, Jesse scanned the ice until he found what he was looking for. An air pocket! After pulling the soldier's mitten off, he immersed the frostbitten hand into the hole in the ice. Steam rose from the icy water. The soldier winced in pain. "You feel that pain? Now you have feeling in your hand."

"B-believe it or n-not, s-sir, the w-water is w-warmer than the air around us right now," gasped the soldier through chattering teeth.

Minutes later, Jesse pulled the soldier's hand out of the water and immediately covered it with the coarse gunnysack cloth while briskly rubbing it from the fingers, clear up to his elbow. "This brings back the circulation of the blood into your hand. It is such sweet, exquisite agony to suddenly have a feeling again, even if it was painful for a few minutes. Now you won't lose your hand, boy."

"Th-thanks, C-Captain!" The gratitude emitting from the soldier's young face said it all.

"Don't mention it!" returned Jesse.

When they returned, Donovan was stalking about the camp, craving a nip from the flask of whiskey he had stashed inside his coat pocket. He went to the river's edge and broke the layer of ice with the kettle and filled it with water. Upon returning, it wasn't just the water inside the kettle sloshing about as Donovan staggered to the fire. "I'm making coffee!" he announced with a slur.

"Remove the coffee grounds and save them for tomorrow; we're running low of coffee already," spoke up Jesse, noticing Donovan's inebriated condition.

Jesse had to relieve himself and disappeared in the bushes also before he turned in for the night. It was very dark as the moon hid behind the clouds. The sudden jolt slammed the breath from him. He rolled on the ground, trying to get up. But the attacker was quicker and was on top of him, pinning him on the ground; he was strong and agile.

Jesse's hand went to his belt but the bowie must have fallen out in the fall. He kneed the warrior in the groin, quickly bringing up the other leg and kicking with both knees; he managed to throw the brave over his head. The attacker landed on his back with a loud thud. They both got up on their feet, facing each other, circling. Each man knowing he had a fighter opposite him!

The warrior dropped to the ground and swept Jesse off his feet. Jesse fell backward, slamming his head on a rock. He was dizzy and saw stars for a few seconds. The attacker was fast. A glistening, murderous knife blade was held to Jesse's throat; one quick, deadly swipe and his life could end right here. The moon came from behind the clouds, temporarily throwing some light on the two fighters. Jesse's eyes locked with his assailant's. Cold! Blue! Like his own. The assailant's long saffron hair hung in Jesse's face. Hair just like his own! The light from the moon revealed the facial features, also similar to his own.

Dizziness was clouding his head, his eyesight unfocused. A sudden flash of *white!* The man on top of him was not a man. Staring back at him with identical, blue, shining eyes was a wolf, a large white wolf. Darkness again fell on the land and the wolf was gone.

Jesse recovered and wandered back into camp. He had a slight cut at his throat, under his chin. The boy had his chance to kill him! But he didn't! That morning he announced to the others, "We're going home!"

They had been riding less than an hour when they saw the lone rider again, riding toward them. Jesse knew it was Little Wolf; the red scarf around his neck whipped in the wind. "I'm going to take him in," he told Donovan, who was still a bit inebriated.

The rider stopped. So did the army. They were about two hundred feet apart, facing one another. Jesse said to Silent Hawk, "Give me a white flag; you and I are going closer, to talk to him. To try to bring him in peacefully! The rest of you, wait here. If there is trouble, Donavon, you know what to do."

Behind him, he overheard Donovan's voice growl, "Damned Injuns, nothin' but bare hide in below zero weather and they don't seem to mind the freezin' cold one bit!"

The two men approached Little Wolf cautiously while waving the white flag. They remained mounted on their horses, facing each other. Jesse signed to him in the Sioux language, letting him know that he came in peace, to talk. Little Wolf was not yet twenty summers, but he looked much older.

He was very thin, haggard, sitting rigid on his horse. His disheveled, corn-silk-colored hair was bound by two eagle feathers, their tips pointing downward. His pale face, an impassive reflection, was entirely void of emotion. Until he saw Jesse before him! A dark scowl quickly crept over the weary, haggard face, revealing his anger, his hate for this man. Jesse signed to him again, noticing the sudden change in his son's eyes, now so cold and distant. Eyes where the whole universe once had dwelled.

"I speak your language, old man!" voiced Little Wolf disrespectfully. Loathing flowed from his cold, blue eyes as he spoke the English language fluently.

"Come with us! We will hunt Spotted Dog and his men together, bring them back to stand trial," persuaded Jesse.

"Spotted Dog is *dead.* So are his men," answered Little Wolf angrily.

"Then come back with me, son! I will see that you will get a fair trial." Jesse had assumed that his son was responsible for their deaths. "You have nothing to fear if you give up."

"I am not your *son!*" spat Little Wolf, his voice dripping with malice.

"And *I* did not kill them!"

"Look, there are thirty rifles pointed at you. You don't have a chance! It doesn't have to end this way."

"I am not afraid of an army of lions led by a sheep; I am more afraid of an army of sheep led by a lion." Little Wolf stood his ground. "It is easy for you to stand here, with your army at your back."

"Yes, you are right, and it takes courage to stand here *alone*," returned Jessie.

"A solitary tree has deeper roots than when it stands with others inside a forest. As an army soldier, you would not understand this. As a Lakota soldier, I have been taught this. Other things I have been taught you will never understand. I have always tried to do what is *right* for my people, even if it means standing alone."

Little Wolf continued speaking with malice. "I used to be far weaker than what I am now. You laughed at me before, when I was that weak little *savage*. Is that not what you called me, *Captain* Burns?" There was an uncomfortable silence between them.

"Now, I am no longer afraid! I am no longer that little boy!" spat Little Wolf. "You should have kicked me harder when I was down because now if I'm not *dead*, I'm not *fucking* done with this fight."

Another uncomfortable silence passed between them. Jesse knew that if Little Wolf made the wrong decision at this point, his son would never be taken back alive.

"Come back with me!" repeated Jesse, knowing the kid might *never* give in. His son's strong words had cut deeply into his heart. He now realized just how much the boy deeply hated him for all these years.

Jesse suddenly noticed the red scarf behind Little Wolf, waving in the wind; the angry warrior had taken it off and tied it to a tree just before the soldiers rode up, thinking he was going to be shot down. The brave warrior stood his ground; he wasn't afraid to die. Weariness and Dejection showed, but a stronghold had infiltrated inside his body, preparing his soul for death.

He was so tired of running and now, there was a little amount of fight left inside of him. He had expected to be shot dead by these army soldiers because, for him, the fight *was* finally over. However, when he had seen the white flag of truce, he was surprised.

Little Wolf thought about it for many minutes, tormented. Fear of dying was never the issue. He solemnly spoke, "Everything I was afraid of has already happened to me. White men are those who are afraid they will end up in Hell. As a Sioux warrior, I have already been there many times. I fought for what I had grown to trust and believe in, to stand and fight in defense of those I loved. But I have lost my family and my beautiful Yellow Bird, my *future*. So now I have nothing left; now I fear *nothing*!"

At that moment, the long-awaited answer suddenly came to Little Wolf. And it had hit him like a big boulder bouncing off his head. How could he be so blind! The number of times this heartless man had called him s*on*! The number of times he stared at him with those cold, uncaring, but *familiar* blue eyes! The many times he had *saved* his life from the army soldiers! Yet truthfully, deep within his heart, Little Wolf had always *admired* this big man. Now he knew why!

The sudden silence that fell between father and son was so apparent; it was as if the whole world had stopped around them. Jesse thought he was gaining no ground in bringing the kid in and the anger he felt was tearing him apart and it showed.

"Don't you be so quick to judge *me*, Boy! Do you think *my* life has been so *fucking* easy either? Do you think you are the only one who has been dragged through hell and back? *You* don't know half of what I have survived, young man!" defended Jesse angrily.

It angered him to see his son so beaten. A broken man! "I am a wolf stuck in a human body!" Jesse confessed. "I am a wolf who wanders the wild lands, a *creature* who stalks in silent shadows, possessing primal strength and astonishing perception seen through a pair of glowing eyes. Man and creature connecting as one! I talk, I smile, I love just like you! And I hurt, just as you do. But it is always hard to sleep at night."

Jesse paused to control his built-up anger, then added, "I also have *chosen* to do the things that you have refused to do and I continue to do the things that you can't. But beware of my silence! The wolf inside me is waiting to come out." A long pause to control his anger, then, "*As a man*, I also *choose* to listen to my inner voice. As you should do so now."

Behind them, impatient groans and shuffling sounds could be heard. A light dusting of large snowflakes began to fall from the gray sky. A cold, blustery wind whipped up; that same penetrating wind that Jesse battled with for many years. He always hated the wind. Jesse also still hated the *waiting.* So silent, immobile, and still indecisive, and unreluctantly unwilling to give in to the white men.

Little Wolf surprisingly blurted out, "I *too* have the blood of the wolf flowing inside my veins! He shows me the hidden path. His Spirit has taught me to walk tall like the trees; live strong as the mountains, and he always howls with me in my joy. But mostly, he guards me when there is danger. He walks beside me in silence, while the summer sun fills my weary body with new energy each day and the light of the moon guides my way by night."

"But these last few days, I have seen no sun and there has been no moon. It is the way of the Wolf Spirit, *my* inner voice, telling me that my fight is finally over. And when my last breath has been taken, I hope that I will have lived and stood for all that I have believed in. I *will* come with you *peacefully,* but only on one condition!" He hesitated, his voice now a mere whisper. "Don't ever expect me to graze with the *sheep.*"

"I promise you, that won't happen, son! And I will always be there by your side from now on." Father and son shook hands on that promise; for the first time, Little Wolf believed he meant what he had said.

"About that red scarf that you discarded, that was your mother's; she wore it when she gave birth to you. I gave it to her on her sixteenth birthday. I recognized it straight away."

Little Wolf changed his mind about the red scarf blowing in the wind directly behind him and he turned to retrieve it from the tree branch.

That's when the rifle exploded from behind Jesse, blowing a hole in Little Wolf's upper back when he turned his back to retrieve that scarf. The bullet was so powerful at that close range, it went clear through to the other side and exited from Little Wolf's shoulder, high enough to thankfully just miss his heart and lung.

Little Wolf slumped forward, falling off Shadow. The shot was meant to be a fatal blow. He had felt something slam into his upper body. He was surprised that there was no pain, only a burning sensation that went through him. He saw a wall of fire in front of him. It was very bright; it burned his eyes. There were no soldiers; there was no sound. There was *nothing*! He closed his eyes and the wall of fire went away. All he heard was an angelic voice singing a death-song from far away. Muffled, like it was being sung underwater.

Jesse immediately turned in his saddle and yelled out the order, "Hold your fire!"

When he turned around to face his son, Little Wolf laid face down on the ground at his horse's feet. "Bring the wagon! Put him in the wagon! Unbridle his horse, leave him behind. Help me! Hurry!" Jesse was yelling orders at the soldiers.

When Donovan bent down to help lift the body, Jesse yelled angrily, "You son of a bitch! You step away from him or I'll kill you! The boy was *coming* in! He was just getting his scarf from the tree."

Before Little Wolf's body was bundled in stiff, cold canvas, Jesse wrapped the red scarf around his son's neck and tied it. The blood-soaked *cocoon* was gently placed on the floor inside the supply wagon.

"If you don't kill Donovan before we get back, *I* might!" threatened Silent Hawk angrily as he mounted his horse.

The army was going back to Fort Wilderness; Little Wolf's horse, Shadow, followed behind the wagon for a long time, knowing his master was inside. Then he finally galloped away. The soldiers rode home in a concluding silence, no one even coughed. There was no more grumbling or the usual complaining. The atmosphere had become very subdued, like a funeral procession.

Captain Jesse Burns rode with his back straight in the saddle; he didn't want his men to see that inside, he was now a beaten man. A *broken* man! He had never felt this way before; he had let the army do this to him. But he had done his job. He had won the fight! Why did he feel no elation, no pride? At least he had given Little Wolf the chance to surrender.

He never thought he would actually take it. He thought the boy's pride would overrule and he would die before giving himself up so easily, as his son's attitude was so much like his own! Did the boy even know who his real father was? And was there a *thread* of love felt by the boy, a moment of caring revealed, toward his father? The boy could have killed him. Jesse would never find out; now his son could possibly ride from one world to another.

They stopped at dusk and made camp. Jesse ate by himself, beans from a tin cup; he would be so glad when he wouldn't have to eat beans anymore. He had made a big decision today and he wanted to think. As for tonight, he just wanted to be left alone. However, Silent Hawk remained very watchful toward Jesse throughout the night.

It was a long way back to Fort Wilderness. Jesse knew that his trail was going to lead far beyond the fort; he was ready to take that trail. His instincts told him that Abigail had left; she probably went back home to her parents. He didn't have to be told. He knew it would have happened sooner or later. What incentive had he given her to make her stay? How could he show his love for Abigail when he always saw Meadowlark's face looking back at him? But he missed his wife!

Her faithfulness! Her stability!

Everyone remained so quiet. So gloomy, like the weather, as another cloudy day awoke from a low, threatening sky that looked like it would soon blanket the land with snow once more. Silent Hawk kept watching his captain with knowing eyes, especially when they passed Sacred Hill late that afternoon. The scout glanced back at the supply wagon that carried Little Wolf's body; he saw nothing unusual. And when they finally reached the fort gates, Silent Hawk noticed that Jesse seemed to be relieved. His captain was home at last. It had been a long trip, a long, *last* trip!

The wagon was parked beside the others that had returned previously. *There was no real rush to reveal its contents,* thought Jesse. Four other details had returned before them, including Colonel Jim McEwan's. He had lost six of his men, had eight wounded, and captured ten unreceptive Indians from the Sioux camp he raided.

As the wagons were emptied, Jesse stood and watched the sadness in the eyes of the captured warriors. Their hands were tied and their feet were chained like criminals as they were led to the stockade. There, they would remain for days until the army decided what was to be done with them. Occasionally, scraps of food were thrown over the top of the barricade as if the soldiers were feeding dogs or wild animals.

At the agency, another group of soldiers stood guard over captive women and children who were lined up outside of the open doorway, patiently waiting for the distribution of handouts of food and blankets. The lines were long and Jesse could overhear one of the agents complain that they weren't able to feed the ones that they already had. "And the government sends us even more," he grumbled.

The white agency worker was arguing with one of the women. "Only flour, coffee, beans, bacon, and one blanket," he repeated tiredly.

"No meat?" she asked, her voice breaking.

"No sugar! No meat, just bacon! Just flour, coffee, beans, bacon, and a blanket," he agitatedly repeated again and then yelled, "Next!"

The woman reluctantly left, carrying the small sack of food and a blanket; three small children clung to her long skirt as she walked back to the reservation, taking with her the rumors of Little Wolf's death. Word traveled fast among the Sioux reservation; their great leader had been killed. "His body lay in the back of a wagon, riddled with bullets," they were told.

The tribe was gathering quickly as the rumor spread. The memories of the elders could recall nothing like it. Every day, the people came; some in groups of twenty or thirty at a time. There were many. Other great leaders came to pay their respects to Little Wolf. Even some Cheyenne people and the Kiowas sat around the many fires that were burning within the perimeters of the Sioux reservation, now flourishing with activity.

A pulsing rhythm of life was suddenly flowing through the crowded camp as the indigenous people made preparations for Little Wolf's funeral ceremony. A crier rode through the mass of tepees, calling out that it was time for the dancing to begin.

Just as the colors of the sunset faded and long shadows fell across the land, the dance started with slow shuffling movements. The quietness seemed to numb their pain. Their feet scuffed the ground, creating swirls of dust around them. Slow, almost disorientating! There was no sound, other than the soft shuffling of moccasins on the ground and the crackling of the wood in the firepit.

The remaining people that were standing off to the side of the dancers gathered closely around them, adding to the large circle. The bonfire suddenly sent wild, disobedient sparks spiraling upwards toward the Heavens. The crowd once subdued as the quietness seemingly numbed their pain, quickly moved back from the bonfire. There was no warning, no signal. The sorrowful chanting began, and it grew louder. Then the drum started!

Thrumm, thrum, thrum, a massive drum that took six drummers to beat on it. The lodge trembled with its quick beat as sweat poured from the bodies of the drummers and smeared their painted faces. The beat of the drum suddenly became faster and the chanting grew louder and everyone danced with a frenzy, a fury. The drumming became a vast heartbeat of the earth itself, brushing and bouncing off the walls of the canvas tepees, magnifying the sound while the dancers moved more quickly now to the insistent beat.

Rattles took up the rhythm and women swayed, chanting a shrill chorus that heightened the sound of the drum. Bursts of sound shook the night air. It was deafening. Sweat from the bodies and smoke from the fire lingered in the air. The dance became wilder, faster as the flames leaped higher.

The dance continued long into the night. The drum pounded on, calling the ancestors in the sky. Urging, demanding an answer or a sign. The dance was life, the drum was life for Little Wolf, who would soon be among his ancestors at the camp in the sky, on his way to *Seyan.*

This celebration of life would have made Little Wolf proud to see the outpouring of love bestowed upon him. He had sometimes felt out of place among his people because of his appearance, even though he was raised as a true Lakota. It had never been easy to stand on his own, always defending, always proving his heritage. But after today, if he could just see all the crowds of mourning people attending his funeral, there wouldn't have been any more doubts. This would have meant so much to Little Wolf.

On the morning of the second day, the drum suddenly stopped. A spirit wind blew across the grasses and bent the branches of the trees. It was time for the procession to go to the burial grounds on Sacred Hill. They climbed steep slopes on dewy grass to reach the top of the burial grounds, where scaffolds of the dead were erected. The women wept and trilled death songs while the slow-moving elders tried to keep up the pace. Six great warriors, honored to be chosen, pulled a travois up the hill. It was laden with some of Little Wolf's personal items to be attached to a scaffold containing his body. However, at the top of Sacred Hill, there was no scaffold for him! There was no body!

The soldiers had finally reached Jesse's supply wagon, the last one left to unload. The wagon doors were flung open, revealing an empty, blood-soaked, canvas sheet. There was no body inside! An empty purple jar of salve rolled across the bare wood floor.

Corporal Drake, the youngest of Captain Jesse Burn's men, ambled over to where Jesse was standing. "I'll be damned! And that looks like the same jar you gave me for my chapped lips, Sir. How do you suppose it got in there?"

"God only knows, soldier!" Corporal Drake still tailed Jesse. "Anything else on your mind, Corporal?" asked Jesse.

"No, Sir! Well, yes, there is, Sir. You saved our lives out there, Captain Burns. And after talking to the men here tonight, I don't think there is any soldier at this fort who doesn't know how you feel about the men who serve under you, Captain Burns. You brought us all home alive. Thank you, sir."

"That was my main objective, son. Why don't you accompany me to the infirmary? I always make it part of my routine after an assignment like this one. Such simple gestures like a caring, reassuring word, a warm touch of a hand, an expression of a superior's appreciation for the courage, sacrifice, and selflessness evidenced by a bloody wound— these are all acts of kindness, courtesy, and respect that these soldiers deserve."

Jesse led young Corporal Drake across the parade grounds and entered into the infirmary. He was weary of the army and it showed, of chasing the many backsides of Indian ponies, of all the *waiting* for orders, the comings and goings only to end up here in the infirmary to visit a soldier who fought hard for his country and then takes his last breath here. A fallen soldier whose funeral is far from home, far from the bosom of loved ones! Laid here to rest eternally in this lonely wilderness, a country where Jesse came to wonder if God could even hear his prayers when the soldier was lowered into the frozen ground after his comrades worked in relays to dig his grave.

Corporal Drake stood beside his captain, staring down at the wounded soldiers. When Jesse spoke, he heard his name being called and kneeled beside the bed, where a doctor was frantically working to save a young man's life. Blood from massive facial wounds flowed down the front of his uniform, a murky, dying-colored black blood. Both eyes were swollen shut, and his mustache was clotted beneath a battered nose. The doctor straightened up and shook his head at Jesse.

"Hey, Doc! Instead of patching soldiers up, why don't *you* join the fightin' army? Captain Burns, maybe you can help me talk the Doc here into signing up," joked the dying soldier, his voice weak from loss of blood.

"Can you believe it, Jesse! Corporal Jackson here wants to know *why* I don't join the god-damned army," the doctor retorted.

"Hey, watch it, Doc! The army's been my whole life," replied the dying soldier. "It's been good for me. *Until now!* I never knew nothin' else."

Young Corporal Drake heard all this as he kneeled beside the bed. Jesse watched the dying soldier's face grow ashen, passive. Corporal Drake also watched the young soldier, just like himself, take his last breath.

Twilight eased over Fort Wilderness. A deep sense of gloom had settled over the entire camp. Perhaps it was nothing more than weariness, battle fatigue. Or maybe just the coming of night as the sun slid down in the west, ending another day of mourning the deaths of more wounded soldiers. Such good men! Some so very young!

Jesse was weary of it all, the army life, the killing, the suffering. The ever-so-exhausting *waiting!* And for what purpose? The land? The ownership? To gain *authority* over the Indians? And he was also tired of sending off reports to his superiors, who had no clue as to the real situation here. Reports that would justify their actions, making the outcomes of battles and the many broken promises look good on paper, defending them if questioned at a later date.

The captain walked down to the creek, wanting to be left alone with his thoughts, Little Wolf's defiant, hate-filled eyes still haunting him But Jesse wasn't alone! Gathered on the grassy creek bank were a large assembly of the soldiers; they were sprawled on the ground and were quietly talking among themselves.

Two of the soldiers held flaming torches, casting an eerie reflection across the still water nearby. The torchlight also emphasized the whiteness of the bandaging on the many wounded soldiers that had been released from the infirmary earlier. It was not hard for Jesse to notice all the solemn faces, the sacrifices they make for the army. The homesickness! Silent Hawk approached Jesse. "Is it true, Captain? Is this your last expedition?" he asked quietly.

"It is true, my friend," answered Jesse.

"It is also mine! May the wind be finally with you, my friend!" Silent Hawk squared his shoulders and slipped away into the darkness.

Jesse left the men alone, also slipping away unannounced and he headed back toward the stable; he saddled his horse. A funeral service was in progress at the reservation. He watched the mourners dance long into the night. And afterward, as he rode back to the fort, thoughts of Abigail stirred up his insides once again.

Suddenly, his mind was made up and he turned his horse around, changing his direction. It was a long ride as he rode south, then easterly, the wind now at his back. He reminisced about the last time he saw her, the last time he made love to her. He had truly *missed her* this time. It hadn't been the cold, nor the quarter rations or the long march, or the fact that McEwan had sent the wrong man to capture the Sioux, the wrong man to do the wrong job, that made him regret going on the expedition this time.

Jesse had never felt this way about leaving Abigail before. Usually, he was in a hurry to get away from her. However, being away this time seemed different; something inside of him had changed how he felt about a lot of things. How he felt about *her!* How she always sheltered him, cared for him, was always there by his side whenever he needed her.

It scared him that he might not be able to return what she always bestowed upon him so willingly. Knowing that he must—and would, stand by her every day, as long as he lived. He had vowed to do that when they got married. But Abigail had known what he did for a living before she married him; the army was his whole life. It was *who* he was. He thought she would understand as she witnessed her mother living through harder times than she. Her father also served in the army years ago. Abigail didn't get to see much of him either as she grew up.

Jesse kept riding easterly toward Abigail. For a brief moment, he worried about the need for a bath, to scour away the heady fragrances of cold sweat, leather, and gun oil but his need to see her erased those immaterial thoughts. When he reached his destination, he raced up the stairs of her parent's house, not wanting to waste any more time. To greedily share what he could of their next few days together before it was too late!

Abigail was asleep when Jesse quietly slipped into her room. He gazed down at her as she peacefully slept. What security, what joy she had brought to his lonely life, to his strange, double soul. An occurrence that he had kept hidden from her for so long. He gently kissed her on the mouth, awakening her. She sat up, clutching the blanket to her breasts and baring her shoulders. He glanced at the soft swell of the tops of those breasts, remembering how kissing and caressing each one brought him such pleasure as he made love to her many times before.

Abigail wrapped both arms around his neck and pulled him close. "Every night, I have prayed to hear your boots come up those stairs. I have missed you so much, my love."

Jesse tucked his nose into the nape of her neck as they cuddled in the warmth of her bed. He kissed her again and again as they made love. They had not left the room, missing both breakfast and lunch on the following day. At supper, he announced that he was hungry. "Bring me back something to eat too," piped up Abigail.

"I'd say that you haven't missed too many meals since you left the fort, my dear Abigail," Jesse joked as he patted her stomach. At his words, he watched her blush and quickly turn her head away.

"Someday soon, I will tell you a little secret," she confessed shyly.

The saying 'parting is such sweet sorrow' is so true, thought Jessie when he left Abigail the next day and returned to Fort Wilderness.

In the mess hall, a party was in progress. It was Christmas Eve. Outside, hunks of beef were sliced off a carcass on a revolving spit over a firepit. There was lots of food and drinks being served.

Colonel James McEwan approached Jesse. "Merry Christmas, Jesse! It's been a great day! Makes me want to stay in the army forever! I love this life and have no plans of giving it up. In fact, we are heading back out the day after tomorrow to capture more of those thieving renegades. Of course, I'll be leading the expedition. And this time, as God is my witness, I'll have the victory that this army needs, to finally bring this bloody war between the white men and the Indians to an end. I had that Indian camp in my grasp during the last raid, until those *damned* cave dwellers showed up," pondered McEwan. "Are you sure you won't change your mind and come with us?"

"No, this was my *last* assignment," stated Jesse firmly.

"You're sure?" prodded McEwan.

"I've never been surer about anything in my whole life." It was hard to look McEwan in the face now. To his Colonel, this was no longer an expedition to round up the wandering nomads and drive them back to the reservations. An expedition to successfully do everything he could to keep as many of his troops alive. Instead, it became a battle, a challenge; a *fight* to defeat and destroy these copper-skinned people.

Over the years, Jesse had seen first-hand all the savagery and cruel tortures suffered and inflicted by both parties. Each one fulfilling some ancient blood-debt on their so-called enemy. Each one defending their land, their rights.

When in truth, the army's so-called *enemy* were just people like himself, people of a different color, a different breed, who were also struggling to survive, just like everybody else. People who lived off the land cultivating their own more primitive lifestyle, so different from that of the white man. If only the Indians would listen to the better way recommended to them. But was the white man's way *better*?

In their eyes, it wasn't a better way. Most of the Indians living on the reservations had witnessed the swollen bellies of their starving children, saw so many of the white man's diseases quickly spread throughout their camps, resulting in rising death rates of their sick and elderly people. Hunting wasn't allowed anymore; thus, they only ate whatever food the white men rationed them and many times, fresh meat and vegetables were rarely on the menu.

Yes! The Indians believed their way was much better than the white man's way, and all they asked for was to keep their small parcel of land and to be left alone to live the same lifestyle carried forward from their ancestors. *For many reasons*, it was hard for Jesse to look into Jim McEwan's eyes on this Christmas Eve and try to remember what good friends they *used* to be.

"I have to go and write my report," stated Jesse coldly. "Stop by my office later and we'll have a toast for all the good times we've spent with each other in the past. It being our Christmas tradition an' all." As Jesse walked away, he muttered under his breath, "a *farewell* tradition!"

"Sure! That'll give me some time to do some of *my* paperwork, too. See ya' later, Jesse."

Colonel James McEwan went to his office and sat at his desk to pen a letter:

Camp Wilderness, North Bay, Ontario, Canada.
Dec. 24, 1903.

My Dearest Abigail,

I miss you so terribly. Many times, I have taken your handkerchief from my shirt pocket and held it to my face, embracing the smell of you for yet another day. With sad regret, I find the fragrance fading from this scrap of cloth that you so lovingly gave to me years ago.

Even when the fragrance is long gone, I will still carry it over my heart where you will always remain. We have been apart for weeks now but it seems like an eternity. In my thoughts, you rode with me whenever I had a dangerous assignment, never leaving my side; you were my guardian angel. My love for you pulses through my veins every minute and as I take this pen in hand and put these words on paper, I only hope that you feel the same way about me.

For years during every Christmas holiday, I sat at your table, supped delicious dinners, and made idle conversation with your husband while restraining myself from taking you into my arms and making love to you in your very own kitchen. Surprisingly, we had kept our affair a secret for a long time; Jesse never suspected.

When I left you, you showed great concern for my well-being. But I had greater concern for yours, darling. I remember the tears you shed when you tried to tell me about the baby you were carrying. You were so afraid that I might not find you attractive anymore, would not desire you. Silly woman! Your condition only excites me more and I find you more beautiful every time I see you. I am truly fascinated by this new life growing inside of your body. I have never been a father before and this is all so new to me. I only pray that the child is not born blonde-haired and blue-eyed.

Ten years has gone beneath my wandering boots and maybe it is time for me to settle down. You will be saving me from a hellish life, a dangerous life in the army; although I do have to admit it, I enjoyed the army's way of life before I met you. Oh, how I wish you were with me when I arrived back at Fort Wilderness yesterday. My heart felt so heavy; my arms so empty without you by my side.

It was a very dangerous mission; four of my men perished, six were wounded. I barely managed to escape, returning unscathed. I had sent Jesse on a mission that no ordinary man would have survived. But he not only survived, he returned as a hero, with every one of his men unharmed. He left with a bunch of greenhorn youngsters and brought them back as soldiers. What man does that?

I am exhausted, but I had to write to you before I went to bed. I have no idea how long this letter will take before it reaches you. I wanted to send you a message, letting you know that I was OK. I pray that you will not suffer from anxiety, worrying about me like you always do as my message could be late in arriving. It grows late and I must go see an old friend for a quick Christmas toast before I turn in. I will send another message by courier next week. Merry Christmas, my love.

Yours truly,
Jim McEwan.

Captain Jesse Burns went to his office and sat at his desk. Little Wolf's gaunt face appeared before him. He wondered where he was right then. Was he alright? Did he make it? If McEwan knew Little Wolf was Jesse's son, he would kill the boy for sure. Jesse bowed his head and prayed for his son; he had never prayed before.

When he finally finished filling out his report, he leaned back in the chair. He was tired. It was late. Suddenly, he thought of Abigail, envisioned her face as well. Something kept bothering him when she stated that she had a 'secret' to tell him. Abigail had never kept secrets from him. He quickly dismissed the subject. It had only been days since they had made love again; it had stirred his emotions more that night than it had done in years. He missed her, still loved her. He had always loved her. And since he came back, he heard that she had gotten herself a new suitor; *supposedly*, someone that truly cares about her.

I just want her to find happiness, he thought at first. But he only learned of her suitor's identity today. Jesse knew that McEwan was no good for her; he would only break her heart. In the past, Jesse had always sworn that he would kill any man that ever came between him and his Abigail. Now, did he have the right to take away the little piece of happiness that McEwan might give her?

Jesse got up off the chair and went over to the window, rubbing a circle free of its frosty glazing with his fist. Below lay a fresh layer of snow on the parade grounds. Only one set of footprints had pocked its pristine 'tablecloth' surface, leading toward his office door.

Far to the east, a full moon could be seen peeking through the parting, darkened clouds. The storm was passing. Even the wind had died. The blizzard was finally over. Jesse also knew Abigail's little 'secret'. She was with child. And the baby she carried was *his*. Possibly a boy. The curse (or the repetitious vision of his offsprings) that had plagued him for most of his life came back to haunt him.

Jesse went back to his desk and sat down again. How many more nights will this vision keep haunting him? How much longer will he be able to keep living with this curse that transforms him from man to beast? This double image? And how much longer will he be able to keep it hidden from Abigail? If he took his own life, would he destroy the curse as well? The man would surely die, but would the spirit of the wolf live on?

On the other hand, if he shot her lover instead, would he hurt Abigail, possibly ruin her chance at happiness with this man? However, did he really want McEwan to raise this child? His daughter? Perhaps his son? To have him grow up like McEwan? A man who, once he tired of a woman, would eventually walk out on both her and the baby? Break her heart?

Jesse had a choice to make. He opened the desk drawer and pulled out the bottle of whiskey hidden inside and drank it down. His hand reached further back inside the drawer; he pulled out the loaded service revolver. He levered open the action and stared into the breech. One cartridge was inside. Only one! One shot a Captain usually saved for himself. Suddenly, there was a knock at the door.

"Jesse, it's me. Jim McEwan." The door swung open.

The mournful howl of a wolf could be heard throughout the fort. Four times it howled; an old Sioux chief told Jesse a long time ago that it represented a sign of death. He was right! The howl had come from *inside* Jesse's office. There was that familiar, feral smell filling the room. The explosion of the shot echoed throughout the fort, piercing the night air. Jesse had made his choice.

BANG!

Epilogue

When Colonel James McEwan trudged through the newly-fallen snow to make his way toward the captain's headquarters, he had two reasons why he wanted to talk to Jesse on Christmas Eve. He was hoping to convince him to join in on the hunt tomorrow to capture more of the renegades and bring them back to the reservation. One, in particular, was Little Wolf; he knew that he was still out there roaming the hills because he had been spotted many times.

With Jesse's help, he felt that they would have a better chance to either bring the evasive rebel in or *kill* him. The other reason was to keep the twelfth-year tradition going and drink a toast as old friends do, to celebrate yet another passing Christmas together. *Even though we both love the same woman!* thought McEwan wickedly.

The shot was suddenly heard throughout Fort Wilderness just after midnight on Christmas day. Colonel McEwan thrust open the office door, fearing the worst. Slumped over the desk was his friend, Captain Jesse Burns, his bloodied head partially blown off from a self-inflicted wound at close range just moments ago. Jesse's service revolver was clutched in his hand as the dissipating cloud of gun smoke still lingered in the room. On the desk was a penned letter written by Jesse; the ink was still damp. Colonel McEwan picked it up and read it:

My dearest Abigail,

I am sorry to end things this way, but I thought it would be the best way for both of us. Over the years, I have suffered with having two souls inside of me and neither would agree on most occasions. My body has been split into two different forms, causing chaos almost every day. I cannot live with this anymore!

When you bore me a son, I destroyed him, fearing that he would be inflicted with my problem. Our marriage fell apart after that. Years later, Meadowlark came into my life and she gave birth to a son just before she died. My son! A boy who grew up hating his father! I tried to destroy him too, but he still lives. I suspect that Little Wolf has my infliction, possessing another spirit inside his body also.

I had one bullet in my gun and when I learned of your affair with my friend, Jim McEwan, it only confirmed my suspicions that I had refused to believe over the years. This bullet was meant to be for him, Abigail. My God, Jim was like a brother to me; we were that close. How could I shoot my own brother? Then I also wondered what killing him would do to you. I just want you to be happy.

You were always a devoted and caring wife at the beginning of our marriage, my rock of Gibraltar. But I feel that I had driven you to look for happiness elsewhere; even though I have my doubts as to whether Jim will be that man who will make you happy.

In my lifetime, I have loved two women. One for each soul. One has died and the other is very much alive, carrying a new life inside of her womb. Yes, Abigail, I guessed your secret you were withholding from me. You were never good at keeping secrets.

Now the question is, is the baby mine? Or is it Jim's? I will never know. But you will know when you gaze into its little face for the first time. The answer will lie within your heart. And if the baby has blonde hair and blue eyes like me, you will know, my love. I love you, Abigail. I always will! Somehow, death seemed like my only consolation to finally bring me peace.

Always and forever, Jesse.

Colonel McEwan folded the letter and quickly shoved it inside the addressed envelope, which was also left on the desktop. He placed it into his breast pocket before anyone else entered the room. He felt like he was going to throw up. *How long did Jesse know? How many Christmases did he suspect I was having an affair with his wife? Yet, he still remained my loyal friend! Hell! He even saved my life once,* thought Jim McEwan regretfully.

An open window framed with a pair of white, billowy curtains quickly chilled the small room. The gust of unfriendly wind bounced off the walls and encircled the desk. Possessively. A Spirit had entered, making its presence known.

As Colonel James McEwan walked toward the window to close it, he immediately detected the feral smell that had sifted through the opening, gushed in by that powerful gust moments earlier, only to get sucked back out and vanish into the blackness of the night. On the window ledge were large paw prints etched in blood. Captain Jesse Burns, the *man* inside the room, was dead, but the spirit of the White Wolf lives on.

The day after Jesse's funeral, Colonel Jim McEwan, with twenty of his best soldiers, headed out to hunt down more of the renegades that still refused to give themselves up. The orders were to kill them if necessary; especially one in particular, the evasive Little Wolf. The soldiers grumbled about going back out in the cold so soon after Christmas, but it did them no good. Colonel McEwan was on a mission and he drove them long and hard that first day and refused to let up until Little Wolf was dead.

On the fourth night, after having captured only four young braves, grievances from the soldiers encircled throughout the campsite; they all felt the assignment could've waited until spring. They were tired. They were cold. Even some suffered from frostbite. But McEwan wouldn't yield to their complaining. And he told them so.

"We are losing more daylight so be ready to move out an hour earlier in the morning. We won't quit until all of those outlaws are apprehended; do you hear me?" he shouted in an enraged voice and the men fell silent around him.

Before sunrise, the soldiers quietly left and headed home, leaving Colonel McEwan to finish the mission on his own.

"Deserters, every last one of them!" shouted McEwan to the trees when he awoke. He stirred the dying ashes in the firepit and then he felt a 'presence' coming from within the bushes directly in front of him. "So ye decided to come back did ye, ye cowardly bunch," he accused, thinking it was his men returning.

That's when he saw the white flash. While keeping low to the ground, the ghostly shadow skulked toward the firepit, and before the Colonel could blink an eye, it suddenly lunged forward, landing on top of McEwan's chest. The powerful blow had pushed him backward into the firepit.

Whatever it was sitting on top of him felt like an anvil, pinning McEwan to the ground with such enormous strength while long, razor-sharp claws dug deeply into his skin and drew blood instantly. He looked into his predator's face and momentarily thought he saw the familiar pair of blue eyes staring back at him before they quickly transformed.

The shiny glowing eyes, now dripping with hatred, were powerful enough to push back the darkness of the abandoned campsite causing an eerie 'Lumosity' to hover like a heavy fog. Shadowy forms silhouetted from the tall, surrounding trees, bent and waved from the gusty wind that had suddenly arisen, blowing away the strong feral smell that filled McEwan's airways earlier, a smell so strong that it almost choked him.

He remembered that smell! The night when Jesse had shot himself in his office, that same smell lingered in the room until the wind from the open window had finally dissipated it also.

"Jesse!" McEwan called out repeatedly. "I was never going to hurt your son. Yes, look in my pocket; I have your letter. I now know Little Wolf is your son! *Jesse*," he kept imploring. "We have always been close friends. For God's sake, please help me!"

The only response to McEwan's plea: the white wolf savagely bit into flesh, ripped open the neck and McEwan's blood spilled onto the freshly fallen snow. Shortly afterward, the wolf limped away.

The legend of white wolf continues to be told.

The young boy, no more than a shadow in size and having bones showing through his skin, was part Caucasian and part Sioux. But he was raised as a Native-American, living in a time-warped era when his people practiced the old ways, depending on the hunt for buffalo for survival. Blessed with saffron-colored hair, fair skin, and sparkling blue eyes, he looked so different from his fellow playmates and was thought by his people that his medicine was strong, his spirit stronger.

Now, whenever the warrior within him awakens, he no longer fears death; a person can kill his body, but they can never kill his soul. There are those who say this warrior with the magical powers is still alive and that he will never die. There are some who believe that the young man's spirit always walks the land where he loved to hunt. While others say that he still lives among them, under a different name, maybe even as a different being. No one has ever seen his dead body lying upon a death scaffold.

Minors and settlers often speak of seeing a lone rider, silhouetted against a clear blue sky, on the hilltop where he was shot. Others speak of sightings of a lone rider wearing a red scarf emerging from a heavy white fog or morning mist, bending the long grasses that have since grown tall, a ghostly figure that leaves a wide pathway of meandering stalks in the fields.

There is even talk of people hearing a prayer chant floating across these same flattened fields after the sun goes to sleep; they hear the rustling sound of the wind whispering his name and the mournful howl of a wolf echoing from the hilltop, silhouetted by a full, yellow moon.

Who is to say he is dead, that he will be there forever? Who is to say that he does not run faster than his own shadow, faster than the wind, or even faster than the big white wolf that always follows him wherever he goes? It is said that he carries the spirit of the White Wolf inside him, a spirit believed to have two faces. His father displayed one face, that of the *Bad Moon*, evil and corrupt. While Little Wolf symbolized the other, the face of the *Good Sun*, vigilant, protective.

The stories continued about the saffron-haired, blue-eyed lad and were retold to the younger generations as they huddled around Lakota campfires, even though the endings were always different. Some people say Little Wolf went back to see his good friends, Jean-Luc and Ilkcaw Fox, who discovered months later that Ilkcaw was finally with child. They became proud new parents to a set of healthy, identical twin boys, both blessed with saffron-colored hair and bright blue eyes.

Other people say they saw both Little Wolf and his horse, Shadow, on Beaker's Bluff, supposedly there to deliver a message to Ruby Long Bottoms, the Witch of the North (Little Wolf was known to always keep a promise). She was the one who gave him his white man's name, 'John Messenger'. Ruby also asked Little Wolf why her daughter, Pretty Flower, hadn't killed him when she had the chance.

"What made her decide to let *you* live?" she queried.

Little Wolf answered her with a grin, "You never shoot *the messengers!*"

For Claude

Those we love don't go away
They walk beside us every day
Unseen, unheard, but always near
Still loved, still missed, but always dear.

Claude Michel Joseph Roy
January 30, 1947 – January 1, 2020

R. I. P.

A Message from the Author

Hi there! My name is D.M. (Donna) Roy and I live in Southern Ontario, Canada, one of God's most beautiful orchards on Planet Earth. I have had a fulfilling career in the financial field and in those forty-five years, I learned a lot about people, 'Experience' being my most predominant teacher.

My 'nine to five' job amply supported me and my family over the years. However, I have always had the desire to write and had hoped someday to become a published author; this longing always persevered inside of me so I did write almost every day, as often as I could, hoping to master the art of being a *good* writer. As I have passed the stage in my life where I am no longer a 'spring chicken', I still continue *and enjoy* writing. Now, I see myself as being more like a soaring eagle who manages to 'fly around the world' each day when I write.

Sincerely, D.M. (Donna) Roy
P.S. If you enjoyed this book, then watch for my next one called *GOOD SUN, BAD MOON,* Book #2 of *The Messengers.*